DECEPTIONS
SOUTHERN SECRETS SAGA, BOOK 1

JEANNE HARDT

Kerry —
Enjoy!
Jeanne
Hardt

CHAPTER 1

"Mercy, it's warm."

Though it did little good, Claire fanned her face, then walked into the church. Dressed in a lightweight pink cotton dress, with as few undergarments as decency allowed, she scanned those in attendance, looking for Beth.

The sun filtered in through multiple windows, highlighting twinkling dust that arose from the wood pews as members took their seats. She breathed in a mixture of earthy smells; from the warm wood structure, to the horses tethered outside. And of course, the assortment of toilet water folks used to cover up their unique bodily smells. Some of which were *far* from pleasant.

Nodding and smiling as she passed by other parishioners, she scooted into the pew beside her best friend, Beth Alexander.

Beth greeted her with a warm hug and a smile that lifted the corners of her chubby cheeks. The girl had always been heavier than Claire, and some said her features were rather masculine and unattractive. But she had a heart of gold and Claire loved her.

Aside from their longtime friendship, they had two things in common—both had similar ash brown hair, but more importantly, they were twenty-five and unmarried.

Claire intended to stay that way.

"Might fine dress, Claire," Beth said, touching the fabric.

"Thank you. Just finished sewin' it last night."

"Don't know how you do it. Reckon every man in this here congregation was watchin' you. You're too purty for your own good."

Claire shook her head. "Why should they look? No sense in lookin' at someone who doesn't care to be noticed."

"My brother's lookin' right now." Beth nodded to the pew across from them.

Claire remained face-forward, but shifted her eyes down the aisle. Gerald, Beth's brother, caught her gaze.

He's lookin' all right.

With cheeks redder than strawberries, he quickly turned away. He was a few years older than her, and many of the town's folk were certain they'd marry. But since it took both parties to agree, it would never happen. Not that he'd ever formally posed the question.

"Why does he do that, Beth?" Claire whispered.

"Do what?"

"Act so shy and nervous 'round me. We've known each other since we were children. He's like a brother to me."

"Y'all are different now. Don't you see that?" Beth patted Claire's leg. "Hush now. Service is startin'."

They rose to their feet as the song leader began a chorus of *Amazing Grace*. Being one of Claire's favorites, she lifted her chin and sang out loud and strong. But during the last verse of the song, Lucy Beecham wandered in and Claire's enthusiasm fell to the floor.

She eyed Lucy's petite frame as she juggled her four stair-step children. She shuffled them to the front pew, directly in front of her—one on each hip and the other two clinging to her legs.

Lucy sat, cradling her infant. Her unwashed, stringy red hair flopped over the back of the pew, accompanied by the dirty face of her four-year-old. He stuck out his tongue and then hid, cowering down.

To make matters worse, Mrs. White sat beside Lucy and immediately produced a fan to air her face. At seventy-five, she'd lost her sense of smell, but was always overheated. With every waft of the fan, the odor in the front pew drifted over Claire, nearly taking her breath.

When the song ended, Claire took her seat, then leaned in toward Beth. "If I had babies, least I'd make sure they were bathed for church." Most folks took their weekly baths on Saturday night so they were fresh for Sunday morning services. Not the Beechams.

Beth's eyes widened. "Be a little more understandin'. I hear she has another one on the way."

Claire crossed her arms in disgust. "Can't that man stay off her? Least long enough so she can catch her breath?" She believed she'd whispered quietly enough for Beth's ears only, but when Lucy turned around and glared at them, Claire's stomach twisted, realizing she'd been sorely mistaken.

"Spinsters!" Lucy snapped.

Claire's mouth dropped open and her heart sank. When she caught Gerald's eye, it made matters worse. His bright red face gave every indication he'd heard Lucy. Whether red from embarrassment for her, or anger, it didn't matter. As loud as Lucy had been, she assumed the entire congregation had heard her.

Lucy turned back to the front and pulled her children close. She stroked the baby's head, then kissed her light tuft of hair.

Reverend Brown raised his hands in the air and with a sound that seemed to come from the bottom of his toes, cleared his throat. "Let us pray!" The congregation fell silent as the minister offered up prayer and supplication.

Claire had grown accustomed to being called a spinster, old maid, and even some names she didn't quite understand. It usually didn't bother her. But something about being addressed this way in church struck her differently.

Yes, she'd provoked Lucy and was sorry for it. Still, she prided herself in her virtue and believed if God intended her to marry, He'd see to it she knew when the proper man was there for her.

"Amen!"

Her mind drifted throughout the sermon. Unlike her time as a child when the former minister, Reverend Thomas, gave his terrifying *hellfire and damnation* sermons. Her mama had always told her he was simply *scarin' away the devil,* but it never eased Claire's discomfort. He'd scared the fire out of *her*, but kept her attention.

Reverend Brown wasn't a bad speaker; she simply had other things she'd rather think about.

I'll apologize to Lucy.

Once the service ended, Claire waited to approach her until they were clear of the others in the congregation. Beth kindly accompanied her for support.

"Lucy, I'm sorry if I hurt your feelin's 'bout your little 'uns," Claire said as heartfelt as she possibly could. "I know it must be awful hard tendin' four of them."

Lucy readjusted the children on her hips and faced Claire squarely. "You ain't got no business tellin' me anythin' 'bout my babies. As for my man, he can get on me whenever he pleases. Least *I* know what it feels like havin' a man 'tween my legs!" She stormed away with her nose in the air.

Claire watched her leave, completely dumbfounded.

"Not a very Christian thing to say, you reckon?" Beth asked, shaking her head.

Claire couldn't help but laugh. "It's a Sunday I'll never forget. Can't remember a word of the sermon, but Lucy's preachin' will be in my head 'til the day I die!"

* * *

Claire tossed and turned, unable to sleep.

Least I know what it feels like havin' a man 'tween my legs . . .

No one had ever said something so sexually bold to her. Everyone knew of her chastity, and she'd always thought of it as a good thing. But Lucy had slapped it in her face. Once the initial shock wore off, it stung.

Maybe I'm truly missin' sumthin'.

Her mama had never talked to her about such things. The whole idea of coupling with a man intrigued her. She'd seen the farm animals mating, and heard the barbaric sounds of the barn cats when the tom would bite the female on the back of the neck, pin her down, and force himself into her. The howling would go on for hours on end. It sounded painful. The female always got the worst end of the situation. Not only did she have to endure being bitten and clawed, but then had to give birth to what had been left inside her.

A vision of Lucy's husband, Frank, biting Lucy on the back of the neck and holding her down popped to mind.

Mercy, no . . .

Shaking her head to wash it away, she shut her eyes tight.

There must be more to lovemakin' than that.

Doubtful she'd ever know. She refused to die of a broken heart as her mama had. The woman's constant words of warning regarding men echoed in her brain.

After almost no sleep, her faithful rooster forced her from the bed. A warm coastal breeze blew through her open windows. Warm, but refreshing.

She trudged through her two-room house and stretched as she moved to the kitchen and opened a jar of canned apricots. Being unwed had its advantages. No one to fuss over for a complicated breakfast. So why did she have no appetite?

Surprised by a loud knock, she grabbed a robe, wrapped herself up modestly, and opened the door.

"Gerald?" Her eyes widened. "What are you doin' here so early? Everythin' all right?"

"Mornin', Claire." He cleared his throat. "Sorry 'bout the inconvenience, but I was hopin' you could see me today. Reckon we could spend some time together?"

"What did you have in mind?"

"How 'bout some fishin'?" With weaving brows and trembling hands, he extended two fishing poles and a bucket of worms.

"Well, all right. Give me a bit to get dressed." She returned inside. Though highly unusual for him to come calling this time of day, she considered him a friend, and it appeared he needed to talk.

He's more nervous than a long-tailed cat in a room full of rockin' chairs.

She peeked out the window and grinned. He was a stout man with a square face, small nose, and closely set eyes. But she'd always admired his thick, curly dusty-blond hair.

Even in her absence, he behaved nervous as a tick. He paced and mumbled to himself, still holding tightly to the poles and bucket.

She came out in a simple, blue cotton dress and sunbonnet. The moment he caught sight of her he nearly tripped over the fishing poles. He clumsily picked up one that he'd dropped, and she could have sworn he whimpered.

They walked to a fishing hole not far away. They'd been there as children, when they frequently went *fishin' an frog-gin'*, but that was a long time ago.

Surrounded by trees, the overgrown pond sat below a high embankment. Claire found a grassy spot to sit, far enough off the water to avoid any possible snakes lurking around the edges. She'd always been cautious, terrified of the dangerous cottonmouths.

Gerald plopped down beside her, then they baited their hooks and waited. Neither spoke.

She stared mindlessly at the water.

Why doesn't he say sumthin'?

She let out a long loud sigh.

"Claire . . ." Thankfully he broke the silence. Obviously still nervous, his hand instantly went to his face. He wore glasses and had a habit of pushing them up on his nose. She'd teased him about it when they were young. As they grew older the teasing stopped, but the habit didn't.

"Yes, Gerald?" She smiled, hoping to ease his discomfort.

"I've been wantin' to talk to you for some time now, but hadn't felt the time was ever right for the talkin'." He wrinkled his nose and twisted his mouth. "I mean to say . . . ah, heck! Why can't I never say the right things 'round you no more?"

"Gerald. We've known each other forever. Why's it so hard to talk to me?" What had happened to her old friend? The one she'd laughed with and shared stories? The one she could talk to about anything?

He scratched the back of his head. "Sorry, Claire. I know I've been actin' like a fool, but it's you. You've changed."

She crossed her arms and tipped her head.

"In a good way!" he quickly added. "But in a way that makes me nervous. Makes me lose my breath." He looked down and away from her.

Just like Beth had said, *y'all are different now.* They certainly weren't children any longer. Truth be told, there were women just a few years older than her who were already grandmothers.

"Come on, now." She nudged his shoulder. "I'm the same Claire I've always been and you're no fool. You're one of the best friends I've ever had."

"But Claire, I don't wanna be just your friend. I . . ." His Adam's apple bobbed as he swallowed hard. "I love you." He took her hand.

She hesitated and almost pulled it back, but changed her mind and let him pull it to his face.

He caressed her fingers with his cheek, then kissed the back of her hand. "Will you be my wife?"

What?

Though he'd been acting unusual, she'd suspected him ill, or deeply troubled about something, but not this. This took her completely by surprise. The parishioners at the Baptist church might have been expecting this, but she never dreamed he'd ever get up the nerve to actually ask her. She knew her answer of course, but how would she tell him?

Silence hung in the air.

"You don't love me," he whispered.

"Oh, no, Gerald. That's not it at all." How could she spare his feelings?

"Then, you *do* love me?" He leaned in with eyes as wide as saucers.

"Course I love you. I've always loved you, but not *that* way." Relieved she'd said it, she let out a heavy sigh. She'd told him *no* without speaking the word.

"Claire." Somehow he'd gained confidence. He pulled his shoulders back and sat tall. "I know I ain't handsome and I ain't got no money, but neither of us is gettin' any younger. I'd be good to you. I'd care for you and keep you company. We wouldn't grow old alone."

"We don't have to grow old alone. We can still be friends. You, an me, an Beth. We'll always have each other. But I can't be your wife. It just wouldn't be right." She stood, brushed off her dress, and started walking away. Staying there with him would only make matters worse.

Pausing, she turned toward him. Her heart ached seeing him sitting there motionless. "I'm so sorry, Gerald."

* * *

Claire tried to get her mind off Gerald. Tending her vegetable garden always helped ease her thoughts.

I broke his heart.

It hadn't been her intent, but she couldn't marry a man she considered a brother, let alone share his bed.

Heaven's no.

She tossed aside a handful of weeds and caught sight of Beth coming down the road. The closer she came, the further Claire's heart sank. More than one heart had been broken that morning.

Claire stood and wiped her hands on her apron, preparing herself for what was to come. Fresh tears streaked Beth's face.

"Why'd you say no, Claire?" Beth sniffled and wiped her nose with a handkerchief. "Marryin' my brother would a been the right thing to do. We'd be sisters. We could look after each other."

Claire's mind spun. She searched for the right words, but didn't know how to say them.

"Claire." Beth kept right on talking. "I know you don't like it when folks call you names. And the things Lucy said were uncalled for. But folks would stop talkin' if you'd take a husband."

"And what 'bout you, Beth? Folks talk to you the same. I'm not tellin' you to go off an marry someone just to make folks stop talkin'." Regardless of whether or not the proposal had come from her brother, her friend had just let her down.

You of all people know how I feel.

Claire took a deep breath and did her best to remain calm. "'Sides, folks don't have to be married to help each other. I'll *always* be here for you."

Beth burst into tears.

"Oh, Beth." Claire reached out and took her hands. "There's no need to cry. I still love you, an Gerald, too. But you gotta understand. I don't love him the way a wife needs to love a husband."

"No, *you* don't understand. Gerald's gone! He left this mornin'. Said he couldn't stay here after all this." She covered her face and sobbed.

It can't be true. He's always lived here. "I'm sure he'll be back. He's just hurtin' right now. Needin' some time."

"You're wrong." Beth trembled as she sucked in air, trying to speak. "He's gone north to live with our uncle. Uncle Henry's wanted Gerald to come work for him for a long time now. Ever since his sons died in the war. Gerald always said no. But he's takin' his offer now. He's gone!"

Claire held her close and let her cry.

Searching her heart, she felt sorry for Beth and knew how lonely she'd be without her brother. The one thing she *didn't* feel? A longing for Gerald. The thought of never seeing him again didn't bother her, which made her feel even worse. Those feelings also reassured her she'd made the right decision refusing him.

Beth blinked slowly. "Go after him, please? I know he'd come back if you asked him to."

"I can't. You know that. I can't let him think my feelin's have changed." *Someday, you'll know I'm right.* "Come on now. I'll walk you home."

They walked arm in arm to the boarding house, where Beth and Gerald had lived since their home had been lost in the war. Their daddy had been killed and their mama had died shortly after from illness.

Since that time, Mrs. Sandborn, the owner, had taken them under her wing and loved them like her own. She was widowed, forty-eight, and silver-haired, and one of the most jovial women Claire knew. The fact she always smelled like freshly-baked bread made her even more likable. Every time Claire hugged her, she felt like she'd just wrapped her arms around a loaf of sunshine.

"Can't believe Gerald's gone," Mrs. Sandborn said with a frown. "I loved that boy. Now I'm gonna hafta hire someone to help 'round here."

So much for the sunshine.

After all Claire's hard work to calm her down, Beth erupted into another loud bawl.

"Ah, heck," Mrs. Sandborn muttered. "Don't know what I was thinkin'."

Claire passed Beth into the woman's arms. "She'll be fine. Take care of her for me."

Mrs. Sandborn nodded, then escorted Beth inside.

As Claire walked the long road home, loneliness crept in. Maybe Beth had been right.

Did I make the biggest mistake of my life refusin' Gerald?

Shaking her head, she clenched her fists, determined to stand by her principles. Though it was unlikely Gerald would be the kind of man her mama had warned her about, if she wasn't true to her feelings, *she'd* be the deceitful one and just as badly mannered as any man that took advantage of a woman.

She raised her head high and smiled.

I did the right thing.

It may have been hurtful, but it had been the only proper thing to do.

CHAPTER 2

Claire pushed off with her bare feet and got the rocking chair moving. Her front porch had always been her favorite spot on hot afternoons. The overhang from the roof, along with numerous shade trees surrounding the house, kept her cooler than most anywhere.

Growing up in the south, she'd become wise to the brutality of the sun and did her best to get her chores done in the early hours of the day.

From here she could see Mobile Bay. The water sparkled in the sunlight. The sunsets were even more breathtaking.

I wouldn't wanna live anywhere else.

She sipped on a glass of sweet tea punch—a recipe her aunt Martha had given her. She abruptly stopped the movement of the rocker.

That man is bound to die of sunstroke.

A tall stranger walked casually down the distant road toward the shore.

He's no southerner.

Someone from the south would've had more sense and at least worn a hat. Intrigued, she set aside her tea and stood to get a better view. His shirt sleeves were rolled up, as were his trousers, all the way to his knees. Even from afar she could tell he was a well-structured man. He had large muscular arms and a broad chest. But from his waist down, he was slender. Without a hat, his head would likely be baked from the heat of the sun, especially since he had a headful of thick dark hair drawing the rays.

Grabbing her sunbonnet, she decided to follow him.

With the stealth of a barn cat ready to pounce on a mouse, she remained some distance behind him. Even his walk caught her interest. He had an air of refinement about him, walking with his shoulders back and his head held high.

A very confident man.

He discovered her pathway to the beach and carefully made his way down. And as he approached the shore, he slipped off his shoes.

You'll regret it.

He hopped around awkwardly making funny little sounds and she covered her mouth to keep from laughing.

Reckon I shoulda told him the sand was hot.

He finally grew some sense and got the shoes back on his feet.

A soft laugh escaped her. "Hey there! You aren't from around here, are you?"

He turned abruptly toward her. His face lit up with a bright smile. "Oh. Hello." He approached her. "I'm not trespassing am I?"

"Course not. This land belongs to God an Alabama. I don't reckon either would mind you bein' here. That is . . . unless you're a Yankee. If you are, you might wanna watch out for Alabama."

He laughed aloud, then softened to a smile. His teeth were near perfect and very white. He had a clean-shaven face and flawless, unblemished skin. Undoubtedly, the most handsome man she'd ever seen.

Definitely not from around these parts.

She dipped her head. "I'm Claire Montgomery."

He bowed slightly at the waist. "I'm Andrew Fletcher. It's a pleasure to meet you, Mrs. Montgomery."

"That would be *Miss* Montgomery." Once again, someone assumed her to be married. He looked to be as old as her, but seemed quite mature. Completely unlike the men she'd grown accustomed to.

"Miss it is, then." He nodded his head.

She grinned and pursed her lips. "You shouldn't be out here in this sun, Mr. Fletcher. It's not good for your health. Aren't you 'fraid a burnin'? " Being close to him now, she could see he was well-tanned and very dark-skinned. She, too, had a dark complexion from a life of living in the sun, but anyone could burn if they stayed out too long.

"I appreciate your concern, but I've never been sunburnt. However, I believe I'll take your advice and find a cool place to put my feet. Any suggestions?" He took a step closer, smiling all the while.

"Lands sakes! You have an ocean of water right in front of you. The sand may be hot, but the water will cool you off." She tapped her finger to her chin. "Then again, you'd still be out in the blisterin' sun. I'd likely come by here tomorrow and find you stretched out and fried like a chicken in a skillet."

He let out a hearty laugh. "So tell me, then, Miss Montgomery, what do people around here do on hot afternoons?"

"As little as possible." Why was it so easy to talk to him? She seldom met strangers here. If she had any sense, she'd run in the opposite direction.

He shook his head, laughing under his breath.

"Now then," she said. "We can stand here bakin' in the hot sun all day, or you could go up the road with me a spell to my place. It's much cooler there and I can fix us some sweet tea punch."

Did I truly invite him to my home?

Inviting a stranger to one's home, *alone*, wasn't wise for a woman to do.

No matter. It's just for a cool drink and some shade.

She was simply being hospitable.

He readily accepted her invitation, and as they walked, she continued to chatter. Somehow she wasn't at a loss for words. Her curiosity about him pushed her on.

"You *are* a Yankee, aren't you?"

"I *am* from the north—*Connecticut*—but live in Mobile now." He answered her with ease. "I've been there about a year."

"Well that helps a might. Least you had sense enough to *move* to Alabama, since God didn't bless you with bein' born here."

He stopped walking, shook his head and grinned. Then he let out a chuckle and they continued on.

"Ease my curiosity, Mr. Fletcher. Why *did* you move here? You seem more of a big city man to me. Granted, Mobile has grown since the war, but nothin' like those cities up north."

"I'm a doctor. There was a need here that I felt called to fill. And I'm glad I came. There are many people in Alabama that can't afford big city doctors. So, I don't always work for pay. At least not the cash kind. Let's just say that people here like to barter. I have more chickens than a man could use in a lifetime."

"You're a doctor?" Her eyes opened wide. "Why, you're still wet behind the ears. I've never seen a doctor that wasn't gray and slightly bent over."

"I'm not that young." The tone of his voice indicated no offense from her question. "I'm twenty-three. Nearly twenty-four."

"And a full-fledged doctor?" *Impressive.*

"I started young. Took an interest in medicine when I was ten years old. My father saw to it that I got the schooling I needed. He hoped I'd stay close to him, but I had other ideas."

"Like Alabama?" She grinned, and when she turned her head to look at him, once again found him smiling at her.

Her heart fluttered. She held her hand to her chest. *That's never happened before.*

When they reached her home, she gestured to a rocking chair on the porch and he sat.

"I'll get that tea." She hurried inside.

Unable to wipe the grin from her face, she bustled around quickly. First, she untied her sunbonnet and flung it onto the sofa, then went to the kitchen.

What am I doin'?

Her heart kept in rhythm with her fast-working hands and feet. Maybe she feared if she took too long he'd leave.

With tea in hand, she returned to him. He'd kicked off his shoes and looked more than comfortable. Steadying her heart, she liked what she saw.

"Now you look more like one of us." She extended a glass. "It's a might warm, but it'll quench your thirst."

Looking up at her, his eyes sparkled. He eyed her hair, then smiled and took the glass. His fingers brushed hers and a tingle crept down her spine. Swallowing hard, she pushed the feeling aside and sat down in another rocker.

After taking a sip of tea, he nodded his approval and licked his lips. "You're not like any of the women I've met in Mobile."

"How so?" She fingered a strand of her long hair. No man had ever looked at it the way he had.

"You have me puzzled. I've met every kind of woman. Rich, poor, educated, and uneducated. *All* people get sick and hurt, so doctors are exposed to some things that are too *delicate* to mention."

"I see. But what's so puzzlin' 'bout *me*?"

"You certainly have the southern drawl, but you speak more eloquently than most."

"Eloquently?" She laughed. "That is one word I am quite certain has never been used to describe me. Fact is, I don't reckon that word has ever been spoken in all a Baldwin county."

"I'm quite serious, Miss Montgomery. You're educated. I'm not used to seeing that here. Tell me more about yourself."

"I find you a might puzzlin' as well, *Dr.* Fletcher. Most folks round here like to talk about *themselves* or share secrets about others. I'm rarely asked to talk about *my*self." She laughed, becoming more comfortable with him. "My mama once told me that gossip was the devil's talk. But if that's true, there are a lot of folks at the Baptist church that converse with the devil."

He laughed freely, lighting up brighter than the hot sun over the distant water. "Tell me more."

What could it hurt? She'd not enjoyed a conversation this much . . . *ever*. "My mama raised me and insisted I get schoolin'. As you said, most people 'round here don't take to bein' educated, but Mama wanted me to have more learnin' than she'd had. I reckon most parents want more for their children than they had growin' up."

His eyes were on her, unmoving. The moment she stopped talking, he made a slight gesture with his hand, encouraging her to go on.

She met his gaze.

No man should be so handsome.

She shook her head and looked away, fearing he'd read into her thoughts. "There was a young school teacher, Miss Eva Carpenter, who came to our town three days a week and taught lessons at the Baptist church. Like you, she took to barterin' for pay. Honestly, I reckon she kept comin' back because of Fred Thomas, old Reverend Thomas's boy. My friend, Beth, and I saw them kissin' one day behind the church." She managed to look at him.

I'm ramblin' like a fool.

He raised his eyes and smiled. "Go on . . ."

He has the kindest eyes.

She swallowed a lump that had worked its way into her throat. "Well. You could say it was the biggest barter of all when the minister married Eva and Fred. She stayed on as teacher for a few more years until the babies started comin'." She paused and fidgeted with the wooden armrest. "And then the war came. That was the end of my education. Least the book learnin' part. Life itself has taught me much more. Well, that an Mama, of course."

"And what of your mother? Where is she now?" He leaned forward, looking her in the eye.

"Buried over yonder." She motioned her head toward the woods. "She passed 'bout four years ago. I've lived alone ever since."

"I'm so sorry." He laid his hand on her knee and she nearly jumped out of her skin.

"Pay it no mind." She forced a gulped whisper.

He withdrew his hand quickly, but his gentleness warmed her. Certainly he'd been offering comfort and nothing more, but his touch ignited something deep within her.

"What of your father?" he asked.

"I'd rather not speak of him," she said harshly, but couldn't help herself. "Some things are best left unspoken."

Why'd he hafta ask 'bout him?

He stood, shaking his head. "I didn't mean to pry." His voice had softened. "It's none of my business. You've been kind, and I know I've overstayed my welcome."

"Forgive me." She let out a sigh. "You just managed to hit a nerve. I didn't mean to be rude. You were simply askin' 'bout my family. Folks 'round here know things 'bout me, and I reckon when you know someone, you know what *not* to talk 'bout. I can't expect a stranger to follow those unwritten rules."

"Even so, I *am* sorry. I just wanted to know more about you. Maybe become less of a stranger." He rested his hand on her shoulder. "May I call on you again tomorrow?"

Oh, my . . .

In no form or fashion was *this* a gesture of comfort. The man was becoming familiar. And for some unknown reason, she didn't mind.

I pray you didn't feel my body tremble.

"There's sumthin' we need to set straight first," she somehow managed to say, while taking a step back.

His brows dipped low. "A problem?"

"Well, Dr. Fletcher. You know good an well that I'm not married, but if you aim to call on me again, I need to know *your* marital status. Is there a Mrs. Fletcher waitin' for you at home?"

Her question must have eased him, because every trace of concern disappeared from his face. "No. I have no one waiting at home for me—aside from my vast number of chickens and horses."

"Horses? You have more than one?"

"Yes. But nowhere close to the number of chickens." He grinned, and her heart tripled in speed. She was beginning to like him more than she probably should.

"Where are you stayin'?" she asked, becoming bold.

"Under the stars." He motioned upward, then nodded toward the road. "I have a horse and buggy not far from here, and I decided it was time to learn how to camp out."

"Camp out?" She giggled. "On the beach?"

"Perhaps." He shrugged.

She bit her lower lip, then grinned. "The sand fleas can be nasty. Just a little helpful hint."

His brow drew in, this time in utter confusion.

She enjoyed toying with this new man in town. "Oh, and yes, you may call on me again tomorrow." Her words were said with confidence, but her belly turned flips.

He put on his shoes and started up the road. When he stopped and looked at her, she waved him on.

Still so many questions left to ask.

CHAPTER 3

Andrew brought very little with him when he left Mobile to come to the bay. He didn't actually have a plan, just needed to get away. After almost a full year in the south, the time had now come to put his mind back in the right place, so he could concentrate on his work.

He'd hoped he'd be able to clear his head with a bit of sea air.

His father had told him about the coast, and he'd always wanted to see it for himself. It had been part of the reason he'd chosen to move to Mobile—being a Gulf seaport. But in the year he'd been there, he'd spent almost no time at the water.

After taking his horse for a drink in a nearby stream, he tethered it to a tree and walked along the road a short distance to get a good view of the bay. He'd considered returning to the beach by Miss Montgomery's house, but didn't want to risk having her see him and think he was over-eager. After all, it'd only been a few hours since they'd parted.

Maybe I am over-eager.

She'd charmed him. Something no woman had ever been able to do.

He breathed in the warm sea air. The gulf coast had a different feel than the Atlantic. Here it felt warm and inviting.

Nothing like the way Father had described it.

The man had called it stifling, but Andrew had a sense of freedom he'd not felt in a very long time. And not just at the bay, but in Mobile as well.

Father can't control my every move here.

He cast aside thoughts of the man and returned them to Miss Montgomery.

"Claire," he mumbled her given name. Would they become familiar enough that she'd allow him to use it? And did he want to become that close to her?

His heart skipped a beat.

Maybe I do.

But if their conversations became more personal, could he bring himself to tell her what he'd done? Terrible at lying, if she happened to ask why he'd come to the bay, it would be difficult to get around the issue.

He bent down and picked up a stone, then pitched it toward the water. Being a long way from the shoreline, there was no chance he'd come close. But throwing stones seemed to help clear his head.

Why should her opinion of me matter?

He didn't need the approval of a simple country girl who was already impressed by his being a doctor. His status captivated every woman he encountered. His mentor at the hospital told him he'd been declared the most promising bachelor in the city by the single ladies of Mobile.

Not one of them had caught his eye. Then he met Miss Montgomery and everything changed. Yes, her opinion of him mattered very much.

With thoughts of her filling his mind, a smile warmed his face. She was lovely, even in her simple outdated sunbonnet and cotton dress. Perhaps that was part of her charm. Not to mention she had wit unlike any woman he'd ever known. Only a brief meeting, and yet . . .

She's something special.

Because she'd indicated the presence of sand fleas, he deterred from his original plan and made a bed in the buggy. Though not very comfortable, the stars made up for it. Being plenty warm, it didn't take long before he drifted off to sleep.

* * *

Claire couldn't sleep. She closed her eyes and pictured the good doctor's chiseled face and dark eyes. Doing so made her heart beat faster. She dismissed her feelings as being *silly* and completely unreasonable, but she couldn't deny them. He'd made an impression on her.

He'd be back tomorrow, but what would she do with him?

Why'd I ever agree to let him call on me?

Clearly, she wasn't in her right mind. She couldn't take him into town. That would spark the best gossip since Jeb Beecham ran off with Widow Blackwell. Jeb had been only fifteen at the time and the widow near thirty.

Folks had a heyday with that one. What would they say if they saw one of the town spinsters with a tall dark stranger?

Lucy Beecham would make up all kinds of stories.

More than that worry, she didn't want to risk Beth Alexander seeing them together. Still getting over Gerald leaving, Beth would never understand why Claire was in the company of another man.

Staying near her home would be best. The closest home to hers was almost two miles away. Unless someone intentionally came to visit, it was unlikely anyone would notice her with him. Folks kept pretty much to themselves until

Sunday services. And taking Dr. Fletcher to services would be completely out of the question.

Maybe the fishin' hole.

Remembering she'd broken a man's heart there, she wasn't so sure. But it would be different with Dr. Fletcher. Besides, there wasn't much else to do.

She decided she'd fry up a chicken, pick some fresh vegetables from the garden, and try to impress him with a picnic dinner. Being an accomplished cook, it couldn't hurt showing off some of her talents. She'd already impressed him with her *eloquence.*

The memory of what he'd said made her smile.

She awoke early, not sure what time he'd be calling. After pumping water from the well, she heated it so she could wash and freshen herself. Then she put on one of her better dresses and proceeded to the garden for vegetables.

Before returning indoors, she had one more thing to do. This was far too important not to share with her mama, so she stopped at the small plot of earth and knelt beside her grave.

"Mama, I've made an impression on a doctor. He's the most handsome man you could ever imagine. He's kind and thoughtful, and he finds me puzzlin', but I *do* think he likes me." She'd been talking like a giddy school girl, but caught herself and stopped. "Don't worry, Mama. I'll be careful."

After doing her morning chores, she put things together for their outing. Straightening up her little home seemed appropriate; though it was doubtful the doctor would ever see the interior. It wasn't proper to invite a single man into her home.

She'd promised herself *and* her mama that she'd keep her head and do things properly. Even if the neighbors couldn't see them, *God* could. Reverend Thomas's sermons still had an effect on her.

While rocking vigorously on her front porch, her heart began to match the pace of the chair the moment Dr. Fletcher came into view. Not wanting to appear over-anxious, she sat and waited for him to reach her before she arose.

She made an attempt to act nonchalant and formal. "Dr. Fletcher." She smiled and dipped her head.

"Miss Montgomery," he replied with a grin and an attempt at a southern drawl. He followed it with a low bow.

She laughed. Definitely not a southern gentleman, but something she believed to be far better. "Did the sand fleas give you a warm welcome last night?" She motioned to the rockers and they both took a seat.

"I decided not to give them the opportunity. I've never been fond of fleas of any sort."

She grinned, but it quickly vanished. Her nerves squelched her playfulness. "Dr. Fletcher." She decided to be forward. "I don't know what your plans were for today, but I was hopin' you might just enjoy stayin' 'round here. I fixed a nice picnic dinner for us. And . . . I hope you won't think it too backwoods, but I thought you might want to go with me to the fishin' hole." She hesitated, watching his expression. Would he find her completely lame?

"I believe fishing is exactly what the doctor ordered." His response seemed a might enthusiastic. More so than she'd expected.

"Now you're tryin' to be humorous. You bein' the doctor an all. Do you always order yourself around?"

"For today, I'll leave that up to you." He placed his hand on her knee.

Her breath instantly hitched. She glanced down at the long capable fingers of a doctor, and then slowly raised her eyes to meet his. They stared at each other for a brief moment, then he pulled his hand away and stood.

"Are you ready to go now?" His voice resonated soft and low.

"Let me get my things." She jumped up and rushed inside to get their dinner, wondering all the while what she'd gotten herself into.

* * *

"You seem at home here," Claire said. "It's strange. You bein' from the city an all." Casting her eyes quickly to the side to get a good look at the doctor, her heart fluttered. His presence overwhelmed her. They sat perched at the edge of the fishing hole in almost the same spot she'd been with Gerald.

"I imagine I've misled you regarding Mobile. Most of my work is done in the city, but I live out of town in what some people would consider the less desirable part of the county."

This made no sense whatsoever. She'd pictured him living in a fine house with two stories and pillars holding up the front. She'd been to Mobile and had seen such houses.

"You're surprised," he said. "I can see it on your face." He lit up with a broad grin. "Trust me, I have other things to tell you that I'm sure you'll find even more shocking." He jiggled his brows and tilted his head, but behind his humorous gesture laid a hint of seriousness.

Undoubtedly, he was attempting to hold her interest, yet she wouldn't care if he just sat there saying nothing at all. He had her completely enthralled.

"I'm not that easily shocked, Dr. Fletcher," she said, pursing her lips. Yes, she was flirting and thoroughly enjoying herself. "So don't think you know so much."

"Miss Montgomery?" He sat up tall. "Would it be terribly difficult for you to call me by my given name?"

Oh, my.

Maybe she'd flirted too much.

Her stomach flipped. "I'll only call you by your given name if you call me by mine." She pinched her lips tight.

Did I truly say that?

His enormous smile confirmed she had. "Very well, then. *Claire.*"

The way he said her name turned her fluttering heart into a chamber holding a flock of wildly flapping birds. "*Andrew.*" His name squeaked out, so she cleared her throat to improve her delivery. "Now, then. You started this. What do you have to tell me that is so very shockin'?"

He became quiet and stared out at the water, fiddling with his fishing pole. "I told you I moved to Mobile because I knew there was a need there." He pitched a stone into the water. Sensing his more serious state of mind, she said nothing and listened. "The truth is, in the south, sickness isn't limited to white people. It's almost impossible for Negroes to find a doctor who will care for them." He paused, looking directly into her eyes.

Her resident birds were instantly silenced.

"So, you doctor the colored folk, too?"

"Yes, I do."

They sat there without speaking. Frogs jumped and croaked, and though her heart had fallen still, the birds in the trees seemed to sing louder.

Concerned, she decided to lower her voice. "You *do* know what the Klan does to folks that help the coloreds 'round here, don't you?"

He stood and turned away from her. "Yes. I've seen firsthand what they do. I pray to God it's something you never have to witness." Every word he spoke grew a little louder.

"I don't understand it! Don't you people realize the inhumanity—"

"Now listen here!" She jerked to her feet and put mere inches between them, ready to spit nails. "Don't you dare include *me* in *you people*! I've never been a part of or condoned the hangin' of a Negro! I may live here and these are my people, but I *do* know the difference 'tween right an wrong!"

"I'm sorry, Claire. I just get so angry at the things I've seen!" He looked down, shaking his head. The tension in his shoulders melted away as he let out a long breath, then reached out and placed a hand on her arm. "I didn't mean to put you in the middle of it, and I certainly never intended to make you angry."

"And I don't mean to get so defensive." She, too, suddenly calmed at his soft touch. "I reckon I have a lot to defend considerin' my heritage. My granddaddy owned slaves." She sat down and motioned for him to do the same. "He grew cotton. Said he needed them. Said the coloreds were uneducated and the only way they could get by was by havin' someone tell them what to do and take care of them."

"I believe a lot of slave owners felt that way. But no man should ever enslave another."

Though she agreed with him, he'd put himself in a dangerous situation. "I see now why your daddy wanted you back in Connecticut. I'd be worried 'bout you, too, if I were him. Any chance *I* could change your mind 'bout this potentially life endin' career move you've made?"

"No." He didn't hesitate to reply. "They've come to trust me *and* depend on me. Not an easy accomplishment for a white man."

"All right, then." She slapped her thighs. "You win." She splayed her arms wide.

"What do you mean?" His brows wrinkled with confusion.

"I want to congratulate you," she said with a half grin. "You've done what I thought you couldn't do. You shocked me. Honestly, I assumed an educated man would have more sense."

She hoped her renewed good spirit would lighten his mood. It couldn't have been easy telling her this secret. He'd placed a great deal of trust in her. No one would want something like this made known.

"You hungry?" she asked, rising again and feeling the need for a change of scenery.

"Starved." He accompanied his reply with a smile, so maybe she'd accomplished what she'd intended.

Bolder than ever, she held out her hand and helped him to his feet.

This man has a very big heart, but not the best common sense.

Even so, she believed him to be one of the finest men she'd ever had the privilege to know.

They spent most of the day together, walking and talking. Time passed quickly until once again he asked permission to call on her the next day.

Of course, she didn't refuse him.

CHAPTER 4

Like the night before, Claire slept little.

As a rule, most people would rather gossip about others than open up to anyone about their own thoughts and feelings. Yet in two days' time, she'd learned more about Andrew than people she'd known her entire life. But something about him bothered her and she couldn't quite put her finger on it.

Once again, rocking on the front porch waiting for him, it suddenly occurred to her. She rocked a little faster. When he arrived, he wasn't even given the chance to say *good morning.* Before he said a word, she confronted him. "Why are you here?"

"Excuse me?" He froze and gaped at her.

"*Why* are you *here*?"

"You said I could call on you again." His words were hesitant. "I—I don't understand."

She waved her hands in the air—not meaning to confuse him. "No I don't mean *here*." She gestured to her porch. "I mean *here*!" She threw her arms wide and outward, trying to make him understand she was talking about *all* of it. Her town. The bay. All of it. "Why would you leave Mobile and come here all alone with no one to stay with and no particular place to go? It makes no sense."

He let out a large breath. "So, I'm welcome, then?" He motioned toward a rocker, asking with his eyes if he could take a seat.

"Course," she said and sat down beside him.

"I came *here* because I needed some time away." He ran his hands along the armrests. "My work can be stressful. As I'm sure you can understand. It had been some time since I'd had some respite."

"Rest what?" She had some education, but had never heard this word.

He smiled. "Rest and relaxation."

"Oh." She thought for a moment. "Makes sense. Still—why here? Why not go north? See your daddy in Connecticut?"

"I wanted to get away. By myself."

She leaned toward him and tilted her head, raising her brows and questioning him with her eyes.

"I came here because my father told me about this place. He'd come here many years ago. Never actually had fond things to say about it and that's part of the reason I wanted to see it for myself. I've found that what my father feels about something is usually the *opposite* of the way I'll feel about it."

"Kinda like your choice in movin' to Alabama." She understood him perfectly. But unlike *her* daddy, at least his hadn't abandoned him. "I'll bet your daddy regrets all that money he spent on your schoolin'."

"No, Father never regretted that. He's a hard man to understand, but he's always been proud of what I accomplished with my education." He scooted deeper into his chair and tilted his head back.

His mood had changed and not in a good way. For the first time since they'd met, she felt she'd intruded. "So, I reckon I sorta spoiled your plans then. You comin' here to be alone an all."

He returned to a more upright position and shook his head, brows weaving. His eyes locked with hers. "No. Not at all, Claire. You've made it worthwhile."

Oh, my.

The warmth of his voice seeped through her. Her eyes remained focused solely on his. They were dark as night, yet warm like the sun.

She wanted to touch him, to be closer to him—closer to this stranger who'd come out of nowhere and mysteriously started changing her life. She didn't understand it, but was certain of one thing—she didn't want him to leave.

For the first time since his arrival, clouds gathered in the distant sky. The winds felt a bit cooler and whistled as they whipped around through the trees, swirling the branches in small circles. A storm was coming, but for now remained quite a distance away.

"Let's explore the shore," he said and reached out his hand.

She willingly took it and their fingers locked together. He gently caressed her with his thumb, moving it slowly along each digit as though he'd never before touched another hand. Such a simple gesture and yet her heart increased its beat.

Hand-in-hand they walked to the shore. With the sun hiding behind clouds, they were able to slip their shoes off and enjoy the sensation of the sand between their toes.

Conversing became less frequent. It seemed unnecessary. They just walked, taking in their surroundings and the joy of being together.

He cleared his throat and broke the silence. "Why did you never marry?"

Though she'd expected the question eventually, it wasn't an easy one to answer. "I might ask the same of you."

"I asked first," he said, grinning.

"I guess that's fair." She pondered her answer, and being that she always said what was on her mind, made it simple. "No man ever turned my head." Saying this had been easier than revealing the whole truth of the matter. No man ever turned her head because she'd been determined not to let them. If she stayed away from men, she could never be hurt by them like her mama had been.

"And what 'bout you?" she asked. "Someone so strong and handsome? I reckon the women in Mobile have been fallin' at your feet."

He laughed and looked down at the sand. His cheeks turned a dark shade of red. The man *had* to be aware of his good looks, so why be embarrassed?

He must not be used to someone so outspoken.

"No woman ever turned *my* head," he finally said, looking straight into her eyes. "Until now."

Her chest tightened and her throat became as dry as a brick. How could she respond?

Feeling emotions unknown to her scared her beyond words. So she did what was safe. "Must be my new dress!" Quick wit had always been one of her greatest talents and a favorite means of escaping difficult conversation. "I made it myself. I'm quite handy with a needle."

He grinned and shook his head. "Well then, we have something in common." He laughed. "Yes, that must be it. The dress."

She playfully tilted her head. "Glad you like it."

"Come to think of it, Claire, I've noticed you've worn a different dress every time I've seen you. That's very unusual for women in these parts. Most have one dress for their day-to-day living and a special Sunday church dress."

"You noticed?" Now he'd impressed her more than she ever thought possible. "I *am* the town seamstress. Most women can sew, but I've made it my profession. It's how I make a livin'. Whenever someone needs sumthin' sewn for a special occasion, they come to me. Folks say I'm gifted with the needle. I'm able to do tiny, even stitches. Sometimes I do simple mendin' work, but I especially like doin' the fine things."

"Ever consider taking some of your things to Mobile? The mercantile would surely take an interest in your dresses."

"Me? In the city? No." The thought made her fidget and she tugged at the fabric of her dress. "Sides, those women wear more layers than we do here. Never could quite understand that. Especially in this heat." She fanned her skirt. "Don't they get their fine things from overseas?"

"Some of it. But the European clothes are very expensive. Your dresses would be more affordable, I'm sure. You'd do quite well."

She considered what he said, but more than anything, she was thankful the subject had changed. Things were becoming a bit too serious. She wasn't ready for the direction their conversation had been leading.

The clouds became heavier and gray. Somehow, the birds knew when the time had come to take shelter and stopped flying overhead.

Claire knew it, too. "We'd best be gettin' back home. Looks like a storm's brewin'."

He squeezed her hand and looked into her eyes. "I hate we have to shorten our time together."

She gulped and nodded.

They walked quickly back to her home, fearing they'd get caught in the rain. Gulf storms were not to be taken lightly. They could come with a rage out of nowhere, beat down trees, tear the roofs off houses, and the worst storms of all could take a life.

"I've been meanin' to ask you," she said. "Where is it exactly you've been keepin' your horse an buggy?"

"Just up the road." He motioned northward. "There's a burned out old farm house there with a fence still standing. I took advantage of the fenced yard. It seemed the perfect place and no one around to mind at all."

"That would be the old Morrison place. There are still reminders of the war wherever you look. They moved to Birmin'ham after they got burned out here. Too many horrible memories and no money to rebuild. I was blessed my house was spared. " She became quiet, recalling her own terrible memories of the war. "You'd best go tend to that horse. You'll need to make sure it has shelter."

"Will you be all right?"

"This isn't my first storm and this old house is strong. Withstood a hurricane or two." She raised her head with confidence. "I'll be just fine. Now go . . ."

"But—"

She placed her hand on his arm. "I'll be all right."

He hesitated before walking away. When he turned back to look at her, she could have sworn she saw regret in his eyes.

He didn't wanna go . . .

CHAPTER 5

The rains came down in torrents. Not in simple drops, but more like solid sheets of water cascading from the sky. It blew sideways and sometimes even appeared to flow upward from the ground, blowing in every direction.

An extremely dangerous storm.

Claire stared out her window as the rain pelted against it. Thunder rumbled far off. No doubt it would get much worse.

Why'd I tell him to leave, knowin' how bad this storm would be?

Andrew had nowhere to go. She had to go after him. Running out into the rain, her dress became instantly soaked and clung to her skin.

Luckily the Morrison place wasn't far. In no time, she spotted Andrew in the distance—reins in hand—trying to lead his chestnut horse to a lean-to by the old farm house.

"Andrew!" she yelled as she ran. "Bring your horse! You can't stay here!"

He, too, was soaked to the skin. "Claire? What are you doing here?"

She stopped in front of him, out of breath, soaked, and covered in mud. "Come with me."

"I'll come, but only to take you back."

He mounted his horse and pulled her up behind him. She held on tightly as the rain continued to beat down, pummeling them like tiny pebbles. At least it didn't take long to reach her home.

He let her down rapidly, but gently. "Go on now. Get back inside. It's not safe out here."

"Don't think I'm lettin' *you* stay out here. That old lean-to won't do."

"Claire . . ." Rain trickled down his face from his hair. "I can't go in your home. It wouldn't be proper."

"Proper?" She frowned at him and shook her head with fisted hands on her hips. They had no time to argue about rules of proper behavior. "Take your horse 'round back. There's a small barn. Then get yourself in here as quickly as you can."

"But Claire—"

"Don't argue!" She stomped her foot. "You'd best get your Yankee tail in here before the storm blows you back to Mobile!"

* * *

Andrew sighed. She was right, but what would he do? Knowing what was proper, and caring about how he came across to her, he didn't want to make a mistake.

He spoke calmly to the mare and led her to the barn. The winds gusted. "There now, Sam. You'll be all right." He stroked her mane, patted her on the nose, then pulled the barn door closed.

Hurrying back to the house, his heart thumped. All those years in school, he hadn't had time for women. And now, right when he needed her, Claire had come into his life. She acted nothing like the women in Mobile who wanted to parade him around on their arms and show him off to their friends. She lived simply. Comfortably. Most important, she was comfortable with herself and who she was.

And she makes me laugh.

He needed to laugh.

His father had been wrong about this place and the people here, and he couldn't be happier that he'd come. He took a deep breath and knocked on her door. When she opened it, he couldn't help but stare.

He gulped. Unable to move.

"Land sakes!" she exclaimed. "Why are you knockin'?" She yanked him inside and shut the door.

The storm may have been raging outside, but he always tried to be a gentleman.

"I put Sam in the barn," he said, making every effort to avert his eyes.

"Sam? I thought your horse was a mare?" Her eyebrows knit in confusion.

"She is. It's actually *Samantha,* but that sounds much too formal for a horse." He grinned uncomfortably, and couldn't even *force* himself to move from the spot she'd pulled him to.

"I've got a rabbit stew simmerin' on the stove. I'm sure you must be hungry." She motioned for him to enter.

Though he kept willing his eyes to wander about the room, they were drawn to her like magnets. Her rain-soaked dress clung to her body, allowing him to see every curve of her form: well-endowed, with a slender waist and perfectly rounded hips.

Yes, he hungered. For more than food. He dare *not* move.

"Andrew . . ." She glanced downward, then jerked her head up, wide-eyed. Instantly her cheeks flushed. "I'd best get out of these wet things. If you'll excuse me. Please *try* to make yourself at home."

She bustled out of the room and went to her bedroom, closing the door behind her.

Thank God.

He bent over and placed his hands on his knees, steadying himself. Then he sucked in a large amount of air and let it out slowly. He had to take control of himself. Being a doctor, he'd seen the bare flesh of a woman, but that was his work. Nothing could be more different. Claire was beautiful in every sense of the word. Being a man, he couldn't help noticing.

Why did it have to storm?

It was late afternoon, and the storm's intensity increased. The winds whistled through small cracks in the woodwork and the rain beat down hard on the roof.

Once Claire left the room, he managed to move from his spot on the floor and shook out his shoulders, finally able to relax.

The smell of the stew filled the air and he realized he *was* hungry. It smelled delicious.

Wandering mindlessly, he gazed at her simple furnishings; a table, two chairs, a wood stove, and a hand-braided rug on the wood floor that lay in front of a stone fireplace. Her home was clean and neat and he felt like he belonged.

When she came out of the bedroom, newly dressed, his heart once again increased its pace. Her hair was down and she was drying it with a towel. It was long, falling nearly to her waist. She'd almost always had it hidden under a sunbonnet. He much preferred it down.

His eyes moved to her feet, which were bare. *Comfortable.*

"Now that's better," she said, smiling at him. "I wish I had some men's things for you. I'm quite sure you wouldn't take much to a dress."

"Not my style. But I do appreciate the offer." He grinned, relaxed by her ease, finding her once again to be playful.

She's so beautiful.

She wiggled her toes. "Might as well get out a *your* wet shoes and socks. And you really should take that wet shirt off. I'd hate to see a doctor get sick. I'll get you a dry towel."

It felt wonderful to slip out of his footwear. And since she'd given permission for the removal of his shirt, he didn't hesitate taking it off. It had been uncomfortable.

"Here you are, Andrew." She extended a towel, then quickly turned her head. Her cheeks had again filled with a brilliant shade of rose red.

"Thank you." He welcomed the towel and patted himself dry, then left it draped over his shoulders.

"Least half of you is taken care of," she said with a coy smile.

She'd rapidly overcome her shyness. Her eyes were now affixed to his bare chest. So he cocked his head and motioned to his trousers, then questioned her with his eyes.

"The rest of you will hafta air dry," she said, clearing her throat.

Probably wise.

She hastened to the stove and ladled out two bowls of stew. Then they sat at the table and ate, barely saying a word. Maybe she'd never shared a meal in her home with a man before.

Darkness set in earlier than usual. The storm had brought heavy clouds that blocked the light from the sun. Soon they'd be in total darkness.

Claire lit a small hurricane lamp on the table. The soft glow sent warmth throughout the house.

The storm hadn't let up, so leaving wouldn't be an option.

He sensed her nervousness. She scarcely talked. *Very unlike her.* Yet they'd been forced into an unforeseen situation. Though she'd invited him in, she, too, was well aware they were doing something highly improper.

After politely thanking her for the meal, he arose and walked to the fireplace. A photograph on the mantel caught his eye.

"She's lovely," he said as he nodded toward the picture. "Your mother?"

She moved to his side. "Yes, that's Mama. Taken just a few years before she died." As she touched the photo, a soft smile warmed her face. "She was very beautiful, but very sad." She looked down, no longer smiling. "She was a good mama though. Couldn't have asked for better."

He put his hand on her shoulder, then brushed her hair back from her face. "You favor her."

She closed her eyes to his touch, but then turned her head and looked away.

She crossed the room and returned to the table. "You've spoken so much of your daddy. I don't recall you ever mentionin' *your* mama."

He sat, lowered his head, then raised it slowly.

It's time to tell her.

"My mother was Cherokee." He'd take his time and choose every word carefully. He needed to watch her reaction, fearing he'd displease her. "She wasn't raised by her people, but was taken in by a wealthy landowner and his wife who lived in Connecticut. My grandparents. She was raised properly, but always wanted to learn more about her people and find some way to help them. She was kind and very giving."

Claire tipped her head slightly to one side. "Go on."

He closed his eyes, visualizing the memory. "She had long black hair. She'd braid it and wrap it on top of her head. Most people treated her well—being married to my father—but there were always those whose prejudice stood in the way." He looked directly at her now. "They couldn't see her for who she was. I think that's what drew me to the Negroes here. She taught me how to see through color."

Claire's eyes showed compassion and encouraged him to continue.

"She became pregnant when I was almost ten years old. Father said it was a miracle—she'd lost other babies—but he was concerned because she was on in years. Still, she was a strong woman and her pregnancy was without complication and full term. When her time came, Father brought a midwife in. I can still remember sitting outside Mother's room with my father waiting to hear the sound of a baby's cry. But it never came."

He stopped. Though harder than he thought it would be, he had to tell her everything. Claire hadn't made a sound—listened so intently she barely passed breath. So he pressed on.

"My mother never cried out. There was too much silence. Father became nervous, and then the midwife came out of the room. There was horror on her face and blood on her hands. She fell to her knees and started crying, saying she was sorry. Then she told us my mother was dead—the child, too. A little girl. My baby sister.

"The baby had been breech and the umbilical cord had wrapped around its neck. With every contraction and every push, my mother had slowly strangled the child. She was stillborn. The midwife pulled the dead child from my mother, then my mother began to hemorrhage. The bleeding couldn't be stopped and her life just slipped away . . ."

Tears trickled down Claire's cheeks. She'd remained still and quiet, giving him all the time he needed. Not saying a single word.

"Father got up and went into her room. He told me to stay where I was. I wanted to see my mother, but he wouldn't let me go in. I don't think he shed a tear—at least, I never saw it. As for me, I couldn't *stop* crying. I sat there watching that bawling midwife, wondering why she couldn't have done something. Father finally came out of her room, and all he said was, *it seems I was never meant to raise a daughter,* and left to arrange a mortician. When he returned home, he told me to stop crying and that I would have to grow up now. He didn't hold me or offer *any* comfort. My mother had been the affectionate one. And she was gone.

"They were buried in the same casket. My little sister was placed in my mother's arms so she could hold her for eternity. That day, I decided to become a doctor. It was the only way I could feel like I was doing something for her. I may have been too young to make such a decision, but that day I was forced to become a man."

Tears streamed down Claire's face. "Oh, Andrew, if your mama could see you now—and all the good things you do for those poor folk—she'd be so proud of you."

"No, Claire. You don't understand." He bent his head. "I failed. I couldn't save her!"

"You were just a boy. There was nothin' you could a done." She reached her hand out to him, but he couldn't take it. Not until he told her the rest.

"I'm not talking about my mother!"

Her eyes widened from his outburst, but until she understood what he'd done, he couldn't make amends. She leaned back in her chair, putting more distance between them. "I'm listenin'."

With the towel she'd given him, he dabbed at the sweat that had formed on his face. "Six weeks ago I was awakened by the sound of someone pounding on my door. I opened it to find a small Negro boy standing there. He looked about eight years old. He begged me to come and help his mama. So I grabbed my bag and a lantern, swung the boy atop my horse and headed into the night. He guided me to a small shanty about two miles down the road. When he pushed the door open, I saw five pairs of eyes staring at me. His brothers and sisters. They'd never been so close to a white man.

"He took me by the hand and led me into another room. His father stood over the bed where his mother lay. She was in labor and crying out in pain. There was fear in her eyes. When she saw me all she said was, *help me.* Her husband told me she'd been pushing for hours, and that she'd never had trouble like this before. Then I saw the baby. He was breech. I told her to stop pushing, so I could try to turn him, but she'd already pushed the life right out of him." He couldn't help himself and began to sob. "The umbilical cord was wrapped around his neck like a noose. All I could do was pull him from her—*lifeless*—and then, just like my mother, the bleeding started. I couldn't save her! I couldn't save her . . ."

He'd seen death before and always knew his limitations as a doctor, but this death brought back the memories of his boyhood and the night his life had been altered forever.

His tears flowed uncontrollably, and as he placed his head in his hands, his entire body shook.

Claire gently raised his head and pulled him to her. He wrapped his arms around her and continued to cry.

Her fingers threaded through his hair, raking it with tender strokes, while cradling his head against her. "Hush now. Shh . . . Andrew, it's all right. It wasn't your fault."

He cried even harder, finally able to grieve for his mother.

She continued to speak soft reassuring words, all the while touching his hair and caressing his face. Bending slightly, she brushed kisses over the top of his head. "It's not your fault," she said over and over again between each soft kiss.

He'd bared his soul to her. Never before had he exposed himself so openly to a woman, but she'd helped him release his innermost feelings. It was the first time he'd talked about the night his mother died. Somehow he knew he could open his heart to Claire and she'd bring him comfort. A weight had been lifted and now he could start moving on with his life.

In his calm, he became fully aware of her holding him. Caught up in his grief, he'd felt nothing but pain. But now that the grief was passing, he felt *her*. Her fingers in his hair. The warmth of her breasts cradling his head. And the sound of her heart beating beneath.

His hands pressed into her back. He brought them to life and caressed her.

Slowly, he turned his head toward her.

Her low-cut dress exposed her bare neckline. Unable to help himself he kissed her flesh, lightly brushing his lips across her skin. Her body trembled.

* * *

Claire could scarcely breathe, wondering how she'd gotten into this situation. Never before had she been alone with a man, and yet here she was with one she'd only known a short while. But he'd been hurting. She'd only wanted to take away his pain.

He'd already become a part of her, and she was becoming alive in a way she'd never been before.

He worked his way to his feet, his lips trailing kisses along her skin as he rose. Blood pumped rapidly through her veins causing her to feel faint, so she reached her arms around him to steady herself.

His body felt strong and firm, his breath warm. She glided her fingertips down his naked back, but then something her mama told her came rushing at her stronger than the winds whipping against the house.

Once you start kissin' a man, you can never go back to just holdin' hands.

Her words finally made sense.

Mama, if you're lookin' down on me now, please close your eyes.

She had no doubt what she wanted. No, not *wanted.* *Needed.* All her life, she'd thought she didn't need a man, but now—the ache her body had for him felt stronger than any pang of hunger or thirst.

"Claire," Andrew whispered and backed away from her. "I'm so sorry—"

"No." She placed her fingers against his lips. "Please don't say it. I want this, too."

A warm smile covered his face as he pulled her closely to him. With a single finger, he traced her mouth, then took her face in his hands. His lips covered hers in a hungering kiss and she welcomed it. She kissed him back with even more fervor. A whimper escaped her. The simple taste of him made her yearn for more.

With an effortless scoop of his arms, he bent down and lifted her off the floor and carried her to the bedroom. Nothing they were doing now made sense, but she didn't care. Her rapidly beating heart led the way. Nothing her mind *or* her mama said mattered anymore.

Thunder rumbled and lightning flashed as the rain continued pounding against her little house. A soft glow flickered from the hurricane lamp in the other room, giving them a faint soft light.

The bedroom curtains were open and as the lightning flashed she could see him. This tall, beautiful man who'd literally swept her off her feet. He set her down gently beside the bed.

The storm outside paled in comparison to the one that raged inside her.

With eyes unmoving from hers, Andrew reached around and untied the bow at the back of her dress. His black pupils burned with hunger and she couldn't deny her own. Drawn to his smooth dark skin, she bent her head and brushed her lips across his neck and chest.

Any moment now, her heart would surely burst. His body beckoned her. *How will it feel pressed to mine?*

His hands moved to the buttons at the front of her dress. She helped him, quivering as their fingers passed over each other. The skilled strong hands of a doctor pushed the dress down over her shoulders and to the floor.

Lightning flashed again, allowing him to see her fully. She felt no shame as she lifted her chemise over her head, then slipped off her undergarments and lay down on the bed. He watched her every move.

He stood over her like something from a dream. How could he be real? Her throat had become dry and her heart couldn't rest. She knew very well what would happen. She wouldn't stop him now, not when she wanted him so badly.

As he removed his trousers and under drawers, lightning flashed again, and she witnessed his full silhouette. Suddenly realizing that when a boy becomes a man *every* part of him grows, she almost gasped, but held it in, not wanting to do anything to spoil the moment.

Nothin' like Rebecca Gentry's baby boy.

She knew so little about men. She just prayed he hadn't seen her body tremble.

He knelt between her legs, then reached out and ran his fingers lightly over her skin, as though memorizing every inch of her body. Then he lowered himself slowly onto her.

His touch increased her desire. Desire she never knew she possessed. She couldn't remove her eyes from his face. He looked almost too perfect.

He caressed her cheek. "I've waited for you all my life. There's nothing to be afraid of. I won't hurt you, Claire." His body pressed against hers. "I'll *never* hurt you . . ." He placed a feather-soft kiss on one eyelid, and then the other, then kissed her lips with tenderness, causing her to melt into the bedding. She grasped his back; his words gave her all the reassurance she needed. And as their bodies joined together, she freed her passion.

* * *

Andrew's heart pounded.

I'm making love to her.

Claire *was* the woman he'd waited for. Every word he'd whispered rang true and from the depths of his heart. In a matter of days, he'd fallen hard. And though he couldn't imagine wanting a woman more, this had to be *real* love, not fleeting desire.

Knowing it to be her first time, he hoped he hadn't caused her pain. He, too, had no experience, but understood and listened to her body. Taking his time, he moved into her as if she was a fragile flower whose petals he didn't want to tear.

Making love hadn't been his intent, but he'd been drawn to her by something completely unknown. And now he was hers forever.

Though he could scarcely see her features as he moved above her, the sounds she made gave him every indication he was pleasing her. But when the storm passed would she regret what they'd done?

He cast aside his worries and focused solely on the moment. Never had he experienced this kind of pleasure. No longer able to hold back, he allowed his release. Her body quivered beneath him. Letting out a low moan, he clasped her tightly to himself, then buried his face in her hair and breathed deeply. The scent of honey filled his nostrils.

Sweet, sweet, Claire.

Her hands moved over his flesh, causing him to shiver and want more. Though they'd paused for a moment, no doubt they'd start again.

Time no longer mattered and sleep had become unnecessary.

Chapter 6

The sun rose and poured light through the bedroom window. The storm had passed.

It was well past ten o'clock when Claire finally opened her eyes to the brightness. The memories of the night began to sift through her mind. They'd made love well into the early morning hours, consumed in each other.

Remembering his warm breath on her skin and his soft lips as they glided over her body, she trembled. There'd only been a brief moment of discomfort, but it wasn't what she'd call *pain*. The emotions she'd felt pushed all of that aside and everything had turned to pleasure.

Now she understood Lucy Beecham.

He'd moved with skill as if he already knew her body. He'd assured her she was his first, and she believed him, attributing his ability to being a doctor and very much familiar with the anatomy of a woman.

Still sleeping, he'd curled up against her. His arm draped over her body and his hand cupped her breast. Understanding his exhaustion, she didn't want to wake him.

With great care, she moved his arm and slipped out of bed. Grabbing her robe and tying it around her, she headed to the door. She wasn't wearing bed clothes and still had *some* modesty.

The moment she opened the door, the sun nearly blinded her. If it hadn't been for the remnants of what the storm had left behind, the bright light could have made her believe there'd never been one. The night's winds had left their mark. Limbs from trees had been scattered across her yard and into her garden. The house had held up—as it always had—though the rocking chairs on the porch had been blown over and pushed some distance away.

"I hope the outhouse is still there," she muttered as she made her way to it. Much to her relief, it had survived undamaged.

Returning to the house, she stopped for water. She wanted to wash and assumed Andrew would as well.

The sound of a horse and buggy approaching stopped her dead in her tracks. "Merciful heavens!" Who'd be coming to call on her?

She prayed Andrew wouldn't wake up and come out of the house to relieve himself.

Seeing Reverend Brown, her heart pumped so hard she lost her breath. What would he think of her when he saw her like this? It was late morning, she wasn't dressed, her hair flew freely—down and tousled—and she looked as though she'd been caught up in the middle of the wind storm.

Would he recognize her lost virtue?

Heat rose in her cheeks.

Just be yourself.

"Mornin' Claire," he said, tipping his hat. Trepidation lay behind his eyes.

He's as uncomfortable as I am.

She decided to call attention to herself first, rather than make him wonder why she appeared this way. "Good mornin', Brother Brown. I'm a bit embarrassed you came by to find me in such a state. The storm kept me up half the night. I couldn't even sleep until the lightnin' stopped. By then it was nearly three in the mornin'."

Lying to a preacher was *not* what her mama had taught her to do.

"Ah . . ." His eyebrows rose. "That's why I stopped by. I got out as early as I could to check on all my parishioners. Make sure no one had been damaged by the storm."

"All's well here, Reverend! 'Cept for a few misplaced tree branches and over-turned rockers. I reckon I can handle those."

"Fine then. I'll be on my way. I have more folks to check on. I'll let you get back to what you were doin'."

If you knew, you wouldn't be so eager.

She gave him one of her best smiles.

"See you at Sunday services!" he said. He tipped his hat and went on his way.

She hastened into the house with the pail of water and slammed the door behind her.

Guilt consumed her.

In a daze, she set down the pail.

Andrew cleared his throat and brought her out of her self-induced fog. "Oh, Andrew! Can you believe it? The preacher just happens to come by the day after I've committed the greatest sin in all my life!"

He moved to her, wrapped his arms around her, and kissed her on the neck. "Good morning to you, too, Claire."

The concern in his eyes melted her heart. The feel of his arms reassured and calmed her. "I'm sorry, Andrew. Good mornin'." Unlike their heated kisses the previous night, she kissed him with tenderness.

"Thank you." He moved toward the door.

"Where are you goin'?" She stepped in front of him and flattened her arms against it.

"To use the outhouse."

"You sure you need to right now?" She grabbed his arm and held him tight.

"Quite sure."

"All right then." She jerked the door open. Holding him back behind her, she scanned the yard, then glanced up the road.

He tapped her on the shoulder. "May I go out now?"

"Fine. Just hurry back."

Shaking his head, he walked out the door.

With her luck, someone else would come to check on her. Someone like Beth.

Her heart thumped as she paced the floor.

Why's he takin' so long?

Her nerves brought out one of her worst habits. She began biting her nails.

Finally, he came back inside.

"What took you so long?" She moved passed him, opened the door again and gazed in both directions. Just to be sure. Closing the door, she let out a relieved sigh.

"I looked in on Sam to make sure she was all right." He crossed to the wash basin and washed his hands and face. "Are *you* all right, Claire?"

No. I'm anythin' but.

She stared at him. He was everything she'd ever thought a man should be.

"Do you love me?" she whispered.

In all the time they'd made love, he'd never once said the words. She needed to hear them now.

"Oh, Claire." He took her hand, raised it to his lips, and kissed it. "I started loving you the first time I saw you on the beach."

"How? Lovin' someone doesn't happen so easy." He hadn't convinced her.

"With you, it was the easiest thing I've ever done. You warmed my heart with your wit and your manner." With one finger he encircled her face, all the while looking into her eyes. "And you're by far the most beautiful woman I've ever seen. Inside and out. Yes, Claire. I love you."

"You're not just sayin' that to make me feel better 'bout what we've done, are you?" Guilt continued to gnaw away at her.

"I wouldn't have made love to you if I didn't love you. I waited a long time to find the right woman to share my life." His eyes didn't waver. "I know we should've waited, but we can't change that now. Can you forgive me?"

His eyes penetrated her soul. "Our circumstances were unusual to say the least. But if you'll recall, I didn't try to stop you. There's nothin' to forgive. I happen to love you, too." Standing on her tiptoes, she kissed his lips, prompting him to pull her close.

A silent stare sparked their desire and they returned to her room and once again made love. With no darkness to hide in, they saw each other completely. Everything was revealed in the daylight.

Claire forgot about Reverend Brown, and Andrew's profession of love set aside her guilt.

* * *

Andrew sat at the table and watched Claire make breakfast, though it was actually time for dinner.

She fried bacon, then made biscuits and gravy. "This'll sweeten things up a bit," she said and placed a small bowl of preserves in front of him.

He took her hand and kissed it.

Having her upset over Reverend Brown's visit caused his heart to ache. He certainly didn't want to damage her reputation. And more than anything, he didn't want her to regret what they'd done.

"I could get used to your cooking," he said, taking another bite of a biscuit.

"Just good ol' country cookin' like my mama taught me." Her smile broadened.

He set down his fork. "Claire, I'm just going to come right out and say this because I've never been surer of anything."

She held a piece of bacon in midair. "You sound serious."

"I am. I want you to go with me to Mobile."

"What?" She gaped at him.

"My house is no mansion, but it's comfortable and large enough for both of us." He paused and closed his eyes, praying she'd say *yes*, then raised his head to look at her. "I want you to be my wife."

She dropped the bacon. "You wanna marry me?"

"Of course I do." *How could she have any doubt?* "I can't imagine being without you. Not now. Not ever."

"Oh, Andrew!" She jumped to her feet, then wrapped her arms around him and held him tight. "Yes, yes! I may be crazed to up an leave the only home I've known." She stopped and swallowed so hard he could hear it. "But yes, I'll marry you."

He lovingly stroked her back, never wanting to let go of her. "You've changed my life. My father was wrong about this place. I've not been so happy in a *very* long time."

"I can say the same, Andrew Fletcher." In a display of excitement, she kissed him all over his face.

He laughed aloud, relieved she felt the same.

With an abrupt halt, she stared at him. "How are we gonna do this?" She released him and paced. "I'll need to let someone know I'm leavin'. They'd be worried if I didn't show up for Sunday services."

She had a very good point. His mind reeled. "Why don't you take Sam into town? Tell a friend that you need some time away, or that you're going to visit family. You *do* have other family near here, don't you?"

"Yes, I do. An aunt up north. She lives 'bout ten miles west of Mobile."

"That's perfect then. I'm sure they'll believe you. Then, after we're married, you can come back and tell them you met me while you were gone. I know they'll be happy for you."

"It'll make for great town gossip. *The old spinster finally nets her a man.* But not all a them will be happy. Remember, you *are* a Yankee." She let out a soft, timid laugh. "But, I reckon that'll work. I best not take Sam though. I could never explain how I got a horse."

"You'd better get going then. It'll take us at least four hours to get to Mobile. The sooner we leave, the better chance we'll have of getting there before dark."

* * *

Claire stopped pacing, but her mind kept on spinning. Had she truly agreed to Andrew's proposal?

What was I thinkin'? I've only known him a few days.

But having lost her virtue to him, she needed to do it regardless. Being completely smitten certainly didn't hurt.

Crossing to him, she gazed into his eyes. "You'd best be here when I get back." His reassuring smile allowed her heart and mind to rest.

So she walked out the door.

She set out on the road she'd traveled many times. The few miles gave her the chance to rehearse the story she'd tell Beth. She'd never want to hurt her friend any further. Knowing that eventually she'd make everything right pushed her forward.

When she reached the boarding house, Mrs. Sandborn stood on the front porch sweeping away some of the leaves and branches the storm had obviously left behind.

"Hey, Mrs. Sandborn!" Claire hollered and waved as she approached.

"Why, Miss Claire! It's so good to see you here." The old woman beamed, set aside her broom, and wiped her hands on her apron. "Miss Beth has been beside herself since Gerald left. Hasn't stopped cryin' for days. It'll be good for her to see a friend."

Some friend . . .

Guilt stabbed her in the heart.

"I'll get her for ya," Mrs. Sandborn said and bustled into the house.

Beth came out and greeted Claire with a strong hug. "I'm so glad you came by. I haven't been myself at all lately." Her eyes looked puffy and red.

"I really am sorry 'bout all that, Beth. I don't know what more I can say to help you feel better."

"Oh, I'll be all right. Eventually. It's just so hard."

"Beth." Claire took a deep breath. Time couldn't be wasted. "I need to go away for a spell. I wanna go an check on my Aunt Martha. Make sure she fared well in this storm."

"You're leavin'?" Beth's eyes began to well with tears.

"Not for good." How could she reassure her? "I promise I'll be back. Just not sure when. Depends on how much help Aunt Martha needs."

Beth let out a long, relieved sigh.

It seemed her friend had believed her, but she had a little more to accomplish. "I was hopin' you could look in on my place for me. Sorta keep an eye on it while I'm gone. It would help me a great deal if you could feed my chickens. Maybe even stay there if you'd like?"

"Course I can." Beth's tears instantly disappeared. "Won't be able to get there 'til tomorrow though. There's still a lot a clean-up to do 'round here."

"That should be just fine. Thank you, Beth." Claire took her hands and gave them a loving squeeze. Things were falling into place better than she'd expected.

She turned to leave.

"Claire?" Beth stopped her. "How you gonna get there?"

Oh, fiddle!

Claire hadn't thought that part through. She'd be riding with Andrew in his buggy, but she couldn't tell Beth. Her mind raced.

Who will Beth never have the chance of seein' in the next few weeks?

And then it came to her. *Old man Jenkins.* He never went to church, kept to himself, and didn't live far from her. He only got out to go to Mobile for supplies. Best of all, Beth was afraid of him. She'd never approach him and question their ride together.

Perfect!

She prepared another lie. "Oh. I saw Mr. Jenkins out cleanin' up his yard. He was fixin' to go to Mobile for a few things. I asked if I could ride along. He said he didn't mind."

"Old man Jenkins?" Beth's eyes opened wide. "You sure you trust him?"

"Oh, Beth. The man's harmless." Lying kept getting easier. "I'd best be goin'. He won't wait all day."

"You be careful now." Beth warned her with a shake of her finger. "I'll see you when you get back. Don't worry 'bout a thing. I'll take good care a your place."

Claire smiled and headed for home.

She'd completed the deception.

CHAPTER 7

As Claire walked home, the anticipation of seeing Andrew again increased her normal pace. She floated on air.

So this is what love feels like.

Love, she'd discovered, was an addictive drug. She wanted more.

Before going into her home, she stopped by her mama's grave.

"Mama, I'm gonna marry me a doctor. I know. I can scarcely believe it myself. Yes, I know Mama, he's a Yankee, but he's the finest man I've ever known, regardless. You were wrong 'bout men, Mama. They aren't all bad." She kissed the tips of her fingers, then touched them to the simple headstone.

When she returned inside, she found Andrew seated comfortably on the sofa. He looked completely at ease in her home.

Her heart fluttered. He'd waited for her. Why had she ever doubted it?

"You're still here?" she asked with a giggle.

"That's what I love about you, Claire." He arose, lifted her in his arms, and spun her around. "I never know *what's* going to come out of your mouth."

"And you never will." She gave him a quick peck on the lips. "Someone's gotta keep you on your toes."

He set her down, but didn't release her. "I'll have you know, I've already bridled Sam. I went up the road and got my buggy while you were gone. You'd better pack your things. If we stay much longer, we may never get out of here today." He winked.

"Now, Andrew Fletcher," she scolded devilishly. "Mind your manners."

It didn't take her long to pack. She took a handful of dresses, underthings, a hairbrush, toothbrush, and her sewing basket. She'd eventually return, so anything else of importance could wait. Since Beth would be watching over her things, she felt comfortable leaving them.

"Nice buggy," she said as Andrew helped her in. It was a one-seater, with a canopy designed to keep the rain off their heads. It appeared to be fairly new and undamaged by the storm.

"Even nicer with someone to share it." He grabbed the reins and gave her the smile she'd grown to love as part of the man she'd soon marry.

As he snapped the reins, she scooted her body next to his and sighed. She couldn't remember a time when she'd been this happy.

Mama was wrong.

The day couldn't be more glorious. The storm had cooled the air and the rain made everything smell fresh. She wouldn't have cared if it still beat down on them. Nothing could ruin this moment in time.

They saw traces of the storm as they went. Mostly branches in disarray and some trees that had been uprooted.

A four-hour ride allowed plenty of time for conversation. With so much left for them to learn about one another, she wasted no time asking questions. Often she'd simply stare at him, unable to grasp that in less than a week, she'd met a stranger, fallen in love, and now was on her way to his home to become his wife.

"I'm curious, Andrew," she said. "That first day we met you referred to me as bein' *eloquent*. What made you say that?"

"You impressed me." He kept his eyes forward, but even his profile reflected his warm smile. "You're quick-witted and smart, and you were one of the first women I met recently who didn't use the word, *ain't*."

"Well ain't I special?" She laughed.

"There. Now you've spoiled it all. I can never think highly of you again." He laughed right along with her.

"Truth be told," she said. "You can thank Eva Carpenter-*Thomas* for the lack of that word in my vocabulary. That was the one thing she wouldn't let us say. Well, that and the *foul* words. Some a the other students didn't care and still used those words. But I was determined not to." She paused, thinking of Beth, and hoped she'd be all right. "I remember goin' home and tellin' my mama that Miss Carpenter said ain't wasn't in the dictionary. Mama argued with me and swore it was. So, I asked her how it was defined, to which she replied, *it means, aren't not*."

They both laughed again, but then she instantly sobered. "I truly do miss her," she whispered.

"I miss my mother, too." Andrew's voice had also softened, and for a short time neither said a word.

* * *

When they arrived at Andrew's home, it had already become dark. Claire sighed, disappointed. She couldn't see the surroundings of her new home-to-be.

No matter. I'll see it tomorrow.

She waited at the entrance of the stable while he un-hitched Sam, then they walked a short distance to the house. It had a simple stoop rather than a large porch—something she'd suggest they remedy.

He opened the door, but stopped her short of going in.

"What's wrong?" she asked. "Didn't you clean up 'fore you left?"

"Maybe not as neatly as you would have, but I *do* know how to tidy up."

"Then, why'd you stop me?"

He lifted her into his arms and carried her through the doorway.

She giggled. "We aren't married yet, Andrew. No need to carry me over the threshold."

"Just practicing." He leaned down and kissed her, cradling her body against his, then walked with ease through the dark house and went directly to the bedroom.

"Now wait just one minute! Don't I at least get a tour of the house?"

"It's dark, Claire. I think that can wait until morning."

"Well, all right then." She wasn't about to refuse him.

He laid her down against the pillows on a bed she found to her liking. Breathing in, his masculine scent surrounded her.

I'm in a man's bed.

Her heart thumped. "Reckon I should take my dress off?"

"I'll help with that." Even in the darkness, she sensed he'd been grinning.

"Andrew Fletcher, what am I gonna do with you?"

"Just keep me on my toes, Claire." His hands easily worked her buttons.

She intended to do just that.

And much more.

* * *

Andrew's eyes popped wide at the sound of the front door opening.

"Hey, Doc! Shore glad you're back. I seen your horse in the barn. I done all you asked while you was gone. Chopped the wood, fed the chickens, and took the eggs to the folks what needed 'em."

Clay.

Clay Tarver, a thirteen-year-old Negro boy who he'd charged with looking after things while he was away. Clay had a desire for learning, so in exchange for the work—along with a small amount of money—Andrew was teaching him to read. Clay had set his sights on becoming a doctor just like *Doc Fletcher.*

Logs thumped onto the floor in the other room.

Andrew lay on the side of the bed closest to the door, and upon hearing Clay speak, he sat up on the edge, yawned and stretched.

Turning to look at Claire, he shook his head at her modesty, but found it endearing. She'd obviously heard Clay and had pulled the covers up over her head. He understood. She was not yet his wife and shouldn't be sharing his bed.

Scolding himself for bedding her before putting a ring on her finger, he intended to make everything right as soon as possible.

Clay's footsteps neared the room, and Claire's body trembled, accompanied with a mouse-sized whimper.

Peeking into the room, Clay grinned. "Sorry if I waked ya, Doc."

The boy was exceptionally tall and skinny, with large ears that were accentuated by a thin face. But his best feature was his incredibly infectious smile. If circumstances had been different, Andrew would have loved to introduce him to Claire, but that wouldn't happen anytime soon.

"Good morning, Clay," Andrew said with deliberate calm. The boy needed to leave before he became aware of Claire's presence.

"Sure was a bad storm we had night for last," Clay rambled on. "Lawdy! Mama hates them storms. In her condition, Daddy don't like her gettin' all upset. Now that you're back, Daddy wants you to look in on her soon as possible. Think you can do that, Doc?"

"Yes, Clay. I'll look in on her today."

"That be right fine a you, Doc. Daddy's been uptight 'bout this baby comin' since what happened to Ms. Lewis." His eyes widened and he clasped his hand to his mouth. Slowly, he lowered it. "Not that anyone blames you, Doc. We's just glad you're back."

"It's good to be back, Clay." He knew the boy felt badly for bringing up Mrs. Lewis. "I'm doing much better now that I've had some rest."

"You look good! That sea air musta worked."

Clay's gaze shifted and his eyes widened. He'd spotted Claire's dress draped over the back of a chair in the corner of the room. His eyes opened even further when he noticed the bulge in the bed. He scratched his head. "Well then. Ummm . . . I'd best be goin'. I'll tell Daddy to look for ya."

"That will be fine, Clay." Andrew remained perfectly calm despite the boy's obvious revelation.

"Bye then, Doc." Clay walked toward the door and paused. "Ma'am," he added. Quickening his pace, he left, mumbling. "You're such a fool, Clay Tarver."

The moment the door shut, a loud groan arose from the mound under the blankets. Andrew chuckled at her discomfort.

She'd been lying on her side covered completely by the bedding. Once the door closed, she rolled over onto her back and flipped the blanket from her face. "Oh, my! I'm gonna die! I'm just gonna shrivel up and lay right here an die!"

"Now, Claire . . ." He still found the situation humorous. "You'll be fine." He couldn't help but laugh.

She sat up straight and put one hand on his shoulder. "I'm glad you find this amusin'. I've never been so embarrassed in all my days!"

"He couldn't even see you."

"That doesn't matter." She covered her face with her hands, shaking her head. "He knew you had a woman in your bed. I reckon that little colored boy will go back to his people and you and I will be all the gossip in Mobile!"

"He's not like that. If he tells anyone *anything,* he may tell his father that Doc Fletcher has finally become a man. Beyond that, no one will know. The Tarvers don't gossip."

"Must not be Baptists!" She flung herself back against the pillows.

"They're good people." He tried to soften her mood. "When you get to know Clay, you'll like him. He's a bit outspoken. Reminds me of someone else I know."

He began to dress, then turned and looked at her lying in the bed pouting. Her long hair fell tousled around her face on the pillow. Exceedingly tempted to undress and stay, he knew he had to leave.

"Where you goin'?" she asked, once again sitting up in the bed. She spoke softly, an indication she'd calmed.

The rumpled blanket covered most of her, but her bare shoulders were enough to nearly change his mind. "I have to go to work at the hospital. There are a lot of people I need to look in on. I've been gone nearly a week and there's no telling what may have come up while I was away."

"So this is what it's like bein' the wife of a doctor? You up an leavin' when I want you to stay?"

"I'll be back just as soon as I possibly can. But before I leave, I have something for you."

He went to a roll-top desk that sat in the corner of the main room of the house, opened a small drawer, and re-moved a tiny box.

Sitting down next to her on the edge of the bed, he opened it with care. It held a ring. As he removed it, he held it with his fingertips, studying it. Many wonderful memories filled his mind.

"This was my mother's," he said, holding it up so she could see it plainly. "My father gave it to me a number of years ago. He said he knew she'd have wanted me to have it, so I could give to someone *I* love."

"It's beautiful, Andrew." She sighed and held her hand to her heart.

"He wanted to give her one of those extravagant rings with large stones, but she wouldn't have it. All she asked for was a simple gold band. But since that wasn't good enough for Father, he had it etched with this tiny leaf pat-tern." He pointed to the fine detail of the ring. "I want you to wear this. Always."

Lifting her hand, he placed the ring on her wedding fin-ger. A perfect fit.

She started to cry. "Oh, Andrew, it's the most wonderful thing I've ever been given. I'll *never* take it off." She wrapped her arms around him and kissed him. "Forgive me for being such a child 'bout Clay. I know everythin' will be fine. I've got the ring on my finger. All we need now is the preacher."

"I've been thinking about that. Why don't we go to the justice of the peace and get the legalities taken care of, and then in a few weeks we can go back to your church and talk to the minister. I want you to have a *real* wedding."

"That sounds just fine." Holding her hand in front of her, she gazed at the ring. "Perfect."

"It's settled then. I'll look into the justice of the peace while I'm gone. You start making your guest list."

"That's easy. I'll put a notice on the church door and invite the whole town. More gifts that way."

"You're keeping me on my toes again, aren't you?" He drew her close and kissed her forehead. "Now, I really do have to go."

"I'll be waitin' right here for you." She patted the bed.

"I'm counting on it." The idea of leaving her made his entire body ache. He kissed her with a kiss he hoped would satisfy her until he returned home. The soft sigh she gave in response made him believe he'd done well. "There will be many more. I promise."

He brushed her hair back from her face. "I love you, Claire."

"I love you, too."

With a huge breath, he grabbed his doctor's bag and left.

CHAPTER 8

The door shut, leaving Claire alone.

Looking around the room, she noticed things she hadn't been aware of the night before. Light poured through the windows, revealing that she'd indeed come to the home of a bachelor. It needed a woman's touch.

The window dressings were just shy of being from a rag basket. And what little furniture he had, desperately needed a good dusting. His home didn't seem much larger than hers, though it had a peaked roof, which allowed a loft overhead for storage.

I'm gonna surprise Andrew and clean up the place before he gets back.

She jumped out of bed—suddenly feeling overly energetic—and quickly dressed.

First things first. A trip to the outhouse.

She'd become familiar with the *little* house already during the night. Andrew had to accompany her there, holding a lantern so she could find her way. She found humor in the situation. Having a man help her to an outhouse was something she never thought she'd experience in her lifetime.

She fanned her face. Another hot July morning. In the daylight, she took in the beauty of her surroundings. Her husband-to-be owned several acres of property.

She strolled by the chicken house—giggling at the large number of occupants—and then walked to the barn and swung open the massive door. The buggy was gone, so she assumed Sam must be as well. In fact, the six-stall barn was completely empty, but the back entrance had been left wide open.

Breathing in the aroma of fresh straw and manure, she followed the rays of sunlight into open air. A large field stretched out before her—fully fenced in—the perfect place for grazing. The field sloped downward toward a sparkling pond, backed by a row of white pine.

Much to her surprise, she saw Sam. Claire called out to her, and she lifted her head and trotted toward her.

"Good girl. I'm gonna be your new best friend." She patted the mare's nose and stroked her mane.

Further away, another mare stood with a colt beside her. The mare was solid black and the colt was also black, but had a white patch across its nose.

"I see you have friends already." Claire attempted to get the attention of the colt, yet it acted a bit skittish.

"I reckon Andrew must have taken your daddy to work today." Since the others weren't eager to make her acquaintance, she gave Sam another pat and headed back to the house.

Four horses . . .

She'd never imagined such a thing. Most people she knew could scarcely afford one.

She grabbed a broom and began to sweep. With her spirit light, her heart burst with joy. *I'm home.*

Holding the broom in front of her, she addressed it as though speaking to someone she'd just met for the first time. "Hello." She attempted to sound very proper and *northern* like Andrew. "I am Mrs. Andrew Fletcher. Mrs. *Claire* Fletcher."

She shook her head. Not quite right. "I am the wife of Dr. Andrew Fletcher and my name is Claire." She held her head very high. "I *do* like the sound a that."

What would Lucy Beecham think when she and Andrew walked down the aisle of the Baptist church?

Lucy won't expect me to have such a handsome man on my arm.

She felt giddy. Would it be wrong to show off her husband? Just a bit?

After sweeping, she scrubbed the floors, dusted, straightened up the bed, and beat the rugs. She found a pretty drinking glass that she used as a vase, picked some flowers, and put a lovely bouquet on the table.

"A little bit a color adds so much."

Standing back, she admired her accomplishments.

Uncertain of how much time had passed, her stomach rumbled. Andrew had a generous pantry fully stocked with assorted canned goods. Preserves, canned fruit, a variety of pickles—including pickled eggs—and miscellaneous vegetables. Most likely not *his* handiwork, but rather that of many a patient who used the goods to barter services.

All that remained to be tidied up was his desk. He had papers strewn about, which was no way for a doctor's desk to appear. Knowing it wouldn't take long to tend, she decided to eat after.

"Andrew, I'm gonna take such good care of you."

An envelope on the desk had a small photograph protruding from it. She pulled out the photo. *Hmm . . . it's rather old.* It had yellowed with age and the edges were worn. It pictured a man and woman on a settee. The woman held a small boy who looked to be about two years old.

Bringing the photo close to her face, she studied the woman and boy. The woman appeared to be Indian.

Andrew as a toddler.

She admired the adorable child who'd grown to be such a handsome man. His mama looked beautiful.

Andrew looks so much like her.

Then, she studied his daddy; the man whom Andrew had described so harshly. He was quite handsome, but rigid and stern without even a trace of a smile. His hands grasped his knees, and he sat completely upright with his chin held high. There was something familiar about him, but she couldn't quite place it. She could have met him someplace before, though highly unlikely.

Curious, she pulled the letter from the envelope. Though uneasy about looking at Andrew's mail, she unfolded the letter. The excellent handwriting indicated it had to have been written by someone well educated.

July 1, 1871

Andrew,

I have much to say to you. I regret that our last days together were filled with disagreement and anger. I understand that you and I will never fully agree with one another on issues of your career. I'm having difficulty accepting your choice in moving to Mobile. You have placed yourself in the midst of people who hate you for where you come from and who you are.

I am thankful that you took my advice regarding your name. As I tried to explain to you before you left, my name is despised by the people where you have chosen to live. The letter you sent me indicated your plans to travel southward to the coast. You will find people there who would harm you, so do not mention your real name.

I hope that in time you will come to understand why I never told your mother about my former wife. I had no intentions of ever telling you of my past, but upon learning of your plans for Alabama, I had no choice but to reveal it.

As I said previously, you are wise to use the name Fletcher. Wear your mother's name well. She would be proud of you.

I am enclosing the photograph of the two of you, which I know you've always cherished. I hope that the next time we meet, you will have forgiven me.

> *Your Father,*
> *John Martin*

What sort of man would sign a letter to his son in such a bold manner?

She gasped, then read his name again and let it sink in.

John Martin, a proud, well-to-do attorney who thought so highly of himself that he had to see his name written.

Even in a letter to his son. It had been scarce more than a legal document to him.

His son . . .

Claire couldn't breathe. All the life, energy, and joy she'd felt moments earlier, vanished. The letter dropped from her hand.

It all hit at once. No wonder the photograph looked familiar. She'd seen a picture of her daddy with her mama, taken before he'd left. She'd come across it in a box of her mama's things after she died.

He's the same man.

John Martin.

Her mama had never spoken the name, but Claire knew it well. She'd asked Aunt Martha about her daddy when she was a young girl. Aunt Martha had revealed it, but made her swear to never let on to her mama that she knew.

After receiving a certificate of divorce, her mama had taken back her maiden name, Montgomery, and went about raising her. Claire had only been a year old when he left, and she, too, had been washed clean of the Martin name.

After that, her mama never spoke his name again. Removing a name, however, didn't remove the painful memories. Her mama's heart had been broken and her spirit crushed. Losing a husband to someone else would destroy any woman.

Claire crumbled to the floor, trying to catch her breath. The room spun. Every bit of air was taken from her body.

I'm gonna be sick.

Her stomach churned and her throat became stone dry.

And then, the tears came.

"Oh, God, what have I done? What have *we* done?" Her body shook. She slapped her palms against the hard wood. "It can't be. No! God, no! It can't be true . . ." Tears streamed from her eyes. "He's my brother! Oh, God! Andrew's my brother!"

She lay down on the floor and buried her head in her arms, sobbing. "God'll never forgive us!" The floor became wet with her tears.

Her heart snapped in two. Unable to understand how she could intimately love someone whose blood she shared, she continued to cry.

Minutes ticked by as she lay there on the floor, wallowing in self-pity. Terrified, not knowing what to do. With great effort she lifted her head and looked around the house.

It's not mine. I don't belong here.

She couldn't stop trembling.

Taking every bit of strength remaining, she pushed herself up from the floor. "I've gotta get outta here."

She went to the desk and rummaged through his things until she found paper and pen. He needed to know she left of her own will, and that she didn't want him to follow her.

Tears dropped onto the paper as she wrote. Her hands shook and her head reeled.

She picked up her daddy's letter from the floor, tucked the photograph inside, and placed it back on the desk. Andrew could never know of their sin. She alone would reconcile with God and spare him the pain.

She stared at her hand—at the ring he'd placed on her finger, which she'd sworn only hours before never to remove. Pulling it slowly off, she kissed it and placed it on the note.

"Goodbye, Andrew . . ."

CHAPTER 9

Claire couldn't go back home. Not yet. But where would she go?

Though she'd told Andrew not to come after her, she knew him well enough to know he'd want answers and wouldn't abide by her wishes. Despite knowing his heart would be shattered, she had no choice in leaving. She felt too ashamed to face him.

If only I'd listened to Mama.

Since she'd told Beth she was going to check in on her Aunt Martha, she decided to go there.

Might as well turn one lie into truth.

It was ten miles to Martha's farm, but she didn't think twice about going. She needed time to think. Time to digest all the events of the past week.

She'd experienced new emotions for the first time. The hardest thing to understand—regardless of what she'd learned—she was still in love with Andrew. That fact alone made her even more disgusted with herself.

The tears finally ceased. Her numb body had dried out and there were no more tears to be shed. She walked along as though in a drunken stupor, taking the steps, but mindless of the things around her. Trudging along, step after step, each one getting her closer to Martha's.

It was mid-morning. She hadn't eaten, but had lost her appetite. The thought of food made her retch. Everything ached but she didn't care.

Nothing mattered.

* * *

When Andrew had walked out the front door that morning, more than anything he wanted to turn around, go back inside, and lose himself once again in Claire's arms. However, he knew he had obligations; the first being a visit to the Tarver's.

He decided to bridle Charger rather than Sam, knowing Sam needed rest. It had been a long week for her on the road.

Charger was a large white stallion he'd acquired through a barter with a patient he'd helped recover from a snake bite. He couldn't have been more pleased with the trade. Not only did he get an exceptional horse, but Charger had also sired a fine colt.

As he hopped into the buggy, he felt light as air. He'd never experienced such joy and sense of hope for his future. Until he met Claire, the world seemed like an ugly place full of despair and hardship. She filled his heart and completed him. Nothing could ruin today.

The Tarvers lived in a small one-room shanty. Elijah Tarver farmed cotton as well as vegetables. He'd grown up a slave, working his hands to the bone, and when given his freedom, worked even harder. He was a large man, nearly six-feet-five-inches tall and weighed almost two hundred seventy-five pounds. His arms were as big around as Andrew's thighs and his hands looked large enough to crush a man's head. But he was a gentle, peaceful man.

He had four children, Clay, age thirteen, Jenny, ten, Samuel, eight, and Joshua, five. His wife, Alicia, was expecting their fifth child—the reason for today's visit.

He'd first met them shortly after his arrival in Mobile. Clay had broken his arm by falling from a large oak tree behind their shanty. It had been a bad break. It took Andrew some time resetting the bone and helping to get the boy healed properly.

Elijah repaid him by offering his services at Andrew's home. He helped with minor repairs and cleared and cleaned some of his property. Once Clay's arm had healed, Clay asked if *he* could work for him, and Andrew happily accepted the offer. The experience had formed a bond between them.

The moment Andrew arrived, Clay greeted him, gaping. "Doc! You're here early."

"I told you I'd be by. Don't look so surprised." Andrew jumped from the buggy, grabbed his bag, and headed for the door.

Elijah opened it, motioning him to come in quickly. His brow wrinkled with worry. "She's over here," he said. He pulled aside a large quilt used as a curtain to separate their sleeping areas.

Alicia sat propped up in bed with sweat pouring from her brow.

"Good morning, Mrs. Tarver," Andrew said, approaching her. "What seems to be the trouble?"

"Doc, if you cain't look at me an tell with your own two eyes, then I'm a might worried 'bout your fitness as a doctor." She grabbed her belly. "I'm gonna have a baby!"

"Now, Mrs. Tarver. You've been through this before and you know you have five more weeks. It's the heat of the summer that's bothering you. I'm sure all you need is some cool water and one of your children to fan you." He gave her a generous smile and patted her hand.

She looked at him crossways. "Sumthin' wrong with you today, Doc? You're a might *too* happy."

Andrew spied Clay with the corner of his eye at the very moment he nudged his father in the ribs and smirked.

Elijah winked. "Leesha, the doc's gotten some good rest lately an feels like a new man. Ain't that right, Doc?"

Andrew's assumptions about what Clay most likely told his father were noticeably correct. "Yes, that's right. And I'd suggest you do the same, Mrs. Tarver. Since I'm here, I'll give you a thorough examination to ease your mind and know everything is going to be just fine."

"Doc, I'm tellin' you. This baby's fixin' to be born!" She shook her finger at him. "I'm havin' all kinds a pain."

"She's been feelin' sumthin' awful, Doc," Elijah said. "I ain't never seen her quite like this."

Not what Andrew wanted to hear. "Clay, get some water for your mother."

The boy wasted no time and did as requested. The other children stood close by, watching wide-eyed, so Andrew pulled the curtain, leaving him and Elijah alone with Alicia.

Andrew rested his hand on her arm. "I'm sure you're just experiencing some preliminary contractions. Not the real ones that will bring on your labor." *I pray I'm right.*

"Talk plain to me, Doc. I's just so 'fraid sumthin's wrong." She looked helplessly at Elijah.

He had no difficulty understanding what *wasn't* being said. Mrs. Lewis had been Alicia's friend, and her death scared her. "Well then, let me take a look." Andrew spoke with calm, and since he'd been visiting her once a month since she believed herself to be pregnant, she'd put her trust in him. But it mattered even more that she *still* trusted him.

After the examination, he determined his assumption to be correct. She'd not started to dilate.

"Mrs. Tarver," he said. "I feel confident you're *not* in labor. There's still some time before your baby's going to be ready to come into this world."

"What 'bout her pains?" Elijah asked, stroking her head.

"That's just the little one letting you know it's there," Andrew replied. The tenderness Elijah showed her warmed him. That's the kind of husband he'd be to Claire.

"It don't hafta do no remindin' far as I's concerned," Alicia said. "Much as it's pokin' an rollin', there ain't no doubt in my mind."

"I'm sure you'll have a healthy beautiful baby. Just like all your other children. You just need a little more time." His heart rested, certain she'd be all right. "I need to go on to the hospital now, but if you need me for any reason, send Clay. I'll either be at home or at City Hospital."

"Fine. I ain't goin' nowhere." Alicia rubbed the large bulge. Her voice had softened. "Thank you, Doc."

He patted her hand, then drew back the curtain.

Clay had been waiting with the water. He sat down beside her on the bed. "Sure glad I don't hafta have no babies."

Alicia rolled her eyes and shook her head, then took the water from him.

Clay looked up at Andrew. "I'll come by later to look after the horses, Doc. If that's a'right. I don't wanna bother you none."

"That'll be fine, Clay. You know you're no bother." Andrew smiled, knowing full well that Clay didn't want to risk walking in on him and Claire again.

Elijah laid a hand on Andrew's shoulder. "Don't know what we'd do without you, Doc. You done so much for us."

"You've done even more for me, Elijah. Your family means a lot to me." Andrew headed for the door.

Once outside, he lifted his face to the sunshine. Such a perfectly beautiful day.

He startled when Elijah tapped him on the shoulder. "Doc, you ain't gotta worry none 'bout me or the boy sayin' anythin' 'bout your woman. He only told me cuz he was happy for ya."

Andrew glanced downward, then looked Elijah square in the eye. "Thank you."

"One thing's for shore. Ain't nuttin' better in life than the lovin' of a good woman."

"I think I've found that out for myself." Andrew climbed into the buggy. The faster he got his work done, the sooner he could return to Claire. "Now, don't you hesitate to send Clay if you need me."

"I will, Doc." Elijah waved him on, and Andrew headed down the road to Mobile City Hospital.

CHAPTER 10

Andrew made his way along St. Anthony Street to the hospital. Knowing he was about to have a confrontation with Klaus Schultz, the hospital administrator, the joy he'd felt with Claire rapidly diminished.

He had no quarrel with the man, but having left his job the way he had, the stern German would likely terminate him. Still, Andrew didn't regret his decision to go. Not only had he been able to get his head together, he'd met the woman he'd share the rest of his life with.

Meeting Claire had been worth losing his job.

After securing his horse and buggy at the hospital livery, he walked the short distance to the main entrance and ascended the steps. The building was spectacular. Reminiscent of a Greek temple complete with tall colonnades, a peaked front, and a full two stories.

Mr. Schultz had been gracious enough to hire him straight out of medical school, but his generosity stopped there. The man followed strict guidelines. And Andrew had broken the rules.

He knocked on the door to his office.

"Come in." His stern voice made Andrew shudder.

With thoughts of Claire and a breath of courage, he opened the door and went in.

Mr. Schultz rose from his chair. He was medium in stature, had graying salt and pepper hair, and a thin mustache. He held himself upright with his chin tilted forward. "Dr. Fletcher, I see you've decided to join our staff once again."

"Sir." Andrew kept his calm. "I know my leave was unplanned, but I assure you it was medically necessary."

"Are you ill?"

"No. I was *becoming* ill. Worn down and in need of some rest. I'm sorry to have inconvenienced the hospital, but I assure you I won't be leaving again anytime soon."

"We've been exceedingly busy and the other doctors have had to pick up your slack. You've done well here, and we need you on our staff." He eyed him in a similar way he might *dissect* a human, taking him apart with an acute stare.

At least he said he needs me.

"Thank you, sir." Andrew stood, unmoving, with shoulders back, waiting for the rest.

"As long as you guarantee you will not leave again *unexpectedly*, I will accept your apology." He tugged at his shirt lapel as if making a point, then sat behind his desk.

"Thank you, sir. I won't disappoint you." Andrew turned to leave.

"There is another matter I must address with you, Dr. Fletcher," Mr. Schultz said, stopping him.

"Yes, sir?"

"There has been some concern regarding the care you've been giving over in Shanty Town." The man looked him directly in the eye. "I'm certain you know what I'm referring to."

"Yes, sir." *Don't challenge me on this issue.* "The care I give to the Negroes is something I do on my own time. It doesn't interfere with my work here."

"I find it hard to believe that you *have* spare time. The hospital can be extremely demanding. Nevertheless, take care that your work with those people does not bleed over into your work here. We don't want them coming to the hospital looking for you, or thinking we're going to take them in. The other patients would be furious if Negroes infiltrated our facility."

Andrew clenched his fists, but knowing where he was, forced himself to remain calm. He couldn't grasp this mentality. The war had ended, but the prejudice remained.

"Yes, sir," he said with strained courtesy. "I understand. I assure you *those people* will not come here."

"I'm counting on it." Mr. Schultz straightened the papers on his desk and spoke without emotion. "You may go now. You have a lot of work to do."

"Yes, sir." Andrew couldn't get out fast enough. He could barely restrain himself from slamming the door. Being reprimanded for his unplanned leave had been one thing, but to be questioned about his care of the Negroes was completely uncalled for. Things were changing in the country, but not fast enough.

Still fuming, he strode down the hall, looking for the one man who understood him. His mentor, Dr. Harvey Mitchell.

The man was an exceptional doctor who shared his views and supported his work with the Negroes in Shanty Town. He'd shared horrific stories of the war and how the hospital had overflowed with soldiers, bleeding and dying. Dr. Mitchell had used his ability to save life and limb, but unfortunately many had still died.

The doctor's reputation at severing limbs wasn't a secret. Andrew prayed he'd never be faced with such a thing, but if he was, he'd been trained by one of the most proficient doctors in the country.

"Let it go, Dr. Fletcher," Dr. Mitchell said as he gripped Andrew's shoulder. "Do your job and Mr. Schultz will have nothing to charge you with."

"But he's so unreasonable. What difference does it make that I treat *those people*—as he called them—in my spare time?"

"It's political. He answers to others who have financial control of the hospital. The people paying your salary. Don't cross him." Dr. Mitchell tipped his head downward and looked at him over the top of his glasses. "Treat your patients here, then go on your way and do what you must elsewhere. Just keep it quiet."

"I will. I never imagined that politics would have a place here. All I want to do is *heal*. Use what I've learned to make sick people well."

Dr. Mitchell shook his head and let out a small chuckle. Not that he'd been humored, it sounded more like disgust. "You're young. You'll find that politics plays a part in everything we do. The war changed the south but we still have a long way to go."

"You don't have to tell *me* that." Andrew sighed. But he needed to stop complaining and get his job done. He had something good waiting for him at home. "Thank you for listening. I'm confident that my life is on course for a positive change."

The man's brows rose. "I'm happy to hear it. Something I should know about?"

"Eventually. Let's just say that my time away proved to be more than beneficial." He grinned and patted Dr. Mitchell on the back.

"Wonderful. I'll look forward to hearing more. Perhaps at Sunday dinner? Margaret would love to have you come again."

Dr. Mitchell's wife was an exceptional cook, but now wasn't the time to accept a dinner invitation. Not until he had things in place with Claire. Then he could take her, too. She'd likely get along well with Mrs. Mitchell.

"Would it be all right if I let you know later in the week? I have a lot to do since I've been away."

"Of course. But please keep it in mind. Margaret's custard can take any man's mind off his troubles."

"You should bring some in for Mr. Schultz. Soften him up a bit."

Dr. Mitchell let out a real laugh this time. "It would take more than her custard to soften a man like him."

The young front desk clerk came running toward them. "Dr. Mitchell! A man was just brought in with a shattered leg! He fell into a well!"

With a quick nod, Dr. Mitchell motioned for Andrew to follow him.

Andrew's day became a blur. After assisting with the emergency surgery—another severed limb—he made his rounds through the hospital checking on patients, updating treatments, and filing reports. Thoughts of Claire had to be set aside so he could focus on work.

By the time he managed to leave, he allowed himself to relax and envisioned Claire. No doubt she'd pulled the rocker from inside to his front stoop.

She'll probably be sitting there rocking vigorously—possibly even darning some socks—and looking absolutely radiant.

He smiled at the thought, but would she be angry that he'd come home late? It was nearly supper time.

Maybe she'll have supper waiting. If not, he'd take her into town and buy her a meal. It was time for him to appear at the local restaurant with a beautiful woman on his arm. He'd introduce her as his fiancée and later as his wife.

He painted a fantastic picture in his mind but also felt guilty. In all the busyness at the hospital he'd been unable to make time to see about the justice of the peace.

She'll understand.

"Come on, Charger," he called out. "Let's pick up the pace. Claire's waiting."

When he arrived home, she wasn't on the front porch. He took Charger to the barn, then returned to the house. As he opened the door, Claire's handiwork made his heart dance. The floors had been swept clean and the table had a striking floral arrangement at its center.

"Claire?"

No answer. He went to the bedroom. The bed had been neatly made and the down pillows had been fluffed. But Claire wasn't there.

Assuming she must have gone for a walk, or perhaps went out to the field with the horses, he headed outside to look for her.

"Claire!"

Where is she?

When he spotted Clay at the chicken coop, he rushed to him. "Clay, have you seen a woman anywhere around here?"

The boy grinned. "No Doc, I ain't *never* seen no woman 'round here. Uh-uh!" He shook his head, grinning all the while.

"No, I don't mean the woman from this morning. I mean *today*. Did you see a woman here *today*?" Though grateful Clay was keeping his secret, he needed answers.

"You gots more than one woman, Doc?"

"No. No, it's the *same* woman. Have you seen her?"

"I din't even really see her this mornin'. Just some bumps under the blanket. I ain't seen no woman at all 'round here. What's wrong Doc? She leave ya?"

Leave me?

That hadn't even occurred to him as a possibility. "No—I don't know—I just need to find her."

"I'll hep ya soon as I finish with these chickens." Clay offered a reassuring smile.

"Thank you. I'm going back to the house. Maybe she left me a note saying where she's gone. Just come on in when you're done here."

Andrew's heart sped up as if preparing for a confrontation. An obvious problem loomed over him.

Returning inside, his heart fell.

Her bag's gone.

His fast-pumping blood caused his head to pound. With a dry throat, he crossed the room to the desk.

His mother's ring sparkled in the fading daylight.

In an instant, his heart seemed to stop beating altogether. He lost his breath. A note lay under the ring.

Andrew,
I can't stay. Please forgive me.
Don't come after me.
Claire

Every bit of life drained from him and he sank to the floor. "I don't understand." He covered his face with his hands, then ran his trembling fingers back through his hair.

Why would she leave? What had he done to cause this to happen?

I shouldn't have laughed at her when she was embarrassed this morning.

I shouldn't have taken her to my bed. I was such a fool. I could've waited. She was worth waiting for.

"God, what have I done?"

Wanting an explanation, he had to go after her. Something out of the ordinary had to have happened.

Why would she put so much effort into straightening up my house, only to leave me?

He may not have known her long, but he knew character well enough to know she'd been genuine. He couldn't have been so easily misled.

Why, Claire? Why did you leave?

The sun would soon set, but that wouldn't stop him. He'd ride Sam. No buggy, just the horse. It would be faster that way. And even in the dark Sam knew the road.

Returning outside, he asked Clay to get her ready.

"Shore, Doc. I'll—" Clay stopped and pointed. "Sumthin's wrong, Doc."

Andrew looked over his shoulder. Jenny ran toward them.

"Doc Fletcher!" she cried out, almost out of breath. "It's Mama! The baby's comin'! Daddy says Mama's all wet!" She came to a stop in front of them, panting hard.

"All wet?" Andrew asked. "Do you mean her water has broken?"

"Yes, yes, that's it! *That's* what Daddy said!"

Why now?

Terrible timing. Andrew's heart was being pulled to find Claire, but his obligation was with Mrs. Tarver.

He had no choice. "Clay, get Charger for me and Sam for you and Jenny. Hurry up now!" He flew to his house to get his bag. Claire would have to wait.

* * *

Upon arriving at the Tarver's, Andrew dismounted and told Clay to tend the horses. He ran to the door and didn't wait for an invitation to go inside.

Alicia's cries of pain wrenched his heart.

Elijah stood at her side holding her hand. "Doc, sumthin's terribly wrong." His voice quivered.

Clay and Jenny rushed in.

"Is Mama all right?" Clay pleaded.

Andrew held up his hands in an attempt to calm the situation. "Clay, take your brothers and sister outside. Your mama will be fine. I promise." Jenny's eyes welled with tears. "It'll be all right, Jenny. Sometimes it's hard to have a baby. Now go with your brother. I'll bring you back in soon." He stroked her hair, then patted her head.

With a timid smile and a nod, she let Clay lead her and their little brothers out the door.

Andrew went to work. "Elijah, please boil some water. I'll need to wash, and we'll need it for the baby when it comes."

"Anythin' else, Doc?"

"That'll do for now. Thank you."

Alicia breathed hard, struggling with her contractions. "You was wrong, Doc! You said it wadn't time! You forgot to tell the baby!"

Andrew pulled her covers back. The blankets beneath her were soaked; proof that her water had indeed broken. He looked toward the stove as if watching the water would help it boil.

How could I have been so wrong?

Once the water heated, he washed thoroughly, then moved to Alicia to check on her progress. "Let's see how far along we are now, Mrs. Tarver."

She cried out again with another contraction. "Get this outta me!" She grabbed his arm and squeezed. Her eyes were wild and wide with desperation.

"Mrs. Tarver." He remained calm. "You need to relax. *Breathe.* It'll make this much easier on you."

"I don't wanna relax none! I wanna push this baby out!"

"You can't push yet. You're not fully dilated. If you push, you'll tear yourself. You've got to give the baby more time."

"I don't wanna do this no more! I's done!" She jerked Elijah's arm. Her eyes blazed and her nostrils flared. "Lijah? You hear me? I's done!"

The enormous man couldn't have appeared more sheepish. His shoulders slumped and he held his hand to his heart. "Leesha, I's so sorry. If I could, I'd have the baby for ya. I hate to see you hurtin'."

"You did this to me!" She smacked him hard on the chest.

Andrew had seen this before. During hard labor, women's emotions oftentimes caused them to rage. Normally mild-mannered Alicia was no exception.

"Elijah," Andrew said. "Why don't you go outside and tend to the children? I'll take care of your wife." *And save you from a few bruises.*

Elijah let out a sigh of relief. "Good idea, Doc. You just call if you need me." He rushed away before Alicia had the chance to lash out again.

"All right, Mrs. Tarver, take a deep breath," Andrew instructed and she obeyed. "Now, the baby has turned and it's almost time for you to push. But I want you to wait until I tell you."

"No! I don't wanna push no more. I's done. I's so tired."

He took a cool rag and wiped her brow. But almost immediately another contraction came.

Checking her again, he determined her dilation had rapidly progressed and she indeed needed to push. "Mrs. Tarver, when you feel the next pains coming on, I want you to push with all your strength. We're almost done here."

"Almost done? You ever tried raisin' five little uns?" She groaned amidst another hard contraction.

"Push, Mrs. Tarver!"

"Uhgrr . . ." Her face scrunched tight as she bore down.

"Good." The head crested. "Again!"

"No!" Though she protested, her body remembered what to do, and she pushed regardless of her dissent.

The shoulders came through and Andrew expelled the tiny baby girl.

Premature.

He'd known all along it had been too soon. He couldn't understand what had brought on the early labor.

He cleaned her face, cleared her nose and throat, and after a good swat on the behind, she began to cry. The teeniest cry he'd ever heard, but a cry nonetheless.

The sound brought in her family.

"It's a girl," Andrew announced with a smile, masking his concern.

Elijah grinned from ear-to-ear, Jenny jumped with joy, and the boys frowned. But they all gathered around to look at her.

"Elijah, get the hot water," Andrew said. "Not just for the baby, but for you and the other children as well. It's important you're *all* clean around the new baby."

"Yessir, Doc." Elijah nodded "C'mon now. You heard the doc." He shuffled them to the kitchen table where he'd set the pan of water.

"We just had a bath last week," Joshua grumbled and Samuel added his disgust. But both succumbed. They'd never cross their father. Andrew had witnessed their respect for him time and again. Of course his enormity may have had something to do with it.

Andrew cleaned the baby and cut the umbilical cord, then wrapped her in a cloth and handed her to Alicia.

Though droopy-eyed and exhausted from the delivery, she sat up and held her close. "Will she live, Doc? She's so small." Tears glistened in her eyes.

"I'll make certain of it. I'll stay here tonight so I can look after both of you."

"You're a good man, Doc." The woman gave him a weary smile. Her gentle disposition had returned.

"I'll fix you a pallet to sleep on," Elijah said and proceeded to gather bedding.

Could he sleep? Not only was Andrew worried about the child, but his thoughts had gone back to Claire. For a brief time, he'd put aside his pain to concentrate on Alicia. But now, it all came rushing back and a dull emptiness consumed him.

CHAPTER 11

Claire rubbed her tired eyes, which were caked with dried tears.

Where am I?

Her shoes had been removed and an incredibly comfortable bed embraced her body.

She breathed in deeply.

Bacon?

Everything struck at once and she started to cry. Softly at first, but then she broke into a hard sob. It seemed her tears weren't completely gone.

Aunt Martha appeared out of nowhere, cradled her in her arms, and stroked her hair. "Sweet, sweet Claire Belle. It's all right. Aunt Martha's here. Shhh . . ."

Dear Aunt Martha. Her *great* aunt. She'd married Claire's granddaddy's brother, Clarence Montgomery. But he'd died a few years back, leaving Martha widowed. She was rather short and plump, and had thinning gray hair, large bulging eyes, and several missing teeth due to her fondness for sweet tea punch and chewing tobacco.

Most folks would be repulsed in her arms, but Claire found comfort. She loved her dearly and snuggled into her embrace.

"My poor, sweet baby girl," Martha lulled. "You need to tell Aunt Martha what happened to ya. You showed up on my doorstep barely walkin'. Thought you was near dead."

"Oh, Aunt Martha!" Claire clung to her.

"Now, now." She stopped patting Claire and huffed. "This don't have sumthin' to do with a man, does it?"

Claire cried even harder.

"Damn men." Martha spat on the floor. "If some man has done gone an hurt you. I swanee! You remind me of your mama. Did you know she came here when that damn John Martin left the two of ya? Course you wouldn't remember. You was just a baby. If your granddaddy had been alive, he'd a put a cap in that boy's head."

The moment she mentioned John Martin's name, Claire wailed.

"Listen to me." Martha's voice softened. "I'm gonna get you some water. All that cryin' is dryin' you up. I'll be right back."

She left the room and Claire leaned back onto the pillows, more miserable than ever.

What would she tell Aunt Martha? She could never tell her about Andrew, so she'd have to tell her a *partial* truth. More than anything, she had to get control of herself and deal with her situation. Regain at least a portion of her common sense.

Martha returned and sat on the bed beside her. "Here now, drink up." She placed the cup in Claire's trembling hand. "I'll help ya."

Martha tipped the cup and Claire swallowed every drop. She hadn't realized just how thirsty she'd become. It had been a long walk to Martha's. Between the heat of the sun and the shedding of tears, she'd plum dried out.

"That's a good girl." Martha took the cup and set it on the dresser. "Now, tell me."

Claire licked her lips, mind spinning. She owed the woman an explanation, but what?

"Forgive me, Aunt Martha. I just don't know what to do." Her eyes filled with tears. Would they ever stop?

"Now. No more cryin'." Martha narrowed her eyes. "You'll make yourself sick."

"I know. I don't feel very well as it is." An appropriate story had come to mind. "And you were right. It was a man." She sniffled.

"I knew it!" Martha hopped from the bed and shook her finger at the ceiling. "The only decent man ever walked this here earth was our good Lord Jesus. The rest of 'em are dog meat!"

Oh, my.

"Martha, how can you say that? What about Uncle Clarence? And your boys?"

"They all left me!" She plopped down beside Claire.

"Uncle Clarence didn't *leave* you. He *died*. He didn't mean to fall off that roof."

"He shoulda been more careful." Martha turned her head and spat again.

"Not *all* men are bad," Claire whispered, thinking of Andrew. "I just reckon you've had some bad luck."

"Ah . . ." Martha's eyes narrowed. "The truth is comin' out." She slapped her knee. "So tell me 'bout this *not-so-bad* man."

Claire had fallen into her trap. She had to tell her *some-thing.* "Well . . ." *Think, Claire!* "You see . . . There's this young man back home. I think you know him. Gerald Alexander?"

Martha wrinkled her nose and looked upward. "Yep, I *do* remember that boy. Had glasses kept fallin' down his nose."

"Yes, that would be Gerald." *What am I doin'?* "He asked me to marry him, but I said *no*."

"You said no?" Martha drew her head back. "You said no, and you're here bawlin' your eyes out over someone you *didn't* wanna marry?"

I've gotta be more convincin'.

"I was just confused over what to tell him. I mean, we'd been friends an all since we was little. And his sister, Beth, is my very best friend."

"Then what's the trouble? Don't you love him?" Martha craned her neck, studying her.

"Course I love him. Always have. But I just don't reckon I can marry him." Whether or not Martha believed her was one thing, but in all truth she'd been honest. The only thing that *hadn't* been true was the reason for her broken heart. "Martha, I need some time to get my head together. Can I stay here with you for a spell?"

"You didn't even hafta ask. Course you can. I could use some help 'round here anyways."

The woman's eyes sparkled. She stood, rubbing her hands together. "Now then. You need to eat sumthin'. It's long past supper time. Aunt Martha's gonna fix you up some good soup and a warm cup a milk. Then you're gonna get a long night's rest. You'll feel better in the mornin'."

Too tired and weak to put up a fight, Claire didn't argue. She felt like a child again in Martha's care. It brought back memories of the time she'd spent here with her mama when the war had come too close to their home on the bay.

Uncle Clarence and Aunt Martha had taken them in until it was safe to return home. Their oldest boy had been killed in the war, and the two younger boys went west. Having Claire and her mama around had eased Martha's loneliness. But that had been a long time ago.

Claire was no longer a child. Her innocence had been given away, never to be regained.

She drifted off to sleep and dreamed of her time with Andrew. How would she ever be able to forget him?

* * *

Andrew had a difficult time sleeping. Though the pallet on the floor felt nowhere near as soft as his bed, it was his mind that wouldn't let him rest.

He got up every hour to check on Alicia and the baby. They were both asleep, but she'd need to feed the baby soon. Though an experienced mother, she'd never had to deal with a premature baby before. The tiny girl was frail and delicate. Each hour of her life could be considered a victory. Andrew intended to *keep* her alive.

When he wasn't thinking about the baby, he thought about Claire. He planned to go after her just as soon as he determined the baby would be all right. It didn't matter what Klaus Shultz would likely say to him. He could lose his position at the hospital, but there were other things in life much more important. There'd be other jobs, but there was only one Claire.

He drifted in and out of sleep, dreaming of her.

The beautiful soft cry of a baby woke him. The curtain had been pulled around Alicia's bed.

"Mrs. Tarver," he whispered. Everyone around him was sleeping. "May I come in?"

"Course you can, Doc." He heard the smile in her voice. "Come look at my little angel."

He pulled the curtain aside to find Alicia sitting up in bed with the baby at her breast. "She's a hungry little 'un. Took right to it."

His spirit lifted knowing the child was eating and doing a good job of it. "She'll be just fine, Mrs. Tarver. You have a beautiful little baby there."

"Looks like her mama." Alicia grinned, then nodded toward Elijah who had slumped over in a chair next to the bed, fast asleep. "You'd think *he* birthed this baby."

Andrew chuckled. "You should let him sleep. The two of you have a lot more on your hands now. I'll leave you to finish feeding her. And when you're done, I'd like to give her a good going over."

"Fine, Doc. An thank you again."

He closed the curtain behind him, then proceeded out the front door. The dawn had barely broken, but it had already started getting hot. Nearly August, it would be some time before the weather turned. He stretched and yawned. It would be a long day.

He was determined to ride to Claire's and could make it in two hours riding Sam. He'd have to push her hard, but she was a strong horse and could manage the exertion. Answers from Claire were necessary. Without them, he could never focus on work.

He took in the scenery around him. The property wasn't bad, but not the best. Elijah had done a fine job of tending the land, but the shade trees were scarce and their little house got hot beneath the cruel sun.

The oak tree further behind the house was quite grand. Old with a thick trunk and branches that reached high into the sky. Moss hung from the boughs. He understood why it had been the tree Clay had fallen from. Its shape made it the perfect climbing tree no child could resist.

He shook his head and smiled. The Tarvers had become an important part of his life.

He walked for a while, giving Alicia time to nurse. Though anxious to leave, he knew it wasn't the appropriate thing to do. Not yet.

When he returned to Alicia, he found her holding the baby on her shoulder, patting her tiny back. "Here, Doc. You can take her now." She held out the baby.

Her small form would have allowed him to easily hold her in one hand, however he held her firmly in both. He carried her into the light. After listening to her heart and lungs and finding them perfectly normal, he noticed a yellow tinge in her eyes. Jaundice was common in premature babies. Her liver hadn't completely developed yet and she'd need to be kept in the light.

When he carried her back to Alicia, Elijah had woken up. He stood by her and stroked her hair with affection. Seeing the two of them warmed his heart, yet also jarred him with pain, reminding him of Claire.

"Your daughter's beautiful," Andrew said, extending the tiny bundle to him.

Elijah's huge hands dwarfed the child even more, and they began to shake. "I . . ." He looked to his wife for help.

She took the baby from him. "It's all right, Lijah. You'll get used to her." Her brows crinkled. "Lijah, what we gonna call her?"

The man shrugged. "Doc, why don't you name her? I's sure you know a real fine name."

"Yes," Alicia added. "You name her, Doc. How 'bout the name of some special woman in your life?"

Claire.

A sharp pang in his chest kept him from speaking her name. "My mother's name was Elizabeth."

Alicia frowned. "Kinda fancy." She mumbled a few things he couldn't understand. "Hmm . . . Liz. Liza. Beth."

Each name that passed her lips didn't seem to suit her. "How 'bout Betsy?"

"Oh. I like that." Elijah beamed. "Betsy Tarver. A might fine name."

Though it wasn't quite Elizabeth, it came close, and Andrew couldn't have been more flattered. But it was time to be serious. "I need to explain something to you about Betsy."

Alicia became rigid. "What's wrong with my baby, Doc?"

He laid a reassuring hand on her arm. "It's nothing serious. I promise you. She has jaundice."

How do I explain it to them?

Elijah's face fell. "She ain't gonna die, is she?"

"No. No. It's nothing that bad. It's just very important that you keep her in the light, *naked*, as much as possible." *How do I make it easier to understand?* "It's like . . ." He grinned, thinking of a brilliant analogy. "It's like cooking a pot roast."

They both gaped at him as if he'd lost his mind.

He rubbed his temples and proceeded as gently as he could. "When a pot roast isn't completely cooked all the way through, you have to cook it a little longer—until it's done. It's like your baby. As if she wasn't quite done cooking yet. You could say she *came out of the oven* too soon." Flustered, he waved his hands in the air. "Just keep her in the light."

"My baby ain't no pot roast." Alicia glared at him.

"Calm down, Leesha," Elijah said, rubbing her arm. "Give the doc a chance to explain."

Offending a newborn's mother was never a wise thing for any doctor to do. "I know Betsy's not a pot roast. She's a beautiful baby girl. And as long as you keep her in the light as much as possible she'll be fine."

"Silliest thing I ever heard," Alicia mumbled. "But I do what you say."

"Thank you." Andrew inhaled deeply through his nose. He'd remind himself never to use this analogy again. "Now, I'm going to have to leave you for a while. I have somewhere I need to go, but I'll be back this evening."

"You sure she be a'right?" Alicia asked.

"Yes, I'm sure. She has a very good mother." Andrew brushed Alicia's cheek with his hand. The gesture prompted a smile he needed.

Elijah accompanied him outside.

"Just keep Charger here with you until I get back," Andrew said. "Sam's much faster and I've got quite a ride ahead of me."

"You goin' after that woman, ain't ya? Clay told me last night you was lookin' for her."

"I hope I can find her."

"You will, Doc. You will." Elijah patted him on the back.

Andrew mounted and sped off to find Claire.

CHAPTER 12

Claire woke the next morning feeling refreshed. The down-filled bed she'd slept on had embraced her body. Leaving the window open all night allowed a breeze to blow through and keep her quite comfortable. She wished she could stay in bed all day, but that would never happen.

Not in Aunt Martha's house.

It was Sunday, but this was one Sunday she wouldn't be going to church. The past week had transformed her into something Lucy Beecham wouldn't recognize.

Claire had always looked down her nose at others whom she thought did ungodly things and had considered herself righteous. But she'd been smacked hard upside the head. Suddenly she understood what it meant to be *human*. From now on she'd leave judgment to God alone.

She lay in bed thinking about Andrew. Replaying everything he'd said and done, she tried to piece together the puzzle that had brought them together. She remembered the night he'd told her about his mama's death and how cold his daddy had been to him.

She also recalled the only words he'd said his daddy had spoken: *It seems I was never meant to raise a daughter*. They made sense now more than ever.

How could Daddy be so unfeeling? Did he ever love anyone other than himself?

The scent of bacon floated into her room.

Aunt Martha's signature perfume.

Exactly what she needed to entice her out of bed. Her stomach rumbled.

She threw on her clothes and went to the kitchen. Passing by her aunt with a cheerful, "Mornin'," she made her way quickly to the outhouse.

Like most other homes, the outhouse had been situated far back behind the main dwelling. She'd heard stories of some of the wealthy folks up north with *indoor plumbing.* Something she believed she'd never have the luxury of, and something she couldn't quite comprehend. Who would ever want *that* indoors?

On the far side of the house was a large barn. The one from which Uncle Clarence had met his end while attempting to repair the leaking roof. Two horses and a milk cow occupied it.

Martha also had a chicken coop, complete with a very loud rooster. Surprisingly, Claire hadn't heard him that morning. She'd been sleeping much too soundly after a very difficult day.

Martha's house was larger than her own home. She had a full kitchen, three bedrooms, and a huge living area. Much too big for Martha alone, but being the only home she'd ever known, she refused to leave. Even long ago after Claire's mama had died and Claire had suggested Martha move in with her. How times had changed.

Claire returned to the kitchen, washed, and offered to help with breakfast.

"I never refuse good help," Martha said and gladly let Claire take over the duty of making biscuits.

Claire couldn't have been more grateful for the task at hand. Even though she believed Martha had accepted her story about Gerald, she feared the woman might start asking more questions. But Martha's unusual silence began to trouble her, and when they sat down to eat at the small kitchen table, Claire decided to be bold and get her talking.

"Aunt Martha? Now that I'm grown, I'd like to know more 'bout my daddy. Is there anythin' you can tell me 'bout him that you haven't already?"

"Lawdy!" Martha grimaced. "That's one man I'd rather forget. But since you asked, I'll tell you what I know."

With a thumping heart, Claire munched on a biscuit and waited.

Martha's lips screwed together like a wrinkled prune. "Your daddy was a selfish, low-down scoundrel who took advantage of your sweet mama, then left her to fend for herself. Poor girl was in love with him. He was good lookin' an smart. All the girls wanted him, but it was your purty mama what caught his eye. Said she reckoned the only way to keep him 'round was to give herself to him. An she did. Biggest mistake she ever made. 'Cept for without him she'd a never had you." Martha reached across the table and pinched her cheek.

Seemed her mama had herself a man before marriage, too. "But why'd he leave? Didn't he love her at all?"

"It was lust—*pure* lust—on his part. He saw a purty thing an had to have it. Least he had the decency to marry her. But then after *you* came along, reckon he got scared. He met some woman when he went to Mobile to take a damn lawyer test. Had to be one a them high-falootin' lawyers. Ran off with the hussy. Just up an left. Damn that John Martin!" Ritualistically, Martha spat on the floor, still cursing him after all this time.

After years of hearing Martha curse, it no longer bothered Claire. Truth be told, if Martha *didn't* curse she'd fear something was wrong with her. "Do you know anythin' 'bout the woman?"

Might as well feel her out on this, too.

"Don't know and don't care to. Any woman who'd take a man from his family needs to rot in Hell."

"What if he never told her he *had* a family?" From the letter she'd read, her daddy *hadn't* told her about them.

"Hell. She *had* to know." Martha slammed her hand on the table. "How could he a kept sumthin' like that from her?"

Claire responded with a slight shrug and continued eating. She ate more than she normally would, making up for the previous day.

"Glad you're eatin' so good." Martha scooted her chair back and stood. "You finish up. I'm gonna get to my chores. Tessie needs milkin'. Come help me when you're done."

"I will. And—Aunt Martha—thank you for bein' here for me. I didn't know where else to go."

"Glad you thought a me, child." She kissed Claire's forehead, then walked away.

* * *

The ride to Claire's seemed to take Andrew forever. Though the trip was much shorter than the one he'd shared with her, time wasn't moving fast enough. He had to see her, *talk to her*, hold her again, and convince her she should never have left.

He needed answers.

He stopped several times along the road so Sam could get fresh water. Luckily, this part of Alabama sported many small ponds and water holes.

As he approached Claire's home, his heart beat faster. He envisioned her there in the storm, pleading with him to come inside, and then standing in front of him with her wet dress clinging to her skin. His desire for her hadn't diminished.

Claire.

She was there in her garden. She had her back to him, then lifted her head as he approached. He started to call out to her, but stopped. Aside from the color of her hair, this woman looked *nothing* like Claire. Truthfully, if she hadn't been wearing a dress, he could easily have mistaken her for a man.

He dismounted and walked toward her. "Good morning ma'am," he said, nodding politely.

Her cheeks instantly turned crimson, and she attempted to wipe away smudges of dirt on her face, only to make it worse. "Mornin' back atcha!" She dropped her head and focused on the ground, all the while fidgeting with her skirt.

"I hate to bother you, but is the woman of the house at home?"

"You mean Claire?" She squinted, gazing upward, then raised her hand attempting to block the sun. Unlike Claire, this woman wore no bonnet.

"Yes, Claire Montgomery."

"How do you know Claire?"

Not a question he'd expected. After all, he thought she'd be here. He concocted a tale. "I was in town recently and was told that she's a seamstress. I asked her to make some shirts for me and I hoped they might be ready."

Please believe me.

"Oh. Makes sense. She makes the finest things in all a Alabama. But I'm afraid she's not here. After that bad storm last week, she went north to check on her aunt. She's old and lives by herself. Claire was worried 'bout her."

Andrew recalled this story. It was what they'd decided she'd tell people when she left to go to Mobile with him. Could she possibly be there now?

"I see. Do you know when she might be returning? I'd like to pick up the shirts as soon as possible."

"Don't know. She asked me to look after her place. Didn't say when she was comin' back."

His heart sank. He couldn't ask where Claire's aunt lived or even her name. It would create too much suspicion. He'd have to return home and come back later. "When you see her, could you please give her a message?"

"Course I can." She tipped her head and batted her eyes.

"Please tell her that Dr. Fletcher came by and that I was very sorry to have missed her." He wanted to say so much more.

"Doctor?" Her eyes no longer fluttered, but popped open wide. "My, oh my! Yessir, I'll tell her."

"Thank you . . ." He gestured with his hand, requesting a name.

"Beth. I'm Beth." She grinned, then nervously chewed her lower lip. "It's nice meetin' you, *Doctor* Fletcher. Don't you worry none. I'll be sure to tell Claire you was here."

"Thank you, Beth." He gave her a respectful nod, then mounted his horse.

He and Sam would return home.

Without Claire.

* * *

Andrew arrived at the Tarver's late that afternoon. Exhausted and disheartened, he wanted more than anything to go home, but had to stop and check in on baby Betsy.

He found Elijah outside tending the garden. A very good sign. If anything had been wrong with the baby or Alicia, the man would have been at their side.

As Andrew dismounted, Clay came immediately to take Sam for water. They exchanged glances, but Clay remained silent. The sadness in his eyes said everything.

He knows I couldn't find her.

Andrew trudged to the garden to talk to Elijah. "How are Mrs. Tarver and little Betsy doing?"

"They's fine, Doc. It's you I's worried 'bout." Elijah plunged his hoe into the loose earth. "You had anythin' to eat?"

No, he hadn't. And until Elijah asked, it hadn't even occurred to him. "No, but I'm not hungry."

"You gotta eat, Doc. I made some stew. I ain't a bad cook. Little uns liked it."

"Thank you. I imagine I could use a bite." He followed Elijah inside.

After washing, Elijah dished up a bowl of stew and set it in front of Andrew at their simple wooden table. He devoured it. The good smell alone had stirred his appetite and it was important for him to eat. "You were right Elijah, this stew is good."

"Thank you. I's gonna go out an check on the children." He left Andrew to finish eating.

"Ain't as good as my cookin'."

Focusing on the food, Andrew hadn't noticed that Alicia was sitting up in bed watching them. She should have been his first concern, but the food had taken precedence. "Well, Mrs. Tarver, you're looking good." The puffiness she'd had under her eyes was gone, and she held Betsy comfortably over her shoulder.

"Nice change since last night. Huh, Doc?" She chuckled. "I kept Betsy in the light like you say. She didn't seem to mind."

He stood from the table and crossed to the bed. "May I see her?" He extended his hands.

Alicia hesitated, studying him like she'd never seen him before. Her behavior seemed odd and completely unlike someone he'd been tending for such a long time. She finally placed the baby in his arms.

He pulled the blanket away from her teeny body and examined every inch of her. Her color looked much better. "She's doing well." With a soft smile he returned her to her mother.

"E-li-jah!" Alicia's abrupt yell caused Andrew to jump.

The man rushed in through the front door. "Yes, Leesha?" He fumbled with his hat and wiped the sweat from his brow.

"Would you mind takin' Joshua outside with you?" The little boy had been sitting quietly on the floor playing with a stack of wooden blocks. "Now that the sun is 'bout to set, reckon you can catch a few lightnin' bugs with him and the other children. I'd like to see Doc Fletcher alone."

"Course I don't mind." The grin he gave Andrew indicated some kind of silent language between the couple.

What's this all about?

"Doc. Come sit over here." She patted the spot beside her on the bed.

He complied, but the situation seemed highly unusual.

Her eyes narrowed. "I knows sumthin's botherin' you an it's eatin' you up inside. I'm no fool. I heard Clay tell his daddy 'bout that woman."

Finally, it made sense. Even Alicia had noticed a change in him.

She laid her hand on his arm. "Don't you worry none. I ain't gonna say nuttin' to nobody, but I wanna tell you this. If she left you, the only way you're gonna have her back is if'n she comes back to you. It ain't gonna do you no good runnin' after her. Now I know it's tearin' you up not knowin' *why* she left. Truth be told, you may never know. That's just the way things is. You cain't kill yourself pinin' over her."

Everything she said sounded logical, but even so, it wasn't possible. He couldn't let it go. "I love her so much. And I was certain she loved me, too."

"Doc, if she truly loved you, she never woulda left. I knows it hurts to hear it, but I care too much 'bout you to see you like this. Give it some time. Maybe she gots cold feet. Maybe she be back. Maybe she won't. But you needs to let her go. If she come back, she's yours to keep."

His eyes filled with tears, but he refused to let them fall, not wanting Alicia to see him cry.

She can't be gone forever. I won't accept it.

Unable to respond, he turned his head and closed his eyes.

"Doc?" Alicia's voice had softened more than ever. "Did Lijah ever tell you how we met?"

"No," Andrew whispered, thankful to have the subject changed.

"Don't surprise me none. He don't like to talk 'bout it much. But I wants to tell you."

Andrew shifted his body, but couldn't look at her. He nodded his head, affirming she had his full attention.

"Lijah an I was both slaves. Never knowed anythin' else. Born into it, we was. We worked for different masters on two different plantations. The fields ran up 'gainst each other, an that was where we met. I spotted his large dark body risin' outta the cotton fields. He was wearin' only pants, an his chest sparkled with sweat. Lawdy, he was a handsome sight. He saw me lookin' at him, an then must a decided he liked lookin' back at me."

After a big smile, she sighed. "Wadn't long for we started talkin' in the fields. Gettin' close as we could 'thout the masters seein' us. I's only seventeen, Lijah was nineteen. We wanted each other in a bad way but slaves wadn't allowed. We'd sneak out in the middle a the night an meet up under the stars. That's where we first lay together—under the stars."

Drawn to her story, he turned to face her. Her eyes lit up with love for her husband.

I thought I'd found that kind of love.

"Well," she continued. "We wadn't together long an I was with child. I hid it for a time. But when my belly got round, my master called me to him an wanted to know who the daddy was. He insisted I tell him. I knew better than to disobey the master. After I told, he went to Lijah's master. An he took Lijah out, bound him to a tree an whipped him. Told him never to see me again. My master was kinder. When my belly got real big, he took me outta the fields an let me work in the house cookin' an cleanin'. When the baby came, he let me keep him. But soon as Clay grew big enough to work, he set him out in the fields."

Her expression changed to one of pain. No longer did her eyes hold the radiance of love. "Mrs. Tarver . . ." Andrew took hold of her hand. "You don't need to tell me all of this. It must be horrible for you to have to remember."

"I never forget. I *wanna* tell you. There's a reason I's tellin' you." She blinked slowly and swallowed hard.

"All right. I'm just concerned for you." He stroked her skin. So much pain lay behind her eyes.

"That's what I like 'bout you, Doc." She tapped his hand, then readjusted the baby in her arms, swaying slowly. "As I's shore you figgered out, Lijah an I din't stop seein' each other. We was as careful as could be, but two years passed an I was with child again. This time, I din't escape a beatin', but it was worse for Lijah. They liked to have killed him with the whip. They only stopped 'cause they needed him. Always was a good worker. He don't work the fields no more 'thout a shirt. Don't want no one to see his scars."

Her breath hitched. She closed her eyes and bowed her head. After a short time, her head lifted and she continued. "This time when my baby came, the master was gonna take it away from me. But God smiled on me an made it a girl. *Jenny.* Master had a daughter who fell in love with her. Thought she was a baby doll. She begged her daddy to keep her, so he did. I nursed her, an the little girl dressed her up. Everyone loved Jenny.

"Lijah wasn't able to see the little uns much. I'd try to bring 'em out to the fields but we was bein' watched. Sneakin' away was gettin' harder an harder, but we found a way. That's what love does. We was never able to marry proper, but we knew in our hearts we was each other's. When I learned I's carryin' a third child, I knew I couldn't say nothin'. They'd a killed Lijah for shore.

"The war had started, an there was rumors 'bout us slaves bein' set free. We had hope. When I told Lijah 'bout the baby, we made plans to run away, though we knew it was dangerous. If we'd a been found, we'd a hung. So we hid an we *stayed* hid until the end a the war, when we knew for shore we was free. Durin' that time, Samuel came into the world. Then three years later when Joshua was born, he was born free. We went through some awful times, but our love kept us strong. Nothin' could tear us apart. That's *real* love, Doc."

She took Andrew's hand and gripped it tight. "*You* deserve real love. Not what you's goin' through now. You see what I'm tellin' ya?"

It couldn't be clearer. He needed a woman who'd always be there for him.

With a heart heavier than ever, he stood, then dipped down to kiss Alicia on the forehead. "Thank you. For everything. It means a lot to me that you shared something so personal. And I understand why. But I can't let her go. Not yet."

"Give it time, Doc." A heartfelt smile from Alicia lifted a corner of his heart.

The baby had fallen asleep, lulled by her mama's soft voice. He cupped his hand over Betsy's head, nodded his thanks to her, then left with a promise to come back soon.

* * *

Andrew returned to his vacant home. As he lay on his bed, he pressed his face into the pillows. Claire's sweet honey scent remained. Emptiness overtook him and he finally allowed himself tears.

Though his mind wouldn't rest, his exhausted body eventually took control, allowing him to sleep.

The next morning he decided to go directly to Mr. Schultz to face his reprimand. If the man intended to terminate his position, he might as well face it head-on.

After another stern, "Come in," from the other side of the man's door, Andrew took a large breath and opened it.

Mr. Schultz looked up from his paperwork. Andrew stood in the doorway expecting to be told to leave.

"Shut the door," the man commanded and rose to his feet.

Andrew obeyed.

"Sit down."

Mr. Schultz pointed to a chair and Andrew once again did as he'd been told. The man remained standing, which allowed him to tower over him.

He's trying to intimidate me.

"Two days ago," Mr. Schultz said. "You offered your assurance that you would not be gone again unexpectedly."

Andrew tried to respond, but the man put his hand up motioning him to be quiet.

"Yet yesterday, we expected you here and you were not." With every word, his voice grew a little louder. "This is unacceptable!"

"Sir, please let me explain."

"Dr. Fletcher, when a man gives me his word and his assurance on a matter, I anticipate being respected enough for it to be carried out!" His jaw lifted upward and he pointed a stiff finger in Andrew's face. "How can I trust you when you so quickly break your word?"

"Mr. Schultz." *Don't challenge my integrity.* "I'm a doctor, and the first responsibility I have is to my patients. I was delivering a premature baby and stayed with the mother until I was certain the child would live." He wasn't about to tell him about his trip to Claire's. Besides, he'd told the truth.

"One of your *Negro* patients?" The man looked down his nose at him.

"What does the race of my patient have to do with my care for them?" Heat pumped through his veins. His face burned with anger.

Mr. Schultz' pointed finger came so close to Andrew's face he could have bitten it. He was tempted to break it. "I specifically told you," the man snarled. "That your work with those people could not interfere with your work here."

"I'd rather lose my job here, than let a perfectly good woman and her child die from lack of proper care!" Andrew pushed aside the man's hand and stood. If he didn't leave now, he'd probably say something he'd regret.

"Sit back down!"

"Why?" Andrew hissed air from his nostrils, breathing hard. He had no desire to listen to anything else the man had to say. "You're just going to ask me to leave. Why should I stay and listen to what I feel is completely unreasonable?" He remained standing.

"Unreasonable? Unreasonable for me to ask you to be responsible to your job here?" Mr. Schultz backed away and returned to his desk. After a long loud sigh, he motioned for Andrew to take a seat.

Andrew hesitated, but out of respect for the man's position with the hospital, he sat.

Mr. Schultz glared, lifting his chin in the air. "I had no intention of terminating your employment today. But consider this a warning. You'd best come every day you are scheduled from this time on or you *will* be terminated. Are we clear?"

"Yes, sir," Andrew replied coolly, then got up and walked out the door, not looking back. If he only had himself to consider, he would've resigned. But he had a responsibility to his patients. He'd deal with Mr. Schultz.

As little as possible.

After all, he wouldn't be going to Claire's again anytime soon. Alicia's story weighed heavy on his heart. She was right. If Claire truly loved him, she'd come back.

* * *

Over the next few weeks, Claire and Martha fell into a routine. They started their mornings early when the rooster crowed, fed the chickens, milked the cow, then checked the garden for any vegetables that may have ripened. They'd start canning soon.

They ate a generous dinner around noon, then in the afternoons they'd sit on Martha's front porch in the swing built for two that had been suspended from the porch ceiling.

They'd sip sweet tea punch and Martha would chew tobacco. She claimed there was *nothin' like the taste of a good chaw an a glass of sweet tea punch*.

Claire had no intention of trying the chaw.

They worked a little more in the afternoon. Sometimes Claire would sew or do other needlework until the sun set. Then they'd eat a light supper and shortly thereafter go to bed. Claire felt right at home, and Martha gave every indication that she hoped she'd never leave.

Martha had one farm hand, George, who came in during the week to help her. He lived just up the road with his elderly parents. He was forty-one and had never married. He didn't talk much, but worked hard. Perfectly suited for Martha who could talk the ear off a stalk of corn.

When George came, he stayed out in the fields and away from Claire. It seemed she made him nervous. He acted shy and could scarcely speak a word to her. She determined women in general were the cause of his behavior, because he acted the same way toward Martha.

His looks were pitiful. He was small in stature and walked with his shoulders hunched forward, which made him appear even smaller. Being mostly bald, he wore a straw hat to keep his head from sunburn. Every day he wore the same coveralls and large boots and usually had a piece of straw dangling from one side of his mouth that he nervously chewed on.

Claire had tried to converse with him, but eventually gave up. As it turned out, it was good that she had. The one day she'd approached him and started a conversation, he'd gotten so nervous he went home early. Martha cautioned her to leave him be. Her aunt didn't want to lose a good hand.

Working with Martha on the farm got her mind off Andrew. At least some of the time. In the late evening while she drifted off to sleep, however, she couldn't get him out of her head. What had he done when he found her note? Did he go after her? Was he completely heart-broken?

If she knew him as she thought she did, she could easily answer her own questions. But she'd had no other choice than to leave the way she did. She'd rather him believe she didn't love him and had changed her mind, than know they'd committed a mortal sin.

Incest isn't forgivable.

She prayed God would have mercy on her. How could she have known that Andrew was her brother?

Eventually, she'd have to go home, but she wasn't ready. Not yet.

CHAPTER 13

Nearly four weeks had passed since Claire arrived at Aunt Martha's, and she'd become restless. She enjoyed her time there, and if given a little *more* time—maybe another ten years or so—she could forget Andrew.

I can't stay here that long.

It was a Tuesday afternoon, the twenty-second of August. Claire looked intently at a calendar that hung on the kitchen wall. She counted the days since her last cycle and the realization hit hard.

I'm two weeks late.

The possibility of pregnancy had never entered her mind. Yes, she knew how that sort of thing happened, and yes, she'd done it. However, they'd only made love six or seven times.

How could I possibly be with child?

She must simply be late due to stress and new surroundings.

After making a sandwich and a glass of sweet tea punch, she went to the front porch to join Aunt Martha for their afternoon ritual.

Martha began chattering about this and that and wasn't paying much attention to Claire. But in turn, Claire wasn't paying much attention to Martha. She had other things to think about.

Setting aside her empty plate, Claire rested her head against her aunt's shoulder. The gentle rocking of the swing soothed her.

"Land sakes child. It ain't time to be snoozin'." Martha's admonishment startled her and she jerked upright.

"Oh, my. I don't know how I fell asleep so easily. I'm just so tired." She followed her words with a loud yawn.

"You was snorin' sumthin' fierce. Maybe you're comin' down with sumthin'." Martha placed her hand against Claire's forehead. "You ain't warm, but you can take it easy this afternoon. Go on in and take you a real nap. I'll wake you for supper."

"Thank you." Claire trudged off to her room, lay down on her bed, and closed her eyes.

Martha woke her as promised and Claire ate a generous meal. Fried pork chops, beans, turnip greens, stewed potatoes, and corn bread. She had second helpings of each.

With fists on her hips, Martha shook her head. "If you *are* sick, you ain't lost your appetite."

They followed up the meal with strawberry shortcake and cream. Claire had two helpings.

"Mercy, child." Martha pulled the cake away as Claire was about to help herself to more. "You keep eatin' like that an you'll end up lookin' like me."

"Don't know why I'm so hungry. I just can't seem to get full." The amount of food she'd eaten had shocked even her. Truthfully, she could eat more but decided to stop. Martha's warning had given her second thoughts.

Feeling tired again, she excused herself to her room. "I don't feel like sewin' tonight Martha. I'm just gonna go back to bed."

"That's fine, dear." Martha's brow furrowed with worry. "I hope you feel better in the mornin'."

* * *

For the first time since the morning after she'd arrived, Claire didn't hear the rooster crow. Instead, the smell of frying bacon woke her up. As the scent filled her nostrils, nausea set in.

"Oh . . . no."

She clasped her hand to her mouth, jumped from her bed, and rushed out the back door wearing only her nightgown. As soon as she cleared the house, she bent over and vomited.

Martha was next to her in no time, holding her hair back. "I'm fetchin' a doctor. I'll send George to Mobile and have one brought out to take a look at you."

That was the last thing Claire wanted. With her kind of luck, George would bring Andrew. She couldn't let that happen. "No, Martha. I'm fine. Truly, I am." And then she heaved again.

"Yep," Martha muttered. "Right as rain."

"It was the smell that affected me. The breakfast." She was trying to convince herself as well as Martha that nothing was really wrong. "Maybe a cup of water would help."

Her nausea passed, and with an empty stomach Claire went inside with her aunt.

Martha pulled out a chair at the kitchen table. "You sit. I'll get your water."

"Thank you. Reckon I'll just have some grits this mornin'. Sumthin' a might easier on my stomach. I hate that you cooked so much."

"Don't worry 'bout that. I'll take a plate to George. I reckon he'll appreciate it." She stacked a plate high with bacon, biscuits, and eggs and headed out the back door.

Claire sipped the water.

Oh, my. What'll I do?

She'd had several friends from church who'd shared what they'd experienced carrying a child. They'd talked about being tired all the time and the morning sickness; how simple smells of certain foods made them retch. She also recalled how emotional they'd been.

It just can't be.

Her hand trembled holding the glass and she abruptly set it down. To still her heart, she set aside the possibility.

Maybe if I don't think 'bout it, it won't be so.

By the time Martha returned, Claire felt a great deal better, and they prepared for their day's chores. They planned to work out in the garden and bring in more vegetables for canning.

Though Martha cautioned her to take it easy, Claire insisted she felt fine.

The hot sun beat down on them. August heat. The sky had no clouds, so there was no relief from the blazing ball of fire. They drank plenty of water to keep themselves hydrated and sat in the shade to rest when they needed it.

Since Claire felt better, she convinced herself she was probably about to start her cycle and that had caused her to feel sick. Wanting to rid her mind of worry, she decided to get Martha talking.

"Martha, is it true I was named after Uncle Clarence?"

"Yep, it's true." She chuckled. "Your mama was might fond a him. He was tickled to death when she named you."

"Funny 'bout baby names. What makes folks decide to choose them an all? Mama never talked to me much 'bout baby things. *The birds an the bees,* so to speak."

What was I thinkin'?

It had just slipped out. She couldn't turn back now. Why on earth she brought up the subject with the one woman who didn't shy away from anything, was beyond her.

"Now, Claire." Martha stood completely upright, then shifted her eyes around the fields as if wanting to be sure they were alone. She then looked Claire in the eye. "You're old enough to know how things work 'tween a man an woman, and if the reason you brought this up has anythin' to do with that Gerald Alexander and your decision *not* to marry him, then let me give you some advice."

I hate myself right now.

They'd spent the last four weeks barely talking about men at all. And she'd been grateful. It had helped cast aside thoughts of Andrew.

Martha cleared a great deal of phlegm from her throat. "If you're worried 'bout takin' care of a man's needs . . ." She narrowed her eyes, then wiggled her brows. "You have nothin' to worry 'bout. Men find ways of satisfyin' themselves without much regard to how you're feelin'. Now that may sound harsh, but for women, it's more 'bout havin' babies than enjoyin' themselves. They just do it for their husbands."

It hadn't been that way with Andrew.

"Now then, is that the problem with this man?" Martha asked. "Has he been pressurin' you to do things?"

"No. Not at all. He's a perfect gentleman. But I don't feel like I *could* do those things with him. He's more like a brother to me." The irony of it all. The man she desired happened to *be* her brother, and the one she could share her life with *felt* like a brother. Things were certainly mixed up.

"Well, now." Martha's face lit up and she clapped her hands together. "If that's all that's keepin' you from marryin' him, then I say marry the man. Those things come in time. It ain't always fireworks on the weddin' night."

Claire sighed. She'd already experienced fireworks. But then everything had fizzled.

"Thank you, Martha. For your honesty. Mama had a hard time talkin' to me 'bout men. She'd been hurt so badly." Though the conversation had been somewhat embarrassing, she still appreciated her aunt's frankness.

"Damn John Martin did it to her. Ruined her for any decent man what might a come along." Martha spat. "I tried to warn her not to get mixed up with a damn northerner!"

Every time Martha mentioned her daddy's name, she always accompanied it with a swear word and a ritual spitting. She truly despised him.

She had good reason.

* * *

The next morning, Martha was once again fixing breakfast when Claire raced through the kitchen and out the back door. She emptied her stomach in the grass, then returned inside.

"I just don't know what's wrong with me, Aunt Martha. I feel fine in the evenin' but sick in the mornin'." She went to the wash basin and ran a damp cloth over her face.

"Sit down, Claire." Like the previous morning, Martha motioned for her to take a seat at the table, handed her a glass of water, then sat herself down. "I reckon there might be sumthin' you ain't tellin' me 'bout Gerald Alexander. That *perfect gentleman* of yours."

"What do you mean?" She'd told her everything about Gerald and what had happened between them.

"Claire." Martha leaned in. Her eyes held not even one drop of humor. "Some things is private 'tween a man an a woman, but I love you an I think you're gonna need some help."

Claire tilted her head and stared at her.

Martha crossed her arms over her chest and huffed. "Claire, are you with child?"

Oh, dear.

She gulped. "Why, Aunt Martha, how can you say such a thing?"

"You're showin' all the signs." Her eyes became narrow piercing daggers, demanding answers. "Tell me truthfully. Did you an Gerald have relations?"

"Oh, Aunt Martha . . . Why—*no.*" She and Gerald had never even kissed, let alone had *relations.* But she couldn't tell Martha about Andrew.

Out of nowhere, the tears came. "Oh, Martha!" she blurted out. "I don't know what to do! I *do* believe I'm with child! My cycle is more than two weeks late. I've never been late in all my life!" She dropped her head down on the table and cried.

"Well, unless you're the Virgin Mary, I'd say you and Gerald had relations!" Martha slapped her hand hard against the table.

Claire wailed. Not only had she tarnished Gerald's name by making Aunt Martha believe him to be the daddy, but the reality of her condition had finally sunk in.

"Damn that Gerald Alexander," Martha grumbled and spat on the floor. Gerald had now joined the ranks of John Martin. "Claire, now you listen here. You're gonna go back home an marry that boy. You said you love him, and he had the decency to ask you to marry him. I won't let you ruin your good name by havin' a bastard child."

The word stung.

This had become all too real. She was going to have Andrew's child and it terrified her. She'd known first-cousins who'd married and their children seemed a little slow-minded. Folks had said it was because their blood relation was too close and it affected their children. What kind of child would she have with a daddy who's her half-brother? She could only pray that the baby would be all right.

"Claire!" Martha tapped her on the head. "Did you hear me? You go marry that boy. That child needs a daddy and you need a husband. Go pack your things. I'm gonna tell George to take you home."

Claire lifted her head and sniffled. "Yes, Aunt Martha." What else could she say? She was trapped, and there was no better solution.

She trudged off to her room to pack.

How can I marry Gerald, carrying another man's baby?

While stuffing items into her bag, she stopped. It all began to make sense.

It would be the most sinful thing she'd ever done, but she had to do it. It would be best for the child. She'd sacrifice her life for the sake of her baby. Her child wouldn't pay for her sins. But Gerald could never know the truth.

Hopefully, the Lord would forgive her for what she was about to do.

CHAPTER 14

Riding all the way home with George wasn't appealing, but Claire didn't have a choice. It was too far to walk.

She hadn't wasted any time packing, and Martha had gone straight to George and told him to harness the team. Martha insisted they leave quickly so George could get back home before dark.

Martha offered to go with her, but she refused. It would make matters worse if Martha insinuated to Gerald something about his defiling of her, and then Claire's plan would never work.

George pulled the buggy to a stop in front of the house. Claire hugged Martha goodbye and climbed in next to him. He scooted as far away from her as he possibly could.

This is gonna be a very long trip.

"Sure you don't want me goin' along?" Martha asked.

"No, Aunt Martha. This is sumthin' I need to take care of myself."

And I want you as far away as possible from Gerald.

"Well, you just remember . . ." She shook her finger. "If that boy don't do right by you, he'll have Aunt Martha to deal with!"

She'd remember.

George clicked to the team, then they headed down the road. Claire turned and waved to Martha, only to see the woman wiping tears from her eyes.

I'll miss you, too.

George ignored her, staring straight ahead, and acted as though she wasn't there at all. All the while, he chewed on a piece of straw.

More than once, she attempted conversation, but found it to be a bad idea. Each time he'd responded with a grunt and no words. So she, too, just sat there lost in her thoughts, going over her plan.

She directed him to their little town and asked him to drop her at the Baptist church. He didn't argue, and nodded as she got out of the buggy—not even bothering to help her down.

"Thank you, George," she said politely.

"Welcome." He turned the team around and left.

My, oh my.

It was early on a Thursday afternoon and the church was empty. Claire walked to the front and knelt down at the altar, then folded her hands to pray.

She decided to speak aloud, though quietly. Maybe God would appreciate hearing her, but she didn't want to risk being heard by anyone else. Though confident she was alone, the things she had to tell God were not things she wanted spoken loudly regardless.

"Lord, it's me—Claire—and I've done some awful things. I always thought I was better than most folks. I tried to remain true to your Word and not be a sinner. But Lord, I *am* a sinner. I was weak, and I gave myself to a man who wasn't my husband. I knew it was wrong, but I did it anyway. I hope you can find it in your goodness to forgive me. I know you've blessed me in so many ways and I thank you for that. But Lord, I need to ask a blessing for this child I'm carryin'. I want it to be healthy and smart. Lord, please make my baby smart."

And then the tears came. Unstoppable heartfelt tears.

"Lord, I know you know everythin'. Even my thoughts. So you know what I'm about to do. I'd like to ask you in advance to forgive that, too. I'm doin' it for my baby. I don't want it to grow up without a daddy, and this is the only way I know how. So, please, Lord. Understand. Thank you, Jesus. Amen."

She arose and wiped her tears. She stared at the cross rising above the altar and remembered what sacrifice had been made for her. Would she have to sacrifice her soul to save her child? She knew she'd do anything for the life growing inside her. Whatever was about to happen, she had to get her head together. She needed to be in the right frame of mind to accomplish what she planned to do.

First things first. She had to find Beth.

She went by the boarding house. Mrs. Sandborn seemed pleased to see her, but told her Beth was at *her* house, so Claire headed home. She'd started to get hungry and promised herself to eat a good meal once she arrived there. She'd make certain she kept her body strong for the baby.

Beth was rocking on the front porch when Claire approached.

The moment Beth saw her, she jumped up and ran to her. "Claire! Oh, Claire. I missed you so much." She wrapped her arms around her and hugged her harder than any bear. "I was gettin' so worried. You've been gone near a month."

Claire laughed; happy to see her friend. "I missed you, too. Sorry I had you worried."

"You didn't walk all the way from your aunt's house, did you?"

"No, her farmhand brought me home. I went to town first, lookin' for you at the boardin' house, then walked from there."

"I'm just glad you're home." Beth pulled her in for another generous hug.

"So am I. Let's go inside. We need to talk, and I'm starvin'." Claire linked her arm in Beth's and they went inside.

Beth had kept the house in perfect condition. But instantly a vision of Andrew standing in the doorway of her bedroom came to Claire's mind. She took a deep breath.

Why do I still want him?

"Beth, I can't thank you enough for takin' care of my home while I was away."

"I was glad to do it. I love this little house." She squeezed Claire's hands. "I'll tend it for you anytime."

"Sumthin' sure smells good." Claire tipped her head back and inhaled deeply.

"I made potato soup. Sit down and I'll get you some." She ladled a bowl full, looking very comfortable in Claire's kitchen. "I've already eaten, but I think you'll like this. 'Specially if you're hungry as you said you was."

They sat together at the table.

"Beth . . ." Time to set the plan in motion. She had to be convincing or it wouldn't work. "I did a lot of thinkin' while I was at my Aunt Martha's and I came to realize sumthin'."

Beth folded her hands on the table, listening.

I'm sorry, Beth. But I hafta do this.

"What I realized is . . ." Claire swallowed hard. "I'm in love with your brother. I miss Gerald so much, an I really need to find him an tell him so." There. She'd said it. Everything had been set into motion and she couldn't turn back now. She forced a smile and waited for Beth's reaction.

Beth's hands quivered and her face turned brilliant red. She jumped out of her chair and into the air. "Thank you, Jesus! Oh, Claire. You don't know how happy you've made me!" She hugged her even harder than before. "We're gonna be sisters. It's just as I always dreamed. You're gonna make Gerald so happy."

Claire wanted to sink into the floorboards. Beth's elation made the lie even worse. "You reckon he still wants to marry me?" She managed to take a few steps back, but Beth's excited energy continued to cover her as much so as her hugs.

"Course he does. It's what he always wanted. You broke his heart when you turned him down. You're the only woman he's *ever* wanted."

"I'm glad to hear that. Can you tell me how to get to where he is? I wanna go there tomorrow. I don't wanna wait any longer." She *couldn't* wait. She could already be four weeks pregnant and had to act quickly.

"He's up north livin' with our Uncle Henry. He's a blacksmith. Has a successful business. Most of his customers come to him from Mobile. He's 'bout a mile north of the city. It's on the main road right out a town. You can't miss it."

Claire dreaded going back there, but it was the only way. "You reckon Mrs. Sandborn would let me borrow her horse?"

"Course she would. 'Specially if I tell her you're goin' after Gerald. She'll be happy, too." Beth beamed, but then knocked her knuckles against her forehead. "In all this excitement I nearly forget to tell you. You had a visitor while you was gone."

"A visitor?" Her heart fluttered, fearing the worst.

"Oh my, yes. Don't know why you never mentioned him. I thought you told me everythin'. He was the finest lookin' man I ever seen. Said he was comin' by to pick up some shirts he asked you to sew. Said his name was Fletcher. *Docto*r Fletcher."

Heat crept up Claire's neck. "Hmm . . . Don't recall a Dr. Fletcher."

"Don't recall? What's wrong with you, Claire?" Beth rolled her eyes. "He's tall, dark-haired, and sumthin' special to look at. Not like any of the menfolk 'round here."

"Oh." She kept a straight face and spoke without feeling. "I *do* remember someone fittin' that description. Yes, he *was* a doctor, come to think of it." Beth *had* to believe Andrew was of no importance to her.

Beth gaped. "How could you forget a man like that?"

"It was some time back when he came by. I assumed he'd forgotten all 'bout those shirts."

"Well, he made me promise to tell you he was here, and he was sorry he missed you."

"Hmm—well then—you kept your promise. He shouldn't have waited so long to come by for his shirts. I gave 'em away thinkin' he'd not return."

How is it that lyin' keeps gettin' easier an easier?

"Gave 'em away? That don't sound like you." Beth shook her head, but then a grin lit up her face, rapidly changing her dour expression. "Ah, heck. What's done is done. Let's get you ready to go see my brother."

"That's a fine idea." *Thank goodness she went back to that conversation.* "If things go as I hope, we'll have us a weddin' real soon."

"Oh, Claire." Beth covered her mouth and looked as if she might cry. "I just can't believe it."

"Me neither. Truly." She had to look away. Never had she lied so much to her best friend, but now it appeared to be her way of life.

And she'd never dreamed she'd be in a position to deceive a man like she planned to deceive Gerald Alexander.

I'm becomin' just like my daddy.

Maybe she had more of him in her than she realized.

Andrew had come for her. He genuinely loved her, but she prayed he'd stop looking for her.

CHAPTER 15

Mrs. Sandborn gladly loaned her horse to Claire. She acted almost as excited as Beth about her plans with Gerald.

I wish I felt the same.

On the ride there, she thought about what she planned to do. It would be the only way to accomplish things quickly and not have suspicion about the child's daddy. If she waited too long, Gerald would never believe the child was his.

She promised herself she'd be good to him, be a fine wife, and take care of him and the baby. Most importantly, she'd never let on that she didn't actually love him. At least not *that* way. He deserved better, but she'd give him all the love she could muster.

The long ride prompted several stops along the way. She'd been getting hungrier and hungrier every day that passed into her pregnancy, so she brought food and ate as she went.

Beth had fussed at her about leaving in the afternoon, saying she should have left first thing in the morning. But Claire told her she felt tired from the long trip the day before, and Beth accepted her explanation and said no more.

She planned to arrive at Henry Alexander's in the evening after sunset. Expecting a full moon, she'd have plenty of light to travel by. But she needed *some* darkness.

I could never do this in the light of day.

The house was easy to find. It was a beautiful two-story home, with pillars adorning the front. The kind of home she'd imagined Andrew would have lived in. Beside the home was a large blacksmith shop. A sign at the peak of the shop read, *Alexander's*, which left no doubt in her mind she'd come to the right place.

Her heart raced as she approached the house, but she'd somehow find a way to hide her nervousness from Gerald. Otherwise, she'd never convince him of her sincerity. The last thing she wanted to do was chew her nails. It would give her away in an instant. She had to remain calm.

I'm doin' this for the baby.

The stage had been set. She wore the dress she'd worn the night she and Andrew had made love—the one with the scooped neckline and button-down front. Andrew seemed to like it and she hoped it would make an impression on Gerald.

She tied her horse to a nearby tree, then crept toward the front door. The house was quiet. She couldn't imagine they'd be in bed so early, but then again, they probably got up at sunrise to start their day.

A soft glow illuminated an upstairs window. She moved closer. Her heart skipped a beat. Through a parted curtain, she could see Gerald sitting at a desk reading a book, using the light from a small lantern.

"Gerald!" She used a forceful whisper, but he didn't budge. She wasn't about to yell outright, not wanting his uncle to hear her.

Picking up a small pebble, she pitched it at the window. It pinged off the glass. Gerald's head jerked at the sound, and he pressed his face to the window.

"Gerald!" She hollered again, this time a bit louder.

Success. He got up and in mere moments came out the front door.

"Claire, what are you doin' here?" He stared at her, utterly confused, as though looking at an apparition, then pushed his glasses up on his nose.

"Gerald, I needed to come. I had to see you."

"Why? I don't understand." He scratched his head. "Sumthin' wrong with Beth?"

"No. Beth's fine. Fact is, she helped me borrow that horse from Mrs. Sandborn so I could get here."

"Well then, come inside an we can talk."

"No. I don't wanna disturb your uncle."

"You won't. He's already sleepin'. Sides, he's deaf as a post." He moved toward the door, motioning for her to follow.

"*No*, Gerald. I don't wanna go in. Come with me." She grabbed his hand and led him toward the stable. He didn't resist, though his hand was damp with sweat.

A few horses snorted as they passed by, then they came to a stall that had been freshly cleaned. A large pile of straw had been mounded up at the back end.

Perfect.

Dropping his hand, she moved toward the straw, then turned to face him. "Gerald, do you still wanna marry me?"

His jaw dropped. "Huh?"

She should have expected this reaction. Keeping her calm, she tried again. "I said, do you still wanna marry me?"

His hands shook. "Oh, Claire. You know I do." Again, he pushed his glasses up his nose.

"Well, *Jerry*, there's sumthin' we hafta do before I can marry you." There'd been very few times she'd called him *Jerry*, but the effect proved to be beneficial. It was a name only she'd been allowed to use and the second she said it, his eyes widened.

Her heart beat out of her chest.

I hafta do this.

"I'll do anythin' for you, Claire. Just tell me what it is."

"You see, I know I can be the kind a wife who cleans the house, cooks the meals, and takes care of you, but I don't reckon I can be the kind a wife who can take care of your *other* needs. Your *manly* needs."

He gulped, then loosened the buttons at his neck. With the back of his hand, he wiped sweat from his brow. "What are you wantin', Claire?" His voice squeaked with more nervousness than ever before.

"I want you to show me I'm wrong. Right here. Right now."

He knows why I'm here.

She reached beneath her dress and removed her undergarments, then lay back on the straw. Not wanting him to turn and run in the opposite direction, she made certain not to expose herself.

"What are you doin', Claire?" He'd leaned in, watching her, but then started violently shaking his head. "No, Claire. This ain't right. It ain't the proper way. I can't do it. If you wanna marry me, we'll go see a preacher and get married in the church like we're supposed to." His breath came out in rapid bursts and he kept his distance.

If she stopped now and waited for a formal wedding, it could be at least another week. This had to be done now.

"Jerry . . ." She cooed his name and his eyes opened even wider than before. "You said you'd do anythin' for me. I hafta know I can do this. I want you to have a proper wife."

Pulling the pins from her hair, she shook it out and let it fall over her shoulders. Then she lifted her skirt enough to expose her bare thighs and unbuttoned the top two buttons of her dress. He now had a proper view of the roundness of her breasts. She was doing all she could to seduce him, and it sickened her.

Determination pushed her on.

He gaped at her, licking his lips. "All right, then. Only cuz you're askin'. But I want you to know I still think it ain't right."

He quickly shut the stable doors. Moonlight poured in through the many open windows of the stalls.

With shaking hands, he removed his trousers. He looked around the stable with wide eyes, as if he feared they'd be discovered.

She could see him plainly. Her seduction had succeeded, proven by his undeniable arousal.

He stood there before her, trembling.

He must think I'm horrid.

Even if he didn't, she thought badly enough of herself for both of them.

As he lay down timidly on top of her, she felt no passion. Maybe it was just as Aunt Martha had said; for a woman it's about making babies, not being satisfied. Still, it had been different with Andrew.

With the exception of his protruding belly, everything about Gerald was smaller than Andrew. His body felt unnatural upon her as he grunted and groaned, attempting to position himself. Droplets of sweat fell from his face onto hers. She closed her eyes and reminded herself not to cry.

As he started to push into her, she let out a small whim-per of pain. He immediately stopped what he was doing.

"Oh, Claire, I'm sorry. I didn't mean to hurt you."

Don't over-do it. This is too important.

He attempted to lift himself off of her, but she yanked him back down. "No, Gerald. It's all right. It's just my first time an all. But please don't stop."

Grabbing his bottom, she brought him closer. He quiv-ered beneath her hands, but her method worked. He went about his business and she relaxed, knowing she'd accom-plished hers.

His release came quick, much to her relief. It was fol-lowed by his entire body violently shaking and then a full collapse upon her. He was quite heavy and for a moment she lost her breath. But then *he* didn't appear to be breath-ing at all.

Oh, my! I've killed him!

She sighed with relief when he gasped for air and rolled off her. How would she ever have explained a death like that to Beth?

"Gerald? You all right?" She shook him by the shoulder. "Was it okay?"

He turned on his side and looked at her with a sideways grin. "Uh-huh."

Having completed her task, she stood and put on her underclothes. "All right, then. I'll marry you." She brushed the straw off her dress and pulled a few strands from her hair.

He remained lying there as if in a daze, but then all of a sudden his eyes popped open wide. He jumped to his feet. "Yeehaw! Claire, you've made me the happiest man in all a Alabama!" He hugged her so tight she couldn't breathe. No doubt he and Beth were brother and sister.

At some point, she probably should have kissed him. But she wasn't ready to. A kiss would be much too intimate.

Sumthin' is dreadfully wrong with me.

She'd try to do better and learn to be affectionate with him, but she certainly didn't feel it now.

Fortunately for her, he didn't even *try* to kiss her.

"You'd better put your pants back on, Gerald." He stood before her half-naked.

"Ah, heck!" He stumbled reaching for his trousers, then faced the opposite direction and got dressed.

She tilted her head, studying the befuddled man. "Suppose your uncle would mind if I spent the night? It's much too late for me to ride home now."

"There's plenty a room. I know he won't mind. There's an extra room upstairs we keep for guests. Bed's already made."

"Then, it's settled. I'll stay here tonight and tomorrow we can go back home an get married." They had no time to waste getting that ring on her finger and the marriage certificate to validate their union.

Gerald huffed. "We can't get married without plannin' sumthin'. We'll need to invite folks. I want it to be memorable."

Just when she thought everything had fallen into place, he wanted a *memorable* wedding.

I thought brides were supposed to be the particular ones.

Her heart raced. "If we go home tomorrow—which is Saturday—we can go to church on Sunday and announce it to the entire congregation. Then we can get married *next* Saturday. That would be September the second. Would that make you happy?"

"Sounds perfect!" He hugged her again. "Claire, I'm gonna be the best husband ever." With newfound bravery, he kissed her on the cheek.

She forced a warm smile.

What have I gotten into?

Taking her by the hand, he led her toward the house. "Wait here, while I tend your horse." He gave her hand a squeeze.

"Fine." Another forced smile.

The moment he left, she nearly crumbled to the ground.

I hafta be strong.

When he returned, he guided her upstairs to a bedroom.

"This is where you can sleep, Claire." He walked in with her.

"Thank you. I'm quite tired." She moved toward the bed and he followed her. "What are you doin'?"

"Don't you want me to lay down with you for a spell?" He'd folded his hands casually in front of himself, looking prim and proper.

"Gerald, we aren't married yet." She pointed to the door.

With his head hanging low, he walked out the door and closed it behind him.

Alone, she removed her dress and climbed into bed. The second her head touched the pillow, silent tears rolled down her cheeks.

What I did to Gerald was wrong.

She cried over the person she'd become. She was losing herself. Perhaps losing her soul. Her heart ached for Andrew. Ached for the kind of love they'd shared if only brief. She wanted *that*.

Not this.

CHAPTER 16

Claire opened her eyes.

Where am I?

It all came rushing in like a slap in the face. The night seemed like a dream to her. Or better yet—a *nightmare*.

She sat up and tried to ignore the instant twist in her belly.

I shouldn't have done that to Gerald.

After shaking her head to clear her thoughts, she took in her surroundings. Regardless of how much she hated what she'd done, she had to move forward . . . for the baby.

Without a doubt, she'd come to a home belonging to someone who didn't hurt for money. Gerald had never mentioned his uncle's wealth.

The bedding was store bought; the bed made of wrought iron. Lovely framed artwork donned the walls; still-life paintings of fruit and flowers.

A vanity sat in the corner of the room made of dark oak. It had a matching stool, padded with a white cushion, embroidered with burgundy roses. The mirror also had roses etched into the glass that were surrounded by a swirling leaf pattern. This room had a woman's touch.

A flashback of the ring that Andrew had given her struck out of nowhere. It had the same leaf design as the mirror.

How long will it take to get his memories out of my mind?

She replaced thoughts of Andrew with those of Gerald. Gerald, her life-long friend. She'd betrayed him and he'd be none-the-wiser as long as she kept her secrets.

What would he say to her after their night in the stable? Would he mention it, or would he act as if nothing had happened?

She didn't want to move from the bed. Not only was it one of the most comfortable beds she'd ever slept on, but staying here meant she didn't have to face the daylight. Or her husband-to-be.

A loud banging came from the hallway. Someone was beating something against the staircase.

What on earth?

"Gerald Alexander! Breakfast is gettin' cold!" The bellowing came from an exceptionally loud man, presumably Gerald's uncle.

Claire threw her covers back.

"Gerald!" Another yell. An *angry* yell.

I shouldn't have stayed here.

Shuffling in the hallway turned her head, then her heart jumped from a rap on her door.

"Claire," Gerald whispered. "You awake?"

She got out of bed, pulled on her dress, then opened the door. Gerald stood there in his pajamas.

"Mornin'," he said with a grin. "You sleep all right?"

"I slept just fine. Thank you." What more should she say to him? This entire situation felt awkward. She'd slept in a stranger's home and he didn't even know she was there.

Running away wasn't an option. She had to make the best of it. "I reckon you should go downstairs, Gerald. Before your uncle gets any more upset."

"Oh, he ain't upset. Beats his cane like that all the time. Like I told you, he's mostly deaf. He usually don't even know he's yellin'."

"Still, I think you should go down and tell him I'm here. I'd feel kinda funny just walkin' in on him."

"Sure, Claire. If that'd make you feel better." His lips curled upward into a smile, then he turned and left the room, leaving the door opened wide.

Nothing about any of this made her feel better.

Moving to the vanity, she sat and gazed into the mirror. *I don't know you anymore.*

Feeling sorry for herself wouldn't do. She had to put on a happy face. After all, she'd just become engaged.

Very little time passed before Gerald flew into her room, wide-eyed. "Claire, you can come down. Uncle Henry wants to meet you. Just make sure when you talk to him, you look straight at him. He reads lips."

"You sure it's all right? Do I look fine?" She turned in a circle. Her dress wasn't pressed and she hoped there wasn't straw stuck in it somewhere.

"You look beautiful, Claire." He took her hands, then leaned forward and kissed her on the cheek.

Why'd he always have to be so sweet? So good?

She'd have to start overcoming her guilt or she wouldn't do him any good at all. "Gerald, don't you think you should get dressed?" He hadn't changed out of his pajamas.

"Wait right here." He did an about-face and went to his room, returning faster than she thought he *could* move, fully dressed.

He escorted her down the stairs and into the kitchen. She took in her surroundings at every turn. The living room was furnished with a large sofa and loveseat, finely upholstered in royal blue fabric. There were enormous bookcases full of books and a huge fireplace with a carved mantel and pillared candles on top of it. A woven rug centered the room, laid atop a fine planked wooden floor.

A portrait of a woman hung over the fireplace. Claire believed her to be Gerald's aunt. Though common-looking, she wore an elegant gown and a beautiful necklace.

The kitchen was nearly as large as the living room, with a huge table and eight chairs, all made of fine wood. The walls had cupboards hung on them, certainly filled with expensive dishes. There was also a sink with an indoor water pump. She couldn't imagine what it must be like not to have to go outside for water. In the corner of the kitchen stood a wood-burning stove with four eyes for cooking—unlike hers, which only had two. She'd never been in such a home.

She smiled politely at the man seated at the kitchen table and was caught off guard by the generous smile she got in return.

"Uncle Henry," Gerald said. "THIS IS CLAIRE!"

"You don't hafta yell, boy. I can hear you perfectly fine." He extended his hand to her. "I'm happy to meet ya, Claire. Gerald's told me a lot about ya." When she set her hand in his, he brought it to his lips and kissed it. Then he looked in her eyes with an enormous smile. Finally, he patted her hand and released her.

No doubt she glowed red. "Thank you, sir. It's a pleasure meetin' you as well."

Henry pulled out a chair for her. "Please, sit down. Have some breakfast."

"You're so kind. But if you'll excuse me, first I have to take care of some *personal* business." She coyly tipped her head.

"Course you do! Gerald, show her to the—well—you know." Henry tossed his head toward the back door.

Gerald stammered something unrecognizable. He gaped at his uncle.

"It's all right, Gerald," Claire said. "I know where to go." She nodded to both of them, then exited through the back door.

Henry's appearance wasn't what she'd expected. She assumed he'd be older. Of course, when she thought of an uncle, she always thought of her Uncle Clarence, her *great* uncle. Henry looked closer in age to her daddy—probably in his early forties. His hair wasn't completely gray and he still had quite a lot of it. He was taller than Gerald and not quite so plump.

And much better lookin'.

Sad 'bout the need of a cane. I'll hafta ask Gerald what happened to him.

Henry had been kind. Probably a little *too* kind. No man had ever kissed her hand that way.

I'm bein' silly. He's simply a very charmin' man.

The outhouse had been well kept, much to her relief. From what she'd learned from Beth, Henry had been a widower for several years. Most bachelors couldn't keep house.

The grounds were also well-tended. Maybe having Gerald around helped. He certainly had done a lot for Mrs. Sandborn.

Abundant trees covered the property and she noticed several horses grazing in the fields. As she cast her eyes in the direction of the barn, her heart thumped. She didn't want to think about last night.

Her stomach grumbled. Luckily, she'd noticed a pot of simmering oats on the stove. Oats gave off very little smell. Had he cooked bacon and eggs, as Aunt Martha had done the previous two mornings, she might have embarrassed herself completely by vomiting in front of her soon-to-be relative. She felt a bit queasy, but nothing like she'd been at Martha's. Perhaps the morning sickness had passed.

She returned to the kitchen and went to the sink to wash. The moment she entered the room, both men stood. She had her back to them, but grinned from ear to ear. The flattering attention boosted her confidence.

After helping herself to some oats, both men grabbed a chair for her. She chose Gerald's and sat down without saying a word. Acting as though she started every morning this way, she sprinkled some brown sugar on her oats, then poured fresh cream over the top and began eating. Even without looking at them, she knew their eyes were on her.

"Claire," Gerald said. "You'll be happy to know that Uncle Henry has agreed to let us live here after we're *MARRIED*!" He directed the last word toward Henry.

Claire dropped her spoon. She'd instantly lost her appetite. How could he make such plans without asking her first?

Not wanting to embarrass Gerald in front of his uncle, she stood. They did as well.

"Gerald?" Claire licked her lips. "May I speak with you privately for a moment?"

"Course, Claire." He pulled his shoulders back and beamed at his uncle, then took her by the hand and led her into the front room. "What's wrong?"

Not wanting to be overheard, she decided to whisper. "I thought we were goin' back home. Back to my house on the shore. I never thought you meant to stay here." This was *not* part of her plan.

"This is where I live now, Claire. I've learned how to make a good livin'. Henry an I have a good business goin'. Fact is, we've considered hirin' help." He took her hands and gently stroked them. "I can provide for you now. I couldn't take care of you proper if we went back home. If you wanna be my wife, then we *hafta* live here."

Claire found this new, more confident, Gerald very appealing. He never once touched his glasses while he spoke, and he'd never looked at her with so much love. She hated the thought of moving away from her little house forever, yet it hadn't been long ago that she'd planned to do so. The fact that the home she'd be moving into was absolutely elegant didn't hurt matters. "You're right, Gerald. This *is* the best choice. Don't know what I was thinkin'."

He kissed her on the cheek. "I promise to make you happy."

They went back to the kitchen and finished eating. And while they ate, they made their plans.

They had one week to prepare.

Claire's clock ticked louder and louder.

CHAPTER 17

"And it doesn't hurt much?" Claire asked Henry, touching her fingertips to his knee.

They were seated comfortably on his sofa, waiting for Gerald to bring the wagon around. Claire decided it would be a good time to get to know Henry better. She made certain to face him squarely so he could read her lips.

"Sometimes," Henry said. He stared at her hand.

She'd made a mistake touching him. His actions gave every indication he found her appealing. It wasn't wise of her to encourage him. She folded her hands in her lap. "So walkin' with the cane helps?"

He nodded. "Sometimes I take medicine. But I ain't never liked to. I get by. Least I didn't lose my leg. A bullet shattered part a the bone. Doctors wanted to take the leg, but I wouldn't let 'em."

"That would a been horrible."

"Yep. But I'd a given both legs if I coulda saved my boys. Did Gerald tell ya they died in the war?"

"Beth did. I'm so sorry, Henry." Instinct made her want to touch him again. To offer comfort. But common sense won and she kept her hands to herself.

Gerald cleared his throat. "Claire, we need to go *now*. I got the wagon ready."

She turned to face him, but then fast as lightning he bolted up the stairs.

"What was that all about?" she whispered, rising to her feet.

"Huh?" Henry asked.

Before she could repeat herself, Gerald returned.

"Sure you're ready, Gerald?" Claire asked. "You ran off so."

"Yep. Just forgot sumthin'. Let's get goin'." He led her toward the door. "I'll be back TOMORROW night Henry." He spoke almost *coldly* toward him.

"I'll be lookin' for ya. You take care of that purty gal of yours now." Henry waved them out the door.

"See you at the weddin' *Uncle* Henry!" Claire shouted and waved goodbye.

Gerald tied Mrs. Sandborn's horse to the back of the wagon for the ride home, then helped Claire up into the seat. A frown remained on his face. "You all right, Gerald? You're a little—*tense*."

"I'm fine! I just didn't like my uncle bein' so . . . well . . . *friendly* with you."

"Oh, Gerald." Claire laughed. "Are you jealous?"

"Well, what'd you expect? I love you, Claire. Henry might be my uncle, but I don't like him lookin' at you the way he does." His mood softened the longer he spoke.

"He's a very nice man and hasn't had a woman around in a long time. I don't reckon he meant anythin' by it. 'Sides, *you're* the man I wanna marry." She gave him a peck on the cheek.

He grinned and looked at the ground. "Reckon I was bein' a bit childish. After last night, I should be actin' more like a man." It was the first time he'd mentioned their time in the stable.

He caressed her cheek and his gentleness warmed her. She tipped her head slightly toward the touch.

"Oh, Claire. I nearly forgot." He reached into his shirt pocket and pulled out a gold band. "This was my mama's. I had it in a wooden box upstairs. I'll put it on your finger for keeps when we get married, but I'd like you to try it on now to make sure it fits."

"So that's why you ran off?" She stared at the simple gold band. Nothing like the ring Andrew had given her.

"Yep." His grin grew.

She held out her hand and he placed the ring on her finger. It was far too big.

He let out a long sad sigh. "Sorry. Reckon Mama had bigger hands than you. Wish I had another ring to give you."

"It's just fine." Sensing his pain, she rested her hand against his face and stroked it with her thumb. "When I get home, I can get some of my knittin' yarn and wrap it around a few times. I'll make it fit."

"You deserve better." He hung his head.

Without thinking, she weaved her fingers into his yellow curls. "I have *you* Gerald. That's all that matters." It wasn't a lie. She genuinely cared for him. *Loved* him. If only she could learn how to be *in* love with him.

He closed his eyes to her touch, then took her hand and kissed it. Without another word, he went around to the other side and climbed up into the wagon.

The ride home couldn't have been more miserable. Had the road always been this bumpy? It had never bothered her before. She thought she'd overcome her morning sickness, but the nausea made itself known. With each turn and bump, she became sicker. She finally asked Gerald to stop the wagon.

As soon as her feet touched the ground, she doubled over and heaved.

"Claire?" He hopped down and went to her side, then rubbed her back until she finished. "I'll get you some water."

He left her side for a brief moment and returned with a jug.

She gladly drank. "Thank you, Gerald. I feel so foolish."

"Foolish for gettin' sick? Pay it no mind."

"Must a ate sumthin' that didn't agree with me. All this jostlin' 'round churned it up. I feel better now. We'd best be goin' on." She had to hide her condition from him as long as she could.

They arrived at the church and found Reverend Brown. He seemed to be thrilled with their news and promised to announce it in church the next morning.

After they returned the horse to Mrs. Sandborn, Gerald asked her if he could stay the night. Of course she agreed. The happiness on her face said it all.

Then they drove on to Claire's to see Beth. Claire had no doubt that the joy on Mrs. Sandborn's face would be nothing in comparison to what they'd see from Beth.

As the wagon neared her house, Beth must have heard them approach. She came out onto the front porch and placed her hand over her brow. Claire giggled, watching her jump up and down.

"She's seen us," Claire said with a laugh.

"Reckon so." Gerald slowed the team, then reached across the seat and took her hand. "I love you."

Tears filled her eyes.

Before she could utter a sound, Beth was all over them. "Gerald! Claire! Oh, my land sakes!" She helped Claire out of the wagon. "Well? Looks like you found him!"

Her enthusiasm could likely wake the dead.

"Sure did, Beth. And we're gonna have a weddin'." Claire hugged her, then Beth hugged Gerald, and finally all three of them embraced at once.

"Well, come inside and tell me all 'bout it." Beth smiled so broadly that her cheeks puffed up to her ears.

They all went inside.

"Yes, Beth," Gerald said. "Claire agreed to me my wife. Can you believe it?" His grin matched his sister's.

They went to sit down at the table, but there were only two chairs. Claire suggested he bring in a rocker from the porch.

Instead, he sat and patted his lap, motioning for Claire to sit. "You just sit right down here."

She hesitated, but the sideways grin he gave her encouraged her to comply. There was something about this new Gerald she'd begun to like.

Beth sat in the other chair, looking at both of them and smiling. "Now—come on—you hafta tell me everythin'."

Claire and Gerald exchanged glances. He had to be thinking the same thing.

No, we aren't gonna tell you everythin'.

They simplified the story and Beth seemed satisfied.

Beth threw together a quick meal of sandwiches and fruit, then Gerald excused himself to go to Mrs. Sandborn's. Before he left, he kissed both of them on their foreheads.

Beth hadn't stopped smiling. It felt good to please her friend, and Claire did all she could to revel in her joy. If she dwelled on the reason behind it, she'd be miserable.

They started talking about the wedding and who they thought would attend.

"Reckon Lucy Beecham might come to taunt me?" Claire asked.

I could probably teach her a thing or two.

Thoughts like that would only get her in trouble. She had to get her mind right.

"Remember what she said that day after services?" Beth covered her mouth. The simple memory brought color to the girl's cheeks.

"How could I forget?"

Claire squirmed in her chair, remembering the words. Recalling *exactly* what it felt like, her body began to warm from the inside out. *Time to change the subject.* "Beth—"

"Claire. While we're on *that* kind of subject . . ." Claire hadn't spoken up fast enough. "I was hopin' I could talk to you woman-to-woman 'bout your weddin' night."

Claire swallowed hard. *So awkward.* Why had Beth become so serious all of a sudden? And why would she *ever* want to discuss what she and her brother might do when they're alone?

"Beth, you know we've always talked 'bout everythin', but that's kinda *personal.*" She hoped Beth would drop the whole thing.

"I know, but it's about Gerald." She obviously had no intention of letting this go. "I just want you to be understandin' of him if he's not able to—well—*you know.* The first time you're *together.*"

Beth struggled with what she was trying to say, but Claire had no idea how to make her friend more comfortable. "You shouldn't worry yourself over this. Gerald an I have been friends for a long time and this is simply the next step. I'm sure he'll be just fine." She didn't have to worry about the man's abilities. All the plumbing seemed to work.

"All I want you to promise me, Claire, is that you'll be *gentle* with him. Understandin'. All right?"

"Course I will." *Why's she so worried?* "Now, can you please stop bein' so serious? We haven't had a sleep-over since we were little girls. I remember how Mama used to fuss at us for gigglin' all night long."

"I remember. Well, we ain't little girls no more. You're gettin' married." Beth giggled.

The mood had lightened, much to Claire's relief.

They spent the rest of the evening going through fabric Claire had in a large sewing box. She had a variety of colors and cloth. Beth insisted the wedding dress be white.

"You hafta wear white. It's a sign of your purity before God."

Hmm . . . highly inappropriate considerin' my condition. Claire kept that feeling from Beth and picked some white eyelet material. She'd have much rather worn blue, but it would've only confirmed what the congregation had always believed—just how *odd* she was.

She could sew an exquisite gown, but would have to get right to it. She also had to fix the ring, but that would only take a moment.

When she laid it down on the table, Beth gasped. "Is that my mama's ring?"

Claire nodded.

Beth's mouth dropped open. "I didn't even know Gerald had it."

"I hafta fix it. It's too big for me, so I'm gonna put some yarn around it to make it smaller." She scanned her sewing basket for the yarn.

Beth picked up the ring, held it in her hand, then slid it on her finger and showed it to Claire. It fit her perfectly.

"I reckon if *I* was marryin' Gerald, the ring would be perfect." Beth sighed. "But sisters can't marry brothers." She laughed heartily.

Claire froze and stared at the floor.

"You all right, Claire?" Beth stopped laughing.

Claire wiped away a tear from her eye. "Yes. Yes, I'm fine. Just got a bit of yarn in my eye." She faced away from Beth and tried to compose herself. Without knowing it, Beth had reopened a wound. Taking a deep breath, she turned toward her. "There. It's fine now. And look. I found the blue yarn I was lookin' for."

She wrapped a small piece of yarn around one side of the ring. After a few loops encircled it, the ring became small enough for her hand. "I've got my sumthin' old an sumthin' blue. My dress will be sumthin' new. Now I just need sumthin' borrowed."

"I'll take care a that. You can wear my cameo. It'll look beautiful with the gown. I'll bring it to the church next Saturday."

Everything was coming together, and Beth had been none-the-wiser of Claire's momentary heartache.

They sewed for a bit, ate, then nestled down into bed. They giggled for a while for old time's sake, then fell asleep.

It had been a long day and Claire was spent. Her emotions were astir and the child inside her slowly grew. It took a lot out of her.

* * *

Beth and Claire got up early the next morning and walked to church.

Gerald stood at the base of the front steps, craning his neck and looking around. He'd been waiting for them. He ran to Claire, picked her up off the ground, and hugged her tight. "I missed you, Claire!"

Parishioners were already filtering into the church and gawked at their public display.

"Gerald," Claire scolded. "People are watchin'."

"Sorry. I wasn't thinkin'. I really did miss you." He took her by the hand and led her inside.

The three of them sat prominently in the front row with Claire in the middle. When Reverend Brown announced their engagement and upcoming wedding, the congregation stirred with instant chatter. It didn't surprise Claire. They'd expected it for some time. *If they only knew the truth.* Now *that* would create *real* chatter. The kind of gossip they'd love to share.

She quickly dismissed her evil thoughts.

As they left the church, they were congratulated by many and everyone promised they'd be there for the happy occasion. The wedding would be at noon on Saturday, the second of September, followed by a hot-dish supper. Reverend Brown had asked everyone to contribute to the meal.

Lucy Beecham was there with her children. Claire had dreaded what she might say, but Lucy didn't say a word. She didn't have to. Instead, she'd passed by Claire and winked. Sometimes a gesture could scream louder than any spoken word.

Gerald departed after they ate a quick meal with Mrs. Sandborn. He had to return to work, but would be back Friday evening with Uncle Henry. He'd spend his last night as a bachelor in the boarding house.

Mrs. Sandborn offered to make their wedding cake. "It will be my gift to you," she said. "Sumthin' sweet for two of the sweetest young people I've ever had the pleasure to know." Claire's façade seemed to be making everyone happy.

Gerald told them goodbye, then pulled her aside.

"Claire, I'll think 'bout you every minute I'm gone. I love you so much." He moved his head forward and puckered his lips.

She turned her head and offered her cheek instead. He gave it a soft kiss and smiled.

"I know. I hafta wait for the weddin' for that first kiss. Right?"

"Yes, Gerald, that's right." *Will I ever be ready to kiss him?*

Beth offered to stay that night at the boarding house so Claire could have her own home to herself. She couldn't have been more grateful. The walk home would be peaceful and familiar. She'd been away much too long.

At first, she swung her arms happily and even whistled. Her heart had lifted. Things had fallen into place more smoothly than she could have hoped. But the closer she got to home, realization struck her upside the head. The coming week would be her last week here.

Within seconds, the tears came.

CHAPTER 18

Over the last month, Claire had cried more tears than she had in her entire lifetime. Her pregnancy made her more emotional, but even if she hadn't been with child, she still would've had a difficult time holding back the tears. Her heart had been split in two.

She did everything in her power to *keep her chin up*, as her mama had always told her to do when things got tough. If only her mama could be here now to assure her she'd done the right thing.

She still experienced morning sickness, but could control the severity by watching what she cooked. The less smell the better.

Long walks on the beach and rocking on the porch helped her dismal mood. It felt good to be home.

She also worked diligently on her gown. The simple, but elegant design had three-quarter-length fitted sleeves, a scooped—but modest—neckline, fitted waist, and a full floor-length skirt. She trimmed the sleeves and neckline in fine lace and made the back button-down with faux pearl buttons.

She also made a matching lace veil. She didn't want to cover her face, but would fit the veil with a comb in her hair. The veil would flow down her back to her waistline. Her hair would be up, as usual, and she'd complete her look with the cameo Beth said she'd loan her.

Likely, Gerald would appreciate how she looked, but she wished Andrew would be the one standing there with her. Every time she thought of him, she scolded herself for doing so. But she couldn't help it. He still held her heart.

* * *

The week flew by. Friday had quickly come. Beth arrived to see Claire's dress and go over last minute details for the wedding.

Amidst laughter and reminiscing, Claire stopped and studied her dear friend. "I'm really gonna miss you when I'm gone."

Beth chuckled. "What do you mean when you're gone? You just came back."

"You know . . . after the weddin' when Gerald and I go back to Mobile."

Beth froze, blinking slowly. "Back to Mobile? What are you talkin' 'bout?"

Claire felt sick inside, seeing Beth so terrified. "Oh, Beth. Didn't Gerald tell you? We'll be livin' with your Uncle Henry."

"No." Beth shook her head violently. "You can't leave me. I thought you was gonna stay right here. That Gerald would be movin' in with *you*. This ruins everythin'."

"Please don't say that." Claire put her arm around her. "I'm sure if you'd like, you could move in with Uncle Henry, too. We could be one big family."

"No." She wouldn't budge. Her body trembled beneath Claire's arm. "I can't do that. My home's here. Mrs. Sandborn needs me. I'll have you know I've been doin' a lot more work at the church. I *can't* leave."

Beth walked away, then stopped at the window and gazed out toward the bay. She fingered Claire's drapery. The girl fidgeted, obviously doing all she could to keep her eyes off Claire.

Why hadn't Gerald told her?

Beth sighed. Aside from her dismal demeanor, the girl seemed at ease here. Completely at home.

At home.

The perfect solution. Not only would it make Beth happy, it would make Claire feel more comfortable about leaving. "Beth, I wanna give you sumthin' as a weddin' gift."

Beth turned to face her with a furrowed brow. "That makes no sense. You're the one gettin' married, not the one to be givin' the gifts."

"Don't matter. I still have a gift for you." This was probably the only *right* thing she'd done.

"All right, then." Beth managed a weak smile. "Where you got it hid?"

"You're standin' in it."

"Huh?" Beth's lip curled.

"I'm givin' you my house."

Beth didn't say a word and her face lost all expression.

"I won't be needin' it anymore," Claire continued. "And I know you'll love it an take good care of it. It's the perfect fit. Not to mention it'll give Gerald an me a place to stay when we want to come for a visit. And I promise we'll visit often. I won't be *that* far away."

Nearly hyperventilating, Beth clamped onto Claire. "Oh, Claire. Tellin' you thank you won't never even begin to express how happy you've made me. But I don't know how else to say it. Oh, my. Thank you." She placed a hand over her mouth, then attempted several large breaths. "I still wish you wasn't leavin', but I understand. Gerald's a lot more confident now that he's makin' a good livin'. I know how important it is for a man to be able to take care a his wife."

Claire pushed an unruly strand of hair from Beth's face. "It's important all right. I'm glad you're happy."

"Happy ain't a good enough word." She gave her the type of hug that only Beth could give.

Finally, something felt truly right.

They finished their work, then decided to sit on the porch for a while and enjoy the waning afternoon.

A horse and wagon approached.

"That better not be Gerald," Beth mumbled. "He ain't supposed to see you before the weddin'."

Claire recognized the wagon, the driver, and the woman sitting next to him. She shook her head. "Believe me, it's not Gerald."

Aunt Martha.

George held the reins and looked as he always did with a piece of straw dangling from the side of his mouth. Aunt Martha was wearing a sunbonnet and blue dress. Aside from the fancy clothes, she was Aunt Martha, chaw and all.

The wagon jerked to a stop. George hopped down and helped Martha out onto the dirt road. She rubbed her bottom and grimaced.

"Like to have killed me!" she fussed.

Claire ran to her and pulled her into an embrace. Beth followed behind her.

"Aunt Martha!" Claire couldn't hide her joy and squeezed the woman's hands. "I can't believe you're here!"

Martha tapped her foot and glared at her. "You married yet?"

"The weddin's tomorrow." Claire beamed, undaunted by the woman's behavior. "Your timin' is perfect."

"Just wanted to make sure that boy done right by ya." Martha spat on the ground at Beth's feet.

Beth's eyes opened wide.

Claire gave Martha a sideways glance and motioned with her eyes to *hush*. "Martha, do you remember my friend, Beth *Alexander?* Gerald's *sister.*"

Martha wrinkled her nose, then stepped closer to Beth. "Oh. Course I remember ya. Didn't recognize ya. You got *fat.*" She patted Beth's belly. "Claire's told me some real *nice* things 'bout your brother." Martha choked a bit getting those words out.

Claire stepped between the two women and draped her arm over Beth's shoulder, leading her toward the house. "Pay no mind to my aunt. She can be a little rough 'round the edges, but she means well. Once you get to know her, you'll find she can be quite a charmer." With a quick glance over her shoulder, Claire once again scolded the woman.

"What did she mean by Gerald doin' right by you?"

"Um . . ." *Oh, my.* "Well . . . by acceptin' my agreement to marry him after I'd already turned him down. You know. Swallowin' his pride an all."

"Oh." Beth turned her head, then whipped it back around again. She put her mouth to Claire's ear. "Does she always spit?"

"Only when I hafta!" Martha hollered. "Ain't nothin' wrong with my hearin'."

Beth's mouth screwed together, but she didn't say a word.

If Claire could get Aunt Martha to behave herself until after the wedding, then all would be well. But it wouldn't be easy.

"Hey, Claire!" Martha stopped them from going further. "Ain't ya gonna tell George goodbye?"

Why should she? The man never spoke. He'd probably care less. Truthfully, she assumed he'd rather never be spoken to at all.

She turned around with Beth and walked back toward the wagon.

Oddly, the man stared at Beth.

What's wrong with him?

"Thank you for bringin' Martha, George," Claire said, keeping her distance.

He nodded, but his eyes remained on Beth.

"Pick me up at the Baptist church at three o'clock tomorrow," Martha said. "George? Did ya hear me?"

"Uh. Yep." He removed his straw hat, dipped his head, and popped the reins. As he drove off, he turned around, once again eying Beth.

Claire leaned back and studied her friend, thinking maybe she'd smudged her dress. But nothing about her looked out of the ordinary.

"What?" Beth asked. "You're lookin' at me funny."

"Not me," Claire said. "George couldn't take his eyes off you."

Martha chuckled. "Now, I have no doubt the man has no sense. Least he's a good, hard worker. Brains ain't everythin'."

"What an ugly thing to say," Beth said with a scowl.

Martha waved her hands and walked away.

"Claire." Beth took one of her hands. "I best be goin' myself. I gotta get back to the boardin' house so I'm there when Gerald arrives. I reckon he's gonna be nervous an I hope to keep him calm."

"Is it because of Aunt Martha?"

"She ain't very kind. But I *do* need to go."

"I'm sorry. I'll have a talk with her."

"Don't make trouble on my count. You got more important things to do." She placed a small bottle in Claire's hand. "Here. I want you to have this."

"What is it?"

"Bath salts. They smell real good. T'morra mornin' when you take your bath, put some in the water. They smell like lavender and will make your skin smell more desirable. Uncle Henry gave 'em to me for Christmas last year. I used 'em once. I reckon they'd suit you better."

Claire examined the bottle, then opened it and inhaled the aroma. "They smell lovely. Thank you."

Martha had mysteriously wandered back to them. She took a whiff and sneezed. "That boy don't deserve ya, Claire."

It would've been better if Martha had gone inside.

Beth pinched her lips tight, breathing hard.

"I really do appreciate this, Beth," Claire said, guiding her away from Martha. "Thank you." She hugged her and said goodbye. "See you in the mornin'. I'll be at the church by eleven. Keep Gerald hid for me, you hear?"

Beth promised she would and left. If Claire had been thinking clearly, she'd have suggested George drive her home. But then again, the girl didn't deserve that sort of torment.

Claire shared her bed that night with Martha. It made for a very long night with little sleep. Aunt Martha's snoring shook the house worse than any storm. Even so, Claire couldn't be happier having her there. Martha was the only soul on earth that knew of her condition.

With thoughts of the man she *wished* she was marrying, Claire closed her eyes and fell asleep.

* * *

Claire woke to a familiar smell. Fried eggs.

Thank goodness I don't have any bacon.

Like clockwork, she got a whiff of the eggs and immediately hopped out of bed and raced out the door.

When she returned inside, Aunt Martha looked her way, shaking her head. "Not how the weddin' day is supposed to start I reckon."

Claire plopped down in a chair. "No! I'm supposed to be happy on my weddin' day. Not vomitin' like a sick cat."

"Should a thought 'bout that 'fore you got all tangled up with that man. Guess you wasn't thinkin' that far ahead."

Claire burst out crying.

"Damn," Martha mumbled, then stood behind her and stroked her hair. "Now, now. Sorry I said it. Sometimes my mouth gets ahead a my mind. You can't change what you done. Now you just gotta make the best of it. Least you chose to get married in the afternoon. You should be right as rain by then. Aunt Martha's gonna heat some water so you can take you a nice bath. Good soak'll be good for ya."

Martha left to pump the water. With a trembling chin and a large dose of self-pity, Claire walked to the barn to get her bathing tub, sniffling all the way. She started dragging it back to the house.

"I'll do that!" Martha scolded. "You don't need to be pullin' on anything big as this. You mind that baby inside ya."

Claire hadn't even thought about the possibility of hurting herself *or* the baby by lifting the tub. She let Martha take it and promised to be more careful in the future.

Martha used some of the heated water to make Claire a cup of hot tea, then started filling the tub. With a mixture of boiling water and some freshly pumped from the well, Claire had a nice temperate bath. She sprinkled in some of the bath salts and the aroma soothed her. Unlike the eggs, the smell didn't make her queasy. Quite the opposite.

While Claire bathed, Martha excused herself to the front porch so Claire could have some privacy.

Claire wanted to stay in the tub forever, forget the wedding, and try to go back in time and change everything. Since that wasn't possible, she set her mind to what she must do. Marry Gerald.

She stared down at her belly. Though she wasn't far enough along to show, she knew the baby was inside. Probably about five weeks. Rubbing her belly with both hands, she caressed the unborn child.

Lord, please make my baby smart. Please make it smart . . .

"I'm your mama," she said and continued rubbing in slow circles. "And no matter what, I'll take care of you an love you. I promise you that."

She'd make this day a happy one.

For Gerald.

She stepped from the water and grabbed a towel to dry off. Beth was right. The lavender made her skin smell appealing. Wanting to make up for the night in the stable, she had ideas for their wedding night. Hopefully, she'd make it a night Gerald would never forget. And in a *good* way.

She put on a simple cotton dress with plans to change into her wedding gown at the church. She'd packed a large chest full of clothing and essentials she'd need at her new house. Since Beth had no furniture of her own, she planned to leave all her furniture behind.

Gerald had given Uncle Henry directions to her home. He'd be there soon to load the chest in the back of the wagon. Then he'd take her and Aunt Martha to the church. They'd leave for Mobile directly after the wedding.

She glanced at the clock. *Nearly ten.* He'd be arriving soon.

She sighed and looked one more time around her little home, then heard the wagon.

Claire told Martha about Henry's hearing impairment as they walked out the door to wait for him. "Just be sure to look right at him when you speak."

Martha nodded, then craned her neck to get a good look at Henry.

He got down, grabbed his cane, and walked toward them.

Martha nudged her. "Not bad lookin', Claire. You sure he an Gerald is kin?"

"Martha," Claire fussed. "Mind your manners."

Henry tipped his hat and nodded, and she introduced him to Martha.

"Pleasure," Henry said with a slight bow.

"Manners, too. My, oh my!" Martha tittered.

Henry paid no mind to Martha's overenthusiasm in his regard. Instead, he smiled at Claire. "You look radiant, Claire."

"I'm not even in my weddin' dress yet." Her cheeks flushed. "Thank you, Henry."

After Martha helped Henry with the chest, he assisted both of them into the wagon. And they were on their way.

When they arrived at the church, they found Beth pacing. Her head popped up as they approached. "Hurry inside, Claire!" She frantically waved her hands. "Gerald will be here any minute!" She yanked Claire's arm and led them to a small room off to the side of the main chapel.

"I get tired just watchin' her," Martha said, pointing to Beth.

"You just rest yourself," Claire said. "I'll have Beth help me with the dress." After their previous encounter, Claire thought it best to keep them separated.

"Think I'll go find me a spot in a pew. I'd like a front row seat for this here weddin'." Martha walked away, followed by a relieved smile from Beth.

"Where's Uncle Henry?" Beth asked.

"Gone to check on Gerald." Claire removed her cotton dress and draped it over a chair.

Beth lowered the wedding gown over her head. "It's beautiful, Claire. You look like an angel. I'll help you fix your hair so we can put the veil on."

When Claire was fully dressed, she turned in a circle. "What do you think?"

"I reckon my brother's gonna die when he sees you." Beth clasped her hands and held them to her breast. "Oh! I'd better go see how he's comin' along. Make sure the groom hasn't gotten cold feet." She turned and started to leave. "I almost forgot!" She threw her hands in the air. "Claire, here's the cameo and I made you this bouquet!"

She shoved a bunch of wild roses into Claire's hands, then placed the cameo around her neck. "Perfect! Oh! I nearly forgot this, too. I need to give Gerald the ring!"

She scuttled out of the room like a cyclone spinning out of control and went to find Gerald.

Martha wasn't the only one tired from Beth's behavior. Claire laughed, watching her go.

This day would never be forgotten.

She gazed at her reflection in a tall stand-up mirror.

What would Andrew think if he saw me this way?

What was he doing at that very moment? She wished she knew.

"Claire?" Reverend Brown knocked on the door, forcing her thoughts to vanish.

With a smile, she invited him in. He proceeded to explain when to come out, when to start walking down the aisle, and to follow his lead when they said their vows. It couldn't be simpler and would be over before she knew it.

Soon, I'll be Mrs. Gerald Alexander.

Oh, my dear Lord . . .

CHAPTER 19

An accomplished pianist, Beatrice Brown, the minister's wife, always played for special occasions. To keep their wedding traditional, they chose the wedding march for Claire's walk down the aisle.

The church overflowed with folks. Events such as this didn't happen every day and in a small town they were celebrated. Everyone came, including Frank Beecham. Of course, food would be served after. Prayer and praise had never interested the man, but his fondness for casseroles frequently drove him to the church.

When Claire noticed him sitting beside Lucy, she assumed he'd come *only* for the supper following. She smiled at them as she passed by. This time, *Frank* winked. Claire quickly turned her head.

The walk down the aisle seemed to take forever. Since she had no one to accompany her, she walked alone. John Martin was the last person she wanted to think about. It'd be better for folks to think he'd died, than to know the truth. Even on this special day, he brought pain to her life.

She focused on Gerald, who had borrowed a suit from Uncle Henry.

He looks quite handsome. Well, as handsome as Gerald can look.

When their eyes met, he pushed his glasses up on his nose.

Yes, Gerald. I'm nervous, too.

Uncle Henry stood next to Gerald, and when Claire took her place, Beth stood beside her.

As the preacher spoke, Claire listened but didn't hear a word. Her mind drifted to another place. She found herself in a dense fog going through the motions and trying to find her way through. She'd gotten herself into a mess and now she had to clean it up.

They said their vows. Yes, she would love, honor, and obey Gerald, *and* keep herself only unto him. From this day forward.

Gerald placed the yarn-wrapped ring on her finger.

"You may kiss the bride," Reverend Brown stated without emotion, as he had many times before.

Claire waited. She smiled at Gerald, but he seemed to be frozen to the floor. She motioned with her eyes for him to do *something*, but he still didn't move. Heat rose into her cheeks.

Just kiss me!

She glanced at Uncle Henry who'd been staring at her like a lovesick puppy through the entire ceremony. He licked his lips.

Oh, my.

If Gerald didn't do something soon, likely Uncle Henry would step forward and kiss her on his behalf.

Gerald's eyes were affixed to the front pew.

Oh fiddle! Aunt Martha's glarin' at him. No wonder he's not doin' anythin'.

Claire took the lead. She bent forward and gave him a quick peck on the lips. She then turned toward the congregation and smiled, expecting to be able to walk down the aisle and exit for the reception.

But her little peck brought Gerald to life. He grabbed her by the shoulders and turned her to face him again. Then he took her head in his hands and pressed his mouth fully on hers in a very hard, tight-lipped kiss.

It completely took her off guard and she stumbled backward. Thankfully, Beth caught her. Gerald turned to the congregation with a large ear-to-ear grin, his body puffed up with pride. Seems he'd staked his claim.

Reverend Brown cleared his throat. "Mr. and Mrs. Gerald Alexander!" The congregation applauded.

Gerald grabbed Claire's hand and whisked her down the aisle. When they reached the end, he lifted her in the air and spun her around.

"This is my wife!" he yelled and they exited the sanctuary.

The fellowship hall was in the basement of the church. It helped to have a cool place for events during the summer and had also been used many times for people to take refuge during a storm.

It had a distinct smell—like an ongoing hot-dish supper. Claire sniffed, then blew out a long breath. Her stomach remained calm. *Thank goodness.* Her queasiness had subsided and she believed she could make it through the rest of the day without becoming sick again.

Gerald's behavior had embarrassed her, but as folks started coming down the stairs and approached them to offer congratulations, no one appeared to have been bothered by it.

He kept his arm linked in hers. She was his now and holding onto her would ensure no one forgot it.

A few of the men wanted to *kiss the bride.* Claire found this to be another unusual wedding ritual. Succumbing, she offered them her cheek and they'd give her a simple sweet kiss. Uncle Henry wanted to kiss her on the lips, but the look Gerald gave him forced the man to follow suit and put his lips to her cheek.

However, when Frank Beecham came into line, Claire's stomach twisted. He had mischief in his eyes.

Claire had caught sight of Frank and Lucy during the ceremony and Lucy had been visibly upset. She had her arms crossed over her chest and her bottom lip stuck out. It may have had something to do with the fact that Frank had his mouth hanging wide open, staring at Claire.

Lucy nodded at her. "I'm happy for ya. Truly." She turned to go to the food line.

Then Frank stepped forward. He grabbed hold of Claire, swung her down in his arms, and kissed her square on the lips. After standing her back up, he looked at Gerald, who scowled and brought up his fists, ready to take a swing at the man.

"Have some fun tonight, you hear!" Frank said, gloating.

Lucy rushed over and smacked him hard on the head. "We're leavin'! *Now!*"

"But I'm hungry," he whined. "All I did was kiss the bride. That's what ya's s'pose to do."

"Not like that!" Lucy grabbed him by the ear and dragged him out of the room. He somehow managed to nab a fried chicken leg on his way out.

Claire had been wrong about who wore the pants in that family. This would be something the members of the Baptist church would talk about for years to come. For now, she had to find a way to calm Gerald.

"I shoulda punched him!" Gerald shook his fists. "He had no right!"

"I'm fine, Gerald," Claire soothed. "Now don't let this spoil things." If only *they* could leave now. Things seemed to be getting worse.

Aunt Martha hadn't come through the line yet, but her turn finally arrived.

Claire held her breath.

Please behave yourself, Martha.

She kissed Claire on the cheek. "You're beautiful, Claire Belle. You be happy now, you hear me?"

"Yes, Aunt Martha. I will be." She returned Martha's kiss. "Martha, you remember Gerald, don't you?"

Martha glared at him. "You better take care a my girl and whoever else may came along."

Claire wanted to crawl under a table.

Why did she hafta say that?

Gerald tipped his head and pushed up his glasses. "I will, Aunt Martha."

Martha slugged him on the side of his arm, scowled, then walked away.

"Why'd she do that, Claire?" he asked, rubbing his arm. "Your aunt have sumthin' against me? She glared at me through the entire service."

"Oh, that's just her way. She's protective of me." Claire fumbled for the right words. "She was just referrin' to the babies we *might* have. That's all."

He leaned close. "I thought maybe you told her 'bout the stable," he whispered through the side of his mouth.

"Course not. No one knows but you an me." *And that's the way it'll stay.*

He let out a long sigh.

Everyone had come through the line, so Claire and Gerald grabbed a plate of food before it all disappeared. The ladies of the church had set up an area for them to eat and they placed a table behind them with a few wedding gifts on it.

The cake was on another table. Mrs. Sandborn did a lovely job. A three-tiered cake with white icing and tiny pink roses.

While they ate, Dorothy White—the oldest member of the congregation—shuffled to their table. She carried a very large folded quilt and laid it down in front of them.

"This is for you two."

Claire ran her fingers over the fine stitches and lovely pattern. "It's beautiful, Mrs. White. How'd you ever find time to make this on such short notice?"

"I started makin' it eight years ago. Everyone knew y'all would get married sooner or later, so I gave myself a head start. Takes me some time to do these things nowadays."

"Eight years ago? Well, that's might fine of you," Claire said with a smile. "Thank you so much."

"Yes, thank you, Mrs. White." Gerald added *his* thanks.

"Glad you two finally got to it! This thing's been gatherin' dust last four years. Glad to get it outta my house!" Mrs. White patted the quilt and a cloud of dust flew into the air. "See what I mean?" She shook her head, then turned and walked away.

"I'll take it out and beat it real good when we get home," Claire said. They moved the quilt away from their food and onto the table behind them.

Gerald began to fidget, which gave Claire the perfect opportunity to suggest they get on their way.

They ceremoniously cut the cake, then Reverend Brown announced they'd be leaving.

Uncle Henry left to prepare the wagon and assisted loading the gifts. Beth had been bustling around, acting as host. She made sure everyone had a good time and got plenty to eat, then directed folks to gather at the church steps to wait for them to come out.

They exited the church quickly and were covered in rice thrown from the onlookers. Gerald hoisted Claire up into the wagon. Henry would be driving, so he got up on the other side of her.

She threw her bouquet over her shoulder. Beth caught it, but passed it off to a young girl standing next to her.

Claire laughed as they rode away.

Married.

Chapter 20

The bumpy ride home jostled Claire just as much as the ride getting there, but she managed to control her nausea. They made the best of the long trip, talking and laughing about their memorable wedding.

"I think you shoulda punched that Frank Beecham!" Henry exclaimed. "He had no right takin' advantage a Claire that way."

"I woulda if his OWN WIFE hadn't done it for me." Gerald laughed. "I feel right SORRY for him."

"So do I," Claire added. "I used to feel sorry for Lucy. I reckon she proved she can take care of herself."

Gerald's face fell and his brows drew in. "I was angry, you know? It may seem funny now, but you're MY WIFE! Don't want no OTHER MAN touchin' you!"

"Now you're talkin', Gerald," Henry said. "You stand your ground. Don't never be afraid to pop-a-man a good one if he messes with your wife."

Sitting between the two of them hadn't been the best idea. Claire understood why Gerald talked louder than normal, but her ears had started to ring. She inched closer to him. Uncle Henry had been sitting a bit too close for comfort.

If he doesn't mind his manners, he could be the one gettin' popped.

The two men continued talking about what happened and Claire began to feel like a piece of property.

So this is what it's like bein' someone's wife?

It would take some getting used to. She sat quietly for some time, lost in thought.

When they arrived home, Gerald and Henry unloaded the wagon, while Claire waited patiently to be helped down. Gerald obviously forgot about her and headed inside. Henry chided him, so Gerald returned to help her.

She gave him her hand and he lifted her down. He again started walking ahead of her toward the door.

Henry shook his head. "Gerald! Carry your wife over the threshold!"

"Huh? Oh, yeah. Almost forgot." He scooped Claire into his arms and carried her inside.

Just like Andrew.

But she'd be set down in a whole different world.

Once inside, Henry excused himself and left them alone. Gerald wasted no time at all and grabbed her face with both hands and kissed her hard.

She forced a smile.

"I love you, Claire!" He bubbled over, acting almost giddy.

"Thank you, Gerald."

What have I done?

Henry returned carrying a small carved wooden box. "This is for you." He handed it to her.

She sat on the sofa—awestruck by the gift he'd given her —and ran her fingers over the fine carving. A similar pattern to the one in the mirror upstairs. The edges had been carved with tiny roses and a swirling leaf pattern.

"Sarah loved roses," Henry whispered. "Had this made for her before we lost our boys. I want *you* to have it now."

"It's lovely, Henry," she said, looking directly at him. "Thank you. I'll always treasure it."

"Open it. There's more inside."

She raised the lid. Inside, she found a porcelain comb and brush set. They, too, were decorated with tiny roses. It also held a small bottle of toilet water nearly full. She lifted it from the box, opened it, and smelled. "Roses." She closed her eyes, enjoying the aroma.

"Yep. Bought them things at the mercantile. Came all the way from Paris, France. Ordered 'em special just for her." He stood there and stared at the floor.

Claire arose and kissed him on the cheek. "Thank you, Henry. This is the most beautiful gift I've ever been given."

Gerald cleared his throat. "Claire, I got a gift for you, too. Been workin' on it all week." He grabbed her by the hand and rushed her up the stairs to the room she'd slept in before. The wrought iron bed had been removed. A full-size pine bed had taken its place. The headboard had been carved with their names.

GERALD & CLAIRE
ALEXANDER
SEPTEMBER 2, 1871

"Thank you, Gerald!" She hugged him tight. "I can tell you worked hard on it. How'd you find time?"

"Stayed up late most nights." He ran his hand over the bed post. His brows drew in. "I wanted us to have a proper bed. You like it?"

"Very much." Seeing his concern, she whispered in his ear. "I'll show you just how much later."

He froze, slowly blinking at her. His cheeks turned several shades of red.

It's gonna be a long night.

Evening approached. They weren't hungry after the large meal at the church, but ate a simple snack of fruit, raw vegetables, and wheat bread with honey. Henry excused himself to his room.

"Gerald, I'm fixin' to get ready for bed," Claire said. "Give me a minute or two before you come up." She kissed him on the cheek and went out the back door to take care of personal business.

When she came back inside, he remained glued to the same spot.

She washed, started up the stairs, then paused and looked over her shoulder. "Remember Gerald . . . a few minutes." She used her softest and most sensual voice.

"All right, Claire." He squeaked out the words.

Determined to do things right by him, she wanted this to be the perfect wedding night. She began by lighting a candle on the nightstand next to the bed. It gave off a soft pleasant glow.

Sitting down at the vanity, she took the pins out of her hair and let it fall over her shoulders. Then she opened the box from Henry and decided to try out the brush.

Such a thoughtful gift.

She dabbed a bit of the rose perfume on her neck. *Subtle*. A pleasant scent. The rest of her skin smelled like lavender.

I hope Gerald appreciates it.

Next to the vanity was a wooden stand that held a porcelain water bowl and a matching pitcher full of water. She poured a small amount into the bowl so she could clean her teeth, wanting to be completely fresh. She hoped her husband would offer her the same courtesy.

She removed her gown and draped it over a chair in the corner of the room. Then she removed everything else and slipped into the bed between the sheets.

The moment she sat down, the bed creaked. She rose up a bit, then let her full weight down. It creaked again.

"Oh, my! The bed squeaks!" Not good.

Least Uncle Henry's hard a hearin'. Hopefully he won't notice.

However, their room lay directly over Henry's. She shook her head.

Will our weddin' night be as eventful as our weddin'?

"Claire?" Gerald rapped on the door.

"Come in," she said in a low, inviting voice.

She'd positioned herself in bed with the blankets pulled up around her. Her hair flowed over her shoulders and onto the blankets. Would he like what he saw?

He shut the door and crept toward her. She patted the bed beside her and he went to her, but rather than climbing into bed, he sat on the edge.

"What's wrong, Gerald?"

"Are you naked, Claire?" He pushed his glasses up on his nose.

"Why, yes I am. I thought you'd like it, this bein' our weddin' night an all."

"I don't reckon I'm ready for you to be naked. I ain't never seen a naked woman in all my life."

"If it makes you uncomfortable, I can put my gown on. Would that help?"

"It would. Thank you, Claire." He let out a large breath.

"You're a very sweet man, Gerald Alexander." She leaned forward to kiss his cheek. As she did so, the blanket dropped, exposing her breasts.

His eyes got as wide as saucers. He sat there with his mouth open, staring at her exposed flesh.

"I'm sorry, Gerald!" She jerked up the blanket, modestly covering herself once again.

He lifted his eyes to her face. Then he pulled the blanket back down again.

"What are you doin'?" His behavior seemed odd. *So unlike him.*

"I decided I like lookin' at 'em. They're nice." He again stared, and this time, licked his lips.

The tides had turned. Heat filled her face. "So you don't want me to put a gown on?"

"Nope."

"Are you gonna get in bed now?"

"Yep."

He went around to the other side. He turned his back to her and removed his pajamas, then slid into bed beside her, lying flat on his back. His weight caused the bed to creak again.

She scooted down and also laid flat back. "The bed squeaks, Gerald."

"Reckon I didn't nail it quite tight enough. I'll fix it t'morra."

"But what 'bout tonight? What if Uncle Henry hears us?" *Spare me the embarrassment, please?*

Regardless of the fact couples were expected to consummate their marriage on their wedding night, she didn't want it to be totally obvious as to what they were doing.

"Don't worry 'bout Henry. Remember, he's deaf as a post."

"I don't think he's as hard a hearin' as he lets on sometimes." She wasn't convinced.

"Just don't think 'bout it."

They laid there without speaking for what seemed like an eternity. She became impatient, not to mention extremely tired. If she lay there too long she'd fall asleep.

"Jerry," she cooed. "You can touch me if you like."

He swallowed hard, then turned on his side facing her. He still had his glasses on.

"Why don't you take those off? You don't sleep in 'em, do you?" She wanted him to relax.

"I wasn't plannin' on sleepin' right now. I'd like to be able to see you."

"Not much to see right now." They'd pulled the covers up to their necks. "Take 'em off. You don't need 'em for what we're gonna do." She reached over and removed his glasses, then placed them on the nightstand.

"Oh, my." He gulped.

"Don't fret, Gerald." She twirled a strand of his hair around her finger and his entire body quivered. "Go on an touch me."

He reached out with a trembling hand and placed it on her waist. He moved it over her body, across her belly, down her side, and then up toward her neck. He'd completely avoided her breasts and wouldn't go any lower than her waistline.

"Gerald, I won't bite you. I'm your wife now. You're allowed to touch me." She continued toying with his hair, trying to help the mood.

Becoming bolder, he moved his hand across her breast. Her nipple instinctively hardened and he jerked his hand away. Then, when he touched her other breast and received the same reaction, he muffled a chuckle.

Wonderful! He's amused.

She laid there with her head on the pillow.

I've married a boy. I need a man.

She'd become his new plaything. Though he'd touched her as intimately as he likely knew how, she didn't feel a thing. No passion and certainly no desire. She'd let him have her, but it meant nothing.

He bent over her and kissed her firmly on the mouth, pressing her head hard into the pillow. At the same time, he pulled her hair with the weight of his shoulder.

This would *not* do. Not wanting to go through the rest of her life with bruised lips and a bald head, she pushed him away.

"Gerald! You're hurtin' me!"

He stopped and drew his head back. "I was just kissin' you. Like I did in church. Figgered you liked it."

"No, I don't like it. But don't be upset. I know you never kissed a woman before. Why don't you let me teach you how to do it more proper?" For his sake *and* hers.

"All right, if it'll make you happy. You know I'll do anythin' for you."

Yes, he'd proven that in the stable.

"Lay back," she instructed.

He obeyed.

"First of all, you need to relax your lips. You've been kissin' me like you're a hammer tryin' to drive a nail." She placed her fingers on the sides of his mouth, then moved them around in a slow, gentle motion. "See what I mean?"

"Uh-huh," he said through pursed lips.

"Now, when you're ready to kiss me, do it softly. Like this." She bent toward him and gave him a light kiss on his upper lip, then another kiss on his bottom lip. Then she put her full mouth over his, moved it gently, and kissed him deeply. His lips responded to hers naturally. Satisfied, she pulled away. "Isn't that much nicer?"

"Uh-huh." Though he hadn't said much, his body reacted, becoming firm against her.

She lay back on the pillow making sure to move her hair to one side and out of his way. "Okay, now *you* try it."

He rolled over to her and kissed her softly, *gently*, just as she'd taught him.

She'd succeeded. There'd be more lessons to come. "Much better."

He nestled his face into her neck. "You smell good." He followed his words with a kiss.

She smiled, grateful for the progress they'd made.

He clumsily climbed on top of her and his whole body shook.

The bed creaked again, but she tried to ignore it and opened her legs to accommodate him.

"What are you doin'?" he exclaimed much too loud.

"Well, it's necessary if you want me." Why was he shaming her? "What's wrong? You act like we've not done this before!"

"Shh . . . not so loud. It's just different with you naked an all. I mean—I like it, but it's different."

"Well then, just close your eyes and pretend we're in the stable and I'm fully dressed. Or I can put my gown on." She wanted this over with.

"No." He softened to a whisper. "I like you like this. Just give me a little time." He grunted while he wiggled around trying to find his way. He eventually found it.

The moment his movement started, the bed began to rhythmically squeak.

Then, the unthinkable happened. Uncle Henry's cane beat against their floor, his ceiling.

Gerald stopped.

Claire sank deeper into the pillow. "You see. He's not as deaf as you think." She couldn't have been more humiliated and covered her face. Though hiding would do no good.

Then the rapping ensued once again.

"Atta boy, Gerald! You keep at it!" Uncle Henry cheered them on.

Gerald puffed up like a proud peacock and continued his lovemaking.

She wanted to die, or at least be taken far away from there. They'd become the percussion section in a lovemaking symphony—the bed creaking and squeaking to every thrust from Gerald.

He seemed oblivious to the sound. He grunted and moaned and without a doubt enjoyed himself.

He was taking much longer than he had before, so she just lay there. She closed her eyes and drifted off to another place where she'd actually contributed to the act. And in no time, she dozed off.

She woke immediately when Gerald's body violently shook over her. He let out a loud groan, and then fully collapsed on her. *So, this is how it'll be.* She'd made her bed and sadly lay in it.

I reckon I deserve this.

Aunt Martha had been right. There were no fireworks. Nothing like the explosive sensations she'd felt with Andrew—sensations she thought weren't possible for the human body. This had been more like the firework that didn't go off. The dud everyone jeered.

He rolled off of her and fell asleep.

She turned over and blew out the candle.

It's like a bad Fourth of July.

CHAPTER 21

Morning came too early. Claire had lain awake in bed for some time after blowing out the candle, feeling sorry for herself and the mess she'd made of her life. Could she ever be truly happy again?

She didn't cry. She wanted no more of that. To be a decent mama she had to get herself together. Gerald wasn't a bad man. He'd be good to her and take care of her.

But I'm not in love with him.

Uncle Henry beat on the stairwell. "Rise and shine lovebirds!"

How could she face him?

I'll act indifferent and go 'bout becomin' the woman of the house. Whether he likes it or not.

Gerald snuggled up to her.

No, not again.

His firm body indicated he'd like more of what she'd given him the previous night.

"We'd better get up, Gerald," she said, hoping to douse his desires. "We don't wanna keep Henry waitin'."

"Ah, shucks, Claire. He'll understand." He pulled her close and planted small kisses across her shoulders.

"Now, Gerald. You don't wanna get too much of a good thing. Save that for later." She thought of a way out. "Sides, nature's callin'." Jumping out of bed, she quickly dressed and headed down the stairs, all the while trying to ignore her husband's protruding lower lip.

She also ignored Henry as she raced out the door to the outhouse, never dreaming she'd be glad to escape there. After staying longer than necessary, she decided she'd better go back inside.

Henry stood at the stove cooking breakfast.

"Hope you like griddle cakes an sausage," he said as she went to the sink to wash. He hadn't started frying the sausage yet and was mixing the batter for the griddle cakes.

"Not too fond of sausage," she lied, looking him straight on. She didn't want him to cook it, fearing the worst.

Her comment made him grin, though she didn't understand why.

"Henry, why don't you let me COOK for you?" She much preferred to anyway. "I want to start EARNIN' MY KEEP!"

"That would do just fine." He flashed an even larger grin. "Haven't had a woman's cookin' in a dog's age."

He sat and started to whistle, while she set to work.

She finished mixing the batter, then instead of sausage she found a jar of peaches. She planned to whip up some cream and top the cakes with the peaches and cream. Not a *manly* breakfast by any means, but a good one.

In time she'd be able to fry food again, but for now she'd attempt to get around it without drawing suspicion.

When Gerald came in and saw her cooking, he smiled, puffed out his chest, and sat down next to Henry. She poured them both some coffee.

Henry patted Gerald on the back. "You caught you a fine wife."

Don't say a word.

Whipping the cream helped relieve her frustration.

"Good coffee," Henry said, but she chose to ignore him. "Just got two new orders for a couple a wagons. That'll keep me busy. Gerald, you'll hafta take care a the shoein' and wheel repair."

Claire sat down beside him. "You know how to do that?"

"Yep. Uncle HENRY taught me. Says I'm GOOD at it." He took a sip of his coffee and smiled at her over the rim of the cup.

"Boy's a natural," Henry said. "Came here with a broken heart, you know?"

She stood and returned to the stove. She didn't like how the conversation had turned.

"UNCLE HENRY!" Gerald slammed down his cup. "Don't TALK 'bout that!"

Henry mumbled something she couldn't understand and she decided to focus on the griddle cakes. Gerald must have told Henry about her declining his proposal, but all of that was in the past, and Gerald obviously wanted to keep it there. A very good thing.

Both Gerald and Henry had second helpings of griddle cakes with peaches and whipped cream. Her cooking impressed them, and there'd be plenty more to come. She'd chosen this life and she'd make it work. She *had* to make it work.

She had plenty of responsibility. Not only would she be preparing the meals for the three of them, but she'd be expected to clean the house, do all the washing, tend the chickens, and milk the cow.

Once the baby came, it would add an entirely new dimension to her daily chores. She wouldn't lack for things to keep her busy. Hopefully, in the evenings after supper, she'd be able to sew and have time to do some of the things she enjoyed.

She feared that for the time being, Gerald would be whisking her off to the bedroom as soon as the sun set. Maybe when her belly started to swell, he wouldn't find her so desirable. Then she'd have a good excuse to deny him. Until then, she'd have to succumb.

* * *

Two weeks had passed since the wedding. Claire and Gerald had fallen into a routine and seemed to be comfortable with one another.

Gerald fixed their bed so it no longer creaked, and Henry behaved himself and didn't beat on the stairwell to wake them in the morning.

Claire wasn't miserable, but far from content. Still, she believed she'd done quite well making good from a bad situation.

The time had come to tell Gerald of her *possible* pregnancy.

It was Saturday morning. Henry had told Gerald the night before that he could take the mornin' off and sleep in for a spell. So Gerald took him up on his offer.

But Claire couldn't sleep. She sat up in bed and looked at her husband, wondering how she'd tell him. He looked so peaceful lying there, completely unaware of her devious plan. She was about to turn his world upside down.

She crept out of bed and went to the kitchen. After cooking some oats, she made a tray to carry up to him. Breakfast in bed would be a good start.

Henry had already gone out to the shop, so she didn't have to worry about him.

She tiptoed up the stairs and into their room. After setting the tray on the vanity, she went to the bed and crawled in next to her husband, then kissed him on the forehead.

"Gerald, wake up," she whispered in his ear.

He rolled over, pulled the pillow over his head, and groaned. "It's too early, Claire. Let me sleep."

"The sun's been up for an hour. I brought you breakfast." She shook his shoulder.

Lowering the pillow, he peered at her with one eye. "You brought breakfast up here? Why?"

"I have sumthin' to tell you." She flashed him a big broad smile.

He inched up and propped the pillow behind his back. "Well? What is it?"

"First of all . . . good mornin'." She kissed him on the cheek.

"I hope you woke me for more than that." He scolded her, but grinned at the same time.

"Course, I did. Gerald, I think we're gonna have a baby," she said and sighed. Now she could stop trying to hide her condition.

His eyes were wide open, staring at her.

"Gerald? Say sumthin'."

"I . . . I . . . How can you be sure? It's so soon."

"I know. But Gerald, I just *know*. See . . . my cycle's late. And I'm never late. It's like clockwork. Always on time. It shoulda started over a week and a half ago, but it hasn't. Oh, Gerald. I'm gonna have your baby!"

"We was only married two weeks ago!" His eyes rolled upward as if doing the calculations in his head.

"Yes, but remember that night in the stable?" She tickled under his chin. "It coulda happened then."

"How could I forget that? I just hope that baby don't come early. Folks might talk. They might figger out what we done."

"No one will ever know 'bout that. Don't you worry. Aren't you happy?"

He took her hands in his and brushed them with gentle kisses. "Claire, you've no idea how happy you've made me. I'm gonna be a daddy!" He brought her into his arms and kissed her lips. "I love you so much. You've made me the happiest man in all a Alabama!"

"You said the same thing to me the night I agreed to marry you."

Thank God, he's happy.

"I meant it then, and I mean it now." He placed his palm against her cheek. "Are you really, truly sure?"

"Yes, Gerald. Quite sure. Women know these things." Of course she was sure. She estimated being nearly two months along. There was no doubt in her mind.

He pushed her hair away from her face and kissed her again. His kisses now were soft and affectionate.

Then he laid her back against the pillows and made love to her. She didn't mind it so much. He'd just tugged on her heartstring.

* * *

They decided to wait a week before telling Uncle Henry the news. They didn't want to take any chances that someone might think the child had been conceived earlier than their wedding night. Especially not Uncle Henry.

Gerald became overly cautious with Claire and any activity she did. He even acted nervous about her hanging the laundry on the line. Of course, she thought he was being silly, but then again, she enjoyed the attention.

"A baby in my home again?" Henry shook his head, then smiled. "It'll be a good thing."

After that day, Gerald and Henry *both* took special care of her. She started cooking whatever they wanted, but after a few mornings of running outside to be sick, they told her *she* could choose the menu.

They decided to make the trip to tell Beth the good news. Henry encouraged them to go, so they hitched up the wagon and headed out early on a late September morning.

Being Saturday, they thought they could get there by dinner time and have the rest of the day with Beth. They planned to spend the night with her, then come back home Sunday afternoon.

Claire became sentimental as they approached her old house. It looked the same. Of course it had only been three weeks since they'd left, but it seemed much longer.

They pulled the wagon to a stop, got out, and went to the door. Claire felt it appropriate to knock since it was no longer her home.

Beth came to the door and nearly fainted when she saw them standing there. She swooned and clutched her chest. "I can't believe you're here!" After catching her breath, she pulled them into a simultaneous hug, then bustled them inside.

Gerald beamed—busting at the seams. "We *had* to come. We have great news!" He nudged Claire, who displayed her own bright smile. She loved seeing him this way. "Claire's gonna have a baby!"

Beth stumbled backward and came to rest in a chair. "You sure? I mean, you was only married three weeks ago."

Beth and Gerald thought very much alike. Beth's eyes rolled upward, obviously doing her own bit of math.

"I know, Beth," Claire said gently. "But I promise you I'm certain. I really am gonna have a baby."

"Have you seen a doctor?"

Since time began, there could never have been a more complex question.

"No, Beth," Claire said, keeping it simple. "There's no need for that. I feel fine. I'm just *late*, and I've had other symptoms, too."

"Sure has," Gerald chimed in. "Been heavin' nearly every mornin' this week."

Beth pulled him to the side. "Oh Gerald, if it really is true, you have yourself a miracle! What with the—"

"Please, Beth. Don't." He stopped her short. His mood instantly darkened.

"All babies are miracles," Claire said, attempting to ease him.

"Yes, they are, Claire." He turned and gave her a kiss on the cheek.

Because something had upset him, she decided to change the subject. "Beth, the house looks wonderful. I knew you'd take good care of it. Do you like livin' here?"

"Yes. Thank you." Beth's fire had also been doused. "Oh, Gerald. Speakin' of the house." She turned to him. "The barn door's comin' off its hinges. Reckon you could take a look at it for me?"

"Sure. I'll go see to it now if you'd like." He moved toward the door, but stopped and kissed Claire before he left.

Claire knew her friend well. She seemed as troubled as Gerald. "What was that all 'bout, Beth?"

The woman waved her hands in the air as if fanning her own flames. "Oh, Claire! I just can't stand it! Please tell me again, are you *sure* you're gonna have a baby?"

"Yes. There's no doubt in my mind."

"Then, your baby truly is a miracle. Gerald would kill me if he knew what I'm fixin' to tell you." She bit her bottom lip and looked around the room like a nervous hen. "Do you recall when we was in school with Miss Eva? Back before the war?"

"Course I remember. But what does that have to do with Gerald?"

"I'm gettin' to that. Do you recall the year he gave you the box a candy for Christmas?"

"Yes. He was the first boy to ever give me a gift. I remember it well. " She smiled, recalling the happy memory.

"He loved you even way back then. You was eleven and he was thirteen." Beth sighed. "Do you also recall how he missed 'bout two weeks a school right before Christmas?"

"Yes, you told me he was real sick. Had to stay home with your mama. Then he came back just before Christmas —when he gave me the candy." She had a vivid memory of that time. Gerald had always been a big part of her life.

Beth took a deep breath. "Gerald wasn't really sick, Claire. He'd been workin' for old man Porter before school, helpin' him with his livestock to earn money so he could buy you the candy. Sent Daddy all the way to Mobile to get it."

"I still don't understand." What did this have to do with their baby?

"See, one mornin' when Gerald was workin', he was helpin' with an old stubborn mule Mr. Porter had. That mule didn't like Gerald an Gerald made the mistake of gettin' up behind him. The mean ol' mule kicked Gerald hard right in the—well—you know. *There*." She pointed to her crotch.

Claire's eyes drew open wide. "Oh, my."

"Yes, Claire. The mule kicked him so hard it sent him flyin' cross the barn floor. Gerald started screamin' an cryin' an Mr. Porter came runnin'. Gerald's pants were drenched in blood. Mr. Porter grabbed him up and ran him to Mama. Then he went an got a doctor. I hadn't left for school yet, an when I heard Gerald cryin' I went in his room. Mama made me leave.

"When the doctor came, he had to put twenty stitches in him. He told Mama Gerald would never be able to have a family. Wasn't even sure if things would work proper for him. If you know what I mean."

Claire nodded. She knew *exactly* what Beth meant.

"Why do you think it took him so long to get 'round to askin' you to marry him?" Beth went on. "He would a asked you when you came back from livin' at your Aunt Martha's—after the war—but he just couldn't do it. Said he didn't wanna deny you a family. Then when you never married, an he figgered you was gettin' too old to have babies anyways, he decided to go ahead an ask you. That's why I wanted you to be patient an gentle with him on your weddin' night."

Claire covered her mouth. Speechless. All she could think about was that night in the stable and how scared Gerald must have been with her begging him to make love to her, wondering if he even could. How could she have done that to him? She'd convinced herself it had been for the baby, and that had made it all right.

She'd said over and over again that the baby was Gerald's. She'd even started believing it herself, only because she wished it so. But this particular lie could never be true. Gerald could never father a child.

"Claire?" Beth placed her arm around Claire's waist. "Please don't tell him I told you. But don't you see I had to? I wanted you to know what a true miracle you're carryin' inside you. God has blessed you, Claire." Beth gave her a gentle squeeze. "I'm blessed, too. I'm gonna be an auntie!"

The front porch squeaked from Gerald's heavy footsteps, but Claire couldn't move.

What have I done?

"Let's go sit outside," Beth said. "We could use a little air." She took Claire by the hand and led her to the porch.

The agonizing heaviness in Claire's heart cut deep. She'd involved Gerald—a decent and innocent man—in her deceptions, tormenting him in a way she only now realized.

He stood at the edge of the porch looking out toward the gulf—at peace and oblivious to the wrong she'd done him.

She walked up behind him, put her arms around him, and kissed his cheek.

He turned to face her. "What was that for?"

"I love you," she said and kissed him again.

This time on the lips.

CHAPTER 22

The end of September approached. The weather was warm—but not *hot*—and one of the most pleasant times of the year in Alabama. Some of the trees had begun to turn colors, but only a few leaves had dusted the ground.

Nearly two months had passed since Andrew had come home to find Claire gone. He'd been going about his day-to-day routine at the hospital, trying to appease Mr. Schultz. His heart wasn't in his work, but he still performed proficiently, arriving on time daily and staying late when the workload warranted. Almost mechanical.

Though he acted gracious to his patients and very kind, he lacked the spark that had been there if only briefly, when his heart felt full and complete.

He couldn't rid himself of thoughts of Claire. He'd taken to heart what Alicia Tarver had told him and knew she was right. But his mind wouldn't allow his heart to be convinced.

He had to try to see her again.

Not knowing why she'd left tore him up inside. He hadn't been eating properly and had lost a great deal of weight. Sleep was almost impossible, and it had become more and more difficult to concentrate at work.

He'd made up his mind to return to Claire's one more time.

After weeks of working non-stop, he had no problem requesting a few days off, and Mr. Schultz granted it.

On an early Saturday September morning, Andrew saddled Sam for another trip down a familiar road.

Will she be there this time?

Several points along the way he considered turning around and going back home, but he kept on. The need for answers outweighed any other impulse he might have.

The closer he got to her home, the heavier his heart became. His throat had completely dried out and his hands trembled holding the reins.

He hoped she'd see him, rush into his arms, and beg forgiveness for ever leaving, but it was highly unlikely. If she'd felt that way, she'd have already come to him.

Those thoughts had plagued him every night since she left. He needed to lay them to rest.

Her house looked exactly the same as the last time he'd been there.

Why shouldn't it?

After tying Sam to a nearby tree, he took slow deliberate steps to her door. As he reached up to knock, his heart thumped hard. The anticipation of her opening the door was almost unbearable.

He knocked.

The door creaked opened.

His heart beat even faster.

"Dr. Fletcher?"

Beth?

His heartbeat subsided. "Yes. Beth, isn't that right?"

"Yep. I'm Beth." She gazed into his eyes—eyelashes fluttering—then stepped out onto the porch.

Though she wore a plain cotton dress, her hair had been pulled up neatly on her head in a tight roll. Her appearance had improved since the last time he'd seen her.

"I reckon you're lookin' for Claire again, huh?" she asked, then motioned to a rocker. "Would you like to sit down for a spell?"

"Thank you." He sat in the very familiar rocking chair. "And yes, I am looking for Miss Montgomery. Is she at home?"

"Well. *Sort*a." She wrinkled her nose. "Would you like some sweet tea punch? I can get it for you." Again, she batted her lashes.

"That would be very nice. Thank you."

How can Claire be sort of home?

Beth went inside and soon came back with two glasses. She extended one to him.

As he took it, his hand naturally brushed hers, causing her face to glow red. She came close to spilling the drink in his lap, so he grabbed it quickly and gave her a polite smile.

She plopped herself down in the other chair.

"So, what do you mean by Miss Montgomery being *sort of* home?" he pressed her.

"Well, you see . . ." She grinned and leaned toward him. "She's at home, but her home ain't here no more."

"She doesn't live here any longer?"

"Nope! She gave *me* this house. Can you believe it? Land an all. Truthfully, she got sumthin' much better." Her eyes widened and she giggled. "Claire married my brother, Gerald. And when she did, she gave me the house. She's my sister now."

Her words might as well have had claws. They'd just ripped his heart from his chest. "Miss Montgomery is married now?"

"That would be *Mrs. Alexander* now. Heck! She an my brother was sweethearts since we was little. He asked her to marry him just before that awful storm we had few months back. Silly girl refused him, but after that time away visitin' her aunt, she realized how much she loved him an came runnin' back here lookin for him. I never seen a woman so lovesick. Course Gerald took her, even after she broke his heart."

Please stop.

He'd heard enough. He wanted to run. To get as far away as he could. He had to remind himself to breathe.

"The most amazin' thing is," Beth rambled on. "Claire's already with child! You bein' a doctor an all, I figger you know how them things happen. They musta got busy real quick." She winked.

He stood and handed her the full glass of tea. "I'm sorry, but I really must be on my way. I'm not feeling very well." Never had he spoken truer words.

"Oh. Sorry to hear it. Did you come by 'bout them shirts? If so, I told Claire you'd been by to get 'em. Hate to tell you, but she said when you didn't come by for 'em, she gave 'em away."

"So you told her I was here?"

"Course I did! She didn't recall you at first, but I reminded her what you look like, and then she recollected. Can't figger how she could a ever forgotten you. I've carried 'round a picture of you in my mind since the last time I saw you." The dreaminess in her eyes made him even more uncomfortable and eager to leave.

"You've been very kind, Beth. But I really must go. It's a long ride back to Mobile."

"Mobile? Why that's where Claire an Gerald live now. They moved in with our Uncle Henry Alexander. He's a blacksmith. Has a shop just north a the city 'bout a mile. If that horse a yours ever needs shoein', you should take her to my brother. He's been learnin' the trade from Uncle Henry and doin' quite well. Or so I've been told. He's makin' good money now, so he can take care a his wife and their new baby like a good husband should."

Claire's in Mobile.

He clutched his chest. What would he do if he ran into her in the city? What would he say? How would he act?

He'd assumed that once he knew why she'd left, he'd be able to move on. But knowing all this didn't help. It made less sense than ever.

"Thank you for the advice." He kept his composure despite being weak-kneed and feeling he'd buckle at any moment. "I'll keep that in mind." He nodded to Beth and turned to leave.

"Want me to tell Claire you stopped by again?"

He stopped, thought for a moment, then shook his head. "No. If she gave away the shirts, she and I have no more business to discuss. Have a good day, Beth." He retrieved Sam and prepared to leave.

Looking over his shoulder, he watched her wave him on, then she guzzled down *his* glass of sweet tea punch.

Andrew dug his heels into Sam, who immediately broke into a full gallop. With each mile that passed, he went further away from the memories of her, yet each mile also drew him nearer to where she now lived.

His heart hadn't been eased. Knowing the truth only made him desire to know more. The answers to his questions created new ones. How could she have so easily deceived him? How could he have believed he was her only love—the first man who'd *turned her head*?

All along there'd been someone else. A childhood friend, whom she'd always loved. That man was now her husband and lover.

Who is this Gerald Alexander?

He'd have to be some kind of incredible man if he'd stolen the heart of a woman like Claire.

She's carrying his child.

Beth's enthusiastic revelation hurt worse than a heavy-handed punch in the stomach.

His mind spun. He'd never loved a woman before Claire. She truly was *his* first love. He'd given her his heart and body, and had every intention of being hers for the rest of their lives. Their time together had been brief, but it meant more to him than anything else he'd experienced in his lifetime.

He shouldn't have gone after her. Not knowing may have been better. Still, he *had* to know.

God! I'm going mad!

He had to talk to someone. Someone who would understand and could possibly help. He headed for the Tarver's.

Clay was outside and came running to him. He grabbed the reins. "You'd best go inside, Doc, and sit yourself down. You look sumthin' awful!"

Andrew dismounted, but didn't respond. He walked to the door and rapped lightly. When Jenny opened it, he walked in. They were all gathered at the table, preparing to eat.

"Sorry to trouble you." Andrew could barely get the words out. "But I didn't know where else to go." He stumbled and fell to the floor.

Elijah jumped up from the table and grabbed him by the arm, lifting him back onto his feet. "How long's it been since you ate, Doc?"

"I don't remember," Andrew mumbled.

Elijah guided him to the table and dished up a plate. "You're *gonna* eat, Doc."

Andrew stared at the food. Chicken, cornbread, stewed

cabbage, green beans, and potatoes. He prodded at it with his fork, then finally managed to move a few bites into his mouth. He slumped over; his confidence diminished. No food could take away this kind of pain.

Alicia cradled Betsy. "Hurry up now." She waved her hand at the children. "And when you're done, go outside an play."

After devouring the few remaining morsels on their plates, the children scuttled out of the house leaving Alicia and Elijah alone with Andrew.

Alicia shook her finger in his face. "Now you listen, Doc. I told you not to go runnin' after that woman. And you did just that, din't you?"

Andrew nodded, but wouldn't look at her. "She's married. She married someone else and she's carrying his child."

Alicia sighed. "Then she was never yours. You're killin' yourself over a woman what doesn't want you. You hafta let her go."

He continued to stare straight ahead without saying a word.

"I don't know what it's gonna take," Alicia huffed. "May hafta have Lijah here give you a swift kick in the tail!"

Andrew shifted his eyes to the man. Elijah grinned and nodded his head.

"Whatever it takes," Alicia continued. "You best snap outta this! No sense wastin' your life away over a senseless woman. I know you're hurtin'. Time will take care a that. For now, you best start eatin' an gettin' some rest or you're gonna end up a patient in your own hospital."

"She's right, Doc," Elijah said. "You're too good a man to let a woman do this to ya. Take your pride back. Be a man." He patted Andrew on the back, bringing him out of his entranced state.

Andrew turned and looked at Alicia, so lovingly cradling her baby, and then at Elijah who was one of the most honorable men he'd ever known.

He arose from the table. "I appreciate everything you've done for me and for trying to help me. But I need to get on home now."

"You sure you're up to it, Doc?" Elijah asked.

"Yes. I'll be fine. And thank you for the dinner." Unable to smile, or display any emotion whatsoever, he headed for the door.

Alicia followed him. "Wait."

She passed Betsy to Elijah, then reached out to Andrew.

He moved instantly to her, allowing her to hold him in a loving embrace. His tears flowed.

"You be just fine, Doc," she whispered. "Just fine."

Andrew held her tightly, comforted by her presence alone. Then he took a large breath to compose himself, thanked her again, and left.

He knew of someone else he could ask for advice in regard to women, and once he got home he'd do just that.

* * *

Why did I cry in front of Elijah?

Andrew had become tired of wallowing in self-pity. Medically, he understood his depression, but just because he could understand it didn't help him overcome it.

He sat at his desk and composed a letter to the man whom he knew had experience with more than one woman and also understood the southern mentality.

He never dreamed he'd seek the advice of his father, but he'd run out of options. Perhaps the man could bring to light something he hadn't seen. Something that would make sense of it all.

September 30, 1871

Dear Father,

I find it very difficult to bring myself to write to you. We have had our disagreements in the past and most of the time do not see eye to eye. However, I have nowhere else to turn and have come to you seeking advice.

You knew of my trip to the coast. You told me it was not a wise decision to come to Alabama at all, and an even poorer decision to seek respite in the area you had once lived. Being that I am hard-headed and determined to make my own way, I went there against your wishes. By your advice I continue to use the name 'Fletcher.' Hopefully that will ease some of your worry.

On my travels, I met a young woman. She was beautiful, smart, and full of life, and I fell for her instantly. After only three days, we found ourselves very much in love. Circumstances brought us together, alone, in the same house. I bedded her, Father, but only upon her consent.

She agreed to marry me and returned with me to Mobile. After only one night here, she left me. When I came home from work she was gone.

I have been tormented ever since. I love her, Father, and cannot understand why she left. I went after her, against my better judgment, only to find she has already married another man and is carrying his child. I was told he had been a long-time beau, whom she had loved for many years. Please help me make sense of this.

I can't eat or sleep and I fear my work may suffer from my grief. Tell me what I need to do. I promise this time I will listen.

Your Son,
Andrew

He folded the letter with plans to post it the next day at work. What sort of advice would his father give? The man was stern, but Andrew believed he loved him and cared about the welfare of his only son. He'd want him to return to Connecticut, but Andrew wasn't ready for that.

He'd grown fond of the people in Mobile and there were many that relied on him. That fact alone encouraged him to get his head on straight.

He made up his mind that from that day forward, he'd get up each morning, eat a good breakfast, and go to work with his chin held high once again. He'd await his father's reply, but in the meantime, he'd start behaving in a way he knew the man would approve of.

Elijah's words, *be a man,* were exactly what he expected his father would say.

CHAPTER 23

Claire had become used to her life with Gerald. She'd fallen into a routine with him and Henry. They appreciated having the care of a woman and especially enjoyed her cooking. They showed their gratitude by thanking her often.

After learning about Gerald's unfortunate accident, she'd developed a new respect for him and took care never to touch him anywhere close to his private parts. If her hand reached even slightly up on his thigh he drew away from her.

Twenty stitches must have caused severe scars, but she'd never tell him she knew. After all, she'd promised Beth she wouldn't.

Another thing this revelation had brought to mind was that the child she carried would be her *only* child. Never again would she have to concern herself over the worry of pregnancy. She found it disheartening that the child wouldn't have siblings. While growing up, she'd always wished she had a brother or sister.

Looking out the kitchen window, she sighed and rubbed her hands over her belly. With just two weeks until Christmas, the weather had turned much cooler. All the leaves were off the oak trees and the branches seemed naked and sad. Snow was rare in Mobile, but the winters usually brought a lot of rain.

They'd shared a very calm Thanksgiving. Just the three of them. But for Christmas, Beth would be joining them. Gerald planned to drive to the bay to fetch her and bring her back to Mobile. Beth would be spending at least a week with them and Claire couldn't wait to have some female company.

She gazed down at her slightly rounded belly. Now in her fifth month of pregnancy, she'd begun to look more like an expectant mother.

The baby would probably arrive the end of April, though she told Gerald it would be the end of May. If folks estimated from their wedding date, then it should be born the first week of June. She'd worried herself sick fearing folks would gossip when the baby came early. She'd have to tell them it was premature.

She had a lot to do to get ready for the holiday. With clear skies and what promised to be a beautiful day, she asked Gerald to drive her into Mobile so she could do some shopping. And since her dresses no longer fit properly, she needed material to sew some new ones. He gladly agreed and planned to find them a Christmas tree while she shopped at the mercantile.

As they drove into town, her hands began to sweat. It was the first time she'd been in the city since her move to Uncle Henry's.

I pray I don't see Andrew.

Being such a large city, it was unlikely. Besides, he probably spent most of his time at the hospital.

Gerald stopped their wagon in front of Parker's Mercantile. He jumped out and then turned to help her.

"Sure you don't want me to go in with you, Claire?" He gently lowered her to the ground.

"You'd just be bored, Gerald. We'll be just fine." She rested a hand on her growing belly, then placed the other on his shoulder. She gave him a quick peck on the cheek. "Now find us a nice Christmas tree."

He grinned and hopped back into the wagon. "I'll be back to fetch you in an hour."

His concern warmed her. She waited to go in until he was well on his way.

Money wasn't a worry—something she'd not yet become accustomed to. Uncle Henry had an account at Parker's and he'd told her to tell Jake Parker to put whatever she wanted on his bill.

As she entered the store, a little bell rang. It hung over the door and jingled, alerting someone of her presence.

"Mornin', ma'am," the man behind the counter cheerfully said.

"Good mornin'." She approached him.

"Anythin' I can help you with?" Uncle Henry had described Jake Parker and she believed this man must be him. He was a southerner through and through, proven by his heavy accent. He appeared to be in his forties, wore a full beard and mustache, and had long sideburns. He had a medium build and average height. She saw nothing especially appealing about him, but he seemed friendly.

"Eventually," she said with a smile. "I'd like to look around a bit. There's so much to look at."

"That there is." He grinned and wiggled his brows. "Just holler if you need me."

Is he flirtin'?

"I'll need you to cut me some material. For some new dresses." She didn't draw attention to her enlarging stomach. No need to tell a complete stranger of her condition.

"Let me know when you're ready." His eyes scanned her from head to foot.

He's flirtin' all right.

She'd do all she could to have as little interaction with him as possible.

The mercantile had everything imaginable—food, tools, dishes, trinkets, and clothing—so she had good excuse to wander from the sales counter. She wanted to buy something nice for Henry for Christmas. Charging it on his account seemed inappropriate. So to compromise, she'd buy some material to make him a new shirt. He'd pay for the material, but she'd put the love and care into making the shirt. That seemed fair.

While she browsed, the bell rang and her heart jumped. Her nerves had gotten the best of her.

Two well-dressed young women entered the store. The dresses they wore had to have come from overseas. They were fine and looked expensive. Trimmed in wide lace and adorned with bustles to enhance their figures. Almost like something that should've been worn to a party, but the women carried themselves as if they wore dresses like these all the time.

The blond woman wore a more conservative blue dress with a high neckline. The redhead, on the other hand, wore a low-cut emerald green dress accentuating her already large bosom.

I reckon she's wearin' a corset.

Everything had been pulled and pushed in the proper direction.

They walked by Claire, giggling, and went to the counter to speak to Mr. Parker.

Claire pondered her plain dress, feeling unattractive. Her bonnet was probably out of style, but she hadn't really concerned herself with that. Until now.

She rubbed her belly and assured herself she was just fine. After all, she was a mother-to-be, and she needn't worry about her outward appearance. She'd already gotten herself a man.

"Has my new hat come in yet, Mr. Parker?"

The question came from the redhead, who spoke like a refined southern belle. She looked radiant, and from the way she carried herself she obviously knew it. Her features were flawless and her hair had been pulled up on her head with the back dropping down in ringlets to her shoulders. Atop her head she wore a cap hat decorated with lace to match her dress. It tied under her chin with a wide satin bow.

Mr. Parker had been sitting behind the counter, but upon seeing the women, jumped to his feet. "Not yet, Miss O'Malley, but I'm expectin' it any day now. You just keep checkin'."

Her blond friend had gone to the window and was gazing out at the street. She was attractive, but paled in comparison to the redhead.

Her eyes lit up with excitement and she waved her arm, motioning for her friend. "Victoria! It's him! It's that doctor I was tellin' you 'bout! Hurry! He's walkin' down the street. You've gotta see him!"

Victoria rushed to her side. "Where, Penny?"

The girl pointed. "Isn't he the most handsome man you've ever seen?"

"Oh my ..." The girl almost purred. "He's more than fine. What did you say his name was?"

"Dr. Fletcher. *Andrew* Fletcher. He works at City Hospital."

Upon hearing his name, Claire's heart stopped. She couldn't catch her breath, but managed to make her way toward the side of the store. Far enough from the window, but near enough to hear their conversation.

"Are you certain he's not married?" Victoria asked. Her voice held restrained calm, but Claire also picked up a trace of excitement.

"Course I'm certain," Penny replied. She'd lowered her voice and Claire had to strain to hear her. "Some folks have said they believe he doesn't like women."

"How can you say such a thing? He most likely hasn't found a woman who's woman enough to spark his interest."

Claire circled her hand over her belly.

If they only knew.

She longed to see him. To gaze once again into his dark eyes. No matter how much she adored Gerald, her heart still belonged to Andrew.

"You're not old enough to do such a thing," Penny scolded. "Your daddy wouldn't have it. That man must be at least ten years older than you."

"Maybe not right now. But give me time. The older I get, the less our age difference will matter. I'm willin' to wait. Looks like he's not in a hurry to find a woman. He might just be waitin' for me, too, and doesn't know it yet." Victoria giggled. One of the most *devilish* sounds Claire had ever heard from a woman.

The thought of Andrew with someone like her made Claire heartsick. But what right did she have to deny him love? Especially from someone as beautiful and refined as Victoria? Andrew was her brother and his happiness should make *her* happy. But she wasn't. She couldn't be. Her heart wouldn't let her.

Sides, Victoria's just a child. How could she ever know how to treat a man like Andrew?

He'd never fall for such a girl, so why be concerned?

She watched the two young women as they continued to giggle and talk amongst themselves. Too busy thinking of Andrew; she no longer heard their words.

Suddenly, a flutter came from deep within her belly. She cupped her hands over it and it fluttered again. The baby moved. It was the first time she'd felt its presence. Just a soft flutter, not a kick or a turn, as if the baby had woken up and realized its existence.

She smiled, thankful for the life inside her, and her thoughts turned to Gerald. She couldn't wait to tell him that she'd felt their baby.

Our baby.

She'd started to believe it.

She selected the cloth she wanted cut from the bolts and told Mr. Parker how much she needed. She also chose a lovely angel ornament that she planned to give Beth for Christmas.

As he cut the material, she asked about the women. They'd left the store shortly after they saw Andrew.

"Oh, that there redhead was Victoria O'Malley. The other was Penelope Hayes. Two fine young women. Victoria's daddy runs the bank. Good folks if you ask me." He stopped in the middle of cutting a long piece of cloth. "How you payin' for this today, ma'am?"

"Please put it on Mr. Henry Alexander's account. I'm his niece, Claire. He asked that you do this for him." She smiled in a way that would convince any man to do her bidding. Jake Parker was no exception and he didn't question her request.

"You must be Gerald's new wife," he said, clearing his throat. "He's one lucky man."

"Thank you, sir. I'm quite fortunate myself. Gerald's a fine husband."

"Reckon he is, ma'am."

Claire gathered up her packages and spied Gerald through the window in front of the mercantile. A large white pine rested in the bed of the wagon. It would be a beautiful Christmas tree.

She loved Christmas. Her mama had made it special. There'd always been a handmade gift for her under the tree, usually clothing of some sort. Her mama had been as handy with a needle and thread as Claire. Claire had learned the skill from her. She hoped she could make this Christmas—and many more to come—just as special for *her* family.

Gerald helped her with the packages, then hoisted her into the wagon.

She beamed.

He gave her a sideways grin. "What you so happy 'bout, Claire?"

"I felt the baby move." She watched his face for a reaction, all the while caressing their unborn child.

"This soon? It's still so tiny in there. How could you feel it?" His brows knit together.

"It may be tiny, but it's very much alive and flutterin' 'round inside me."

"Makes it more real, don't it? Must be kinda strange feelin' sumthin' like that inside. It don't hurt none does it?" His genuine concern charmed her.

"Course not." She laughed. "Let's go home. I wanna tell Uncle Henry."

With a happy spring, Gerald hopped into the seat beside her. She kissed him on the cheek and they headed home.

* * *

Andrew walked briskly toward the mercantile on his way back to the hospital. The winter air chilled him to the bone, so he pulled his long, black frock coat tightly around his body. He clutched his doctor's bag, thankful to be done with the house call.

The sound of laughter made his heart skip a beat.

Claire?

A wagon pulled away, and he was certain he recognized her sunbonnet and her undeniable laughter.

He'd done well over the past few months keeping the promise he'd made to himself. He'd started each day with as positive an attitude as he could muster. But seeing and hearing her brought everything back.

He needed to know more.

Since he'd become a regular customer at the mercantile, Jake knew him well and greeted him with a simple nod.

"Jake?" Andrew wasted no time. "Do you know who those people were that just drove away? I believe they made a purchase."

"Sure do. That there was Gerald Alexander and his wife. Think she said her name was *Claire*. A might fine lookin' woman to be married to a man like Gerald. If I do say so myself. That boy's looks could curdle milk."

Andrew responded with a frown. The man's comment had been far from polite.

"Not that looks are everythin'," Jake quickly added. "Reckon he's a fine man. Has a good business goin' with his uncle just outside a town."

Andrew turned and started to leave.

"Ain't you buyin' sumthin' today, Doc?"

"No, not today. I'll stop in again another time. Thank you, Jake."

Walking out the door, the little bell rang overhead. He gasped, but not from the sound. He'd only seen the back of her head and she still made him lose his breath.

Andrew returned to the hospital to finish his day's work. As he passed the receiving desk, the young desk clerk stopped him, waving an envelope.

"Dr. Fletcher!" She smiled, wide-eyed, and handed him the letter. "I'm sorry the envelope is tattered. Not sure how it happened. Seems it had a rough time getting here."

"Thank you." A quick glance affirmed it to be the reply he'd been waiting for from his father. It appeared it had taken a side trip halfway around the world to get to Mobile. He'd been waiting for two and a half months. Mail was slow, but generally not *this* slow.

Knowing his father had a tendency to upset him, he tucked the letter into his coat pocket with plans to read it later.

That evening, he made himself comfortable at his desk and retrieved the letter from his pocket. With light flickering from a lantern, he inhaled deeply and read.

October 21, 1871

Andrew,

I must say your letter caught me by surprise. I have given your situation a great deal of thought, and though you may not like what I have to say, I am going to be blunt. You asked my advice and therefore I will give it.

First and foremost, I regret you are tormented over the choices you made in aligning yourself with a woman of lower stature. That being said, you need to grow up and start behaving as a man, not a lovesick boy.

So, you bedded this woman, and now you are in love with her? I think not. What you are feeling is not love, but the desire to once again have the pleasures of the flesh. You now know what it feels like to be with a woman. That is what you need, not necessarily that particular tart.

Trust me when I tell you this. All women feel the same in the heat of lovemaking, and the end result is no different. What you must do is find another woman. This time, find one of stature and sophistication, not a southern whore as you found on the coast.

You may find my words disturbing, but from what you told me, this woman already had intentions to wed another, yet she lay with you. That, my son, is a whore, and you have no business bedding whores! You made it clear to me in the past that prostitutes are beneath your stature and yet you bedded something much worse.

In my opinion, she was toying with you. You were her plaything. A final tryst with a fine-looking man before she committed herself to a life of drudgery married to a backwoods farmer, or perhaps someone even more despicable. You should not so easily trust women from the south. I know this from my personal experience.

You should return to Connecticut at once. I know of many fine ladies who would be exceptional prospects for marriage. Or, if you are not interested in marriage at this time, they would accommodate you, regardless. If you choose to remain in Alabama, find a decent woman to satisfy your needs. If she is respectable, do not mention your activities with the other woman. A woman of stature would not accept a man who'd lowered himself as you have.

Grow up, Andrew. Forget the whore and move on.

Your Father,

John Martin

Andrew tightened his fist around the letter, crumpled it, and threw it on the floor. Why had he ever thought he could go to his father for sound advice? The disgusting words written on paper cheapened the love he had for Claire.

How dare he call her a whore!

He may have promised the man he'd take his advice, yet all his letter had accomplished was to infuriate him and make him want to defend Claire. His father didn't know her, yet he cast judgment without full knowledge of the person Andrew knew her to be.

Trying to set aside his feelings for Claire, and look at the situation through the eyes of an outsider, he reminded himself what he'd written. Though he hated to admit it, the man had just cause to come to these conclusions. Claire had betrayed him by vowing her love, when all along she'd loved someone else.

Was she using me? Was our intimacy a cheap thrill for her?

He shook his head. It couldn't be true. His father had to be wrong.

Without a doubt *he* felt more for *her* than mere pleasure. He loved her *and* wanted her. Claire was something special, unlike any other woman.

Different, but no longer his.

I have to give it one more try. Attempt to find answers.

He'd make a trip to see the blacksmith.

CHAPTER 24

When Claire and Gerald arrived home, they shared their news with Henry.

"I remember when Sarah told me Hank moved in her belly," he said, wiping away a tear. "Nothin' like it."

Seeing his pain tore at Claire's heart. The poor man had experienced more loss in his lifetime than anyone ever should. "I didn't mean to make you sad, Uncle Henry." She looked to Gerald for support.

Gerald almost spoke, but Henry raised his hand and cut him off before he had the chance. "I ain't sad," the man said, smiling. "For the first time in a long time I'm happy. And it's all thanks to you, Claire." He placed his arm over Gerald's shoulder. "Don't know how you ever did it, but bringin' Claire here has made both our lives better." He slapped him on the back, then reminded him they had work to do.

Gerald kissed her on the cheek, gave her belly a pat, then followed Henry out the door.

She hoped Henry's compliment had to do with her cooking and cleaning, but she feared it to be something more.

Setting aside her fears, she hid away some of the material she'd purchased. She bought enough to make both Gerald and Henry new shirts and would make time to work on them while they were busy in the shop. It would be difficult to hide, but she could manage. She'd learned how to keep a good secret.

* * *

The eventful day had come to an end.

Claire sat in her room at the vanity brushing her hair and preparing for bed. Gazing at herself in the mirror, she thought about Andrew and the women in the mercantile.

Will he ever have a woman like Victoria?

Out of the corner of her eye she noticed that Gerald had come up behind her. He took the brush from her hand and drew it through her long hair. No one else had brushed her hair since her mama died. Gerald was gentle and the sensation warmed and relaxed her. This type of stroking made cats purr.

"Oh, my, Gerald. That feels wonderful." She closed her eyes and delighted in every stroke.

"Glad you like it," he whispered, bringing his mouth close to her ear.

After drawing it through her hair a few more times, he set the brush on the vanity. Then he returned his attention to her and pushed aside her hair, exposing her neck. Tiny kisses on her bare skin indicated his intentions. Already feeling sensual, she'd willingly comply.

She envisioned Andrew, just like she had many times before. She imagined him touching her. Kissing her.

They crawled into bed and she laid back, ready to let him have his way with her.

Then she felt the flutter again.

"Gerald!" Sensuality went out the window. "It moved again! The baby moved!"

He put his hand on her belly and frowned. "I don't feel it."

"Maybe it's cuz it's so tiny and what I'm feelin' is deep inside. I'm sure that once it gets a little bigger you'll be able to feel it kick just fine."

He rested his head on her stomach.

"What are you doin'?" she asked with a laugh.

"Gettin' to know my child." Turning his head, he planted tiny kisses all across the width of her belly. Then he pulled his head slightly back. "I love you." His words had been directed at the baby. "You don't know me yet, but I'm your daddy."

She found his action endearing and it warmed her to the core. Unable to help herself, she ran her fingers through his thick curly hair.

He rose up even further to kiss her on the lips. "I want you Claire, but do you reckon it's still all right? I mean . . . the baby's gettin' bigger and movin' now. I wouldn't wanna hurt it."

She could easily decline him and he wouldn't think poorly of her. "I reckon it would be all right." For some reason, she didn't *want* to deny him. "Just one more time."

She didn't have to say another word.

* * *

Gerald shook Claire by the shoulders and woke her. She opened her eyes to find him leaning over the top of her.

"Who's Andrew?" he asked with weaving brows.

She pushed her head hard into the pillow. Could he tell that her heart had just stopped beating?

What should I say?

Though barely awake, hearing Andrew's name perked her right up. "What do you mean, Gerald?"

"You was talkin' in your sleep. All you kept sayin' over and over again was *Andrew, Andrew, Andrew.*"

"I did? That's rather odd." *Think fast Claire!* "Oh. I know what it musta been. I'd been thinkin' lately 'bout baby names and that was one of the names I was considerin' for a boy. But I don't reckon I like it so much."

"Well you was sure sayin' it enough." Gerald perched beside her on the bed and stared directly into her face with his arms folded across his chest.

Does he believe me?

She gulped.

"You know, Claire." He tapped his finger to his chin. "I kinda like that name. Andrew Alexander sounds sophisticated. They say a name can make a man. Come to think of it, I had a great-grandfather named Andrew Alexander. I think it's a fine name. We'll hafta keep that in mind. If it's a boy, that is. Not such a good name for a girl." He grinned.

"Oh, I don't know, Gerald. I'd kinda hoped we'd name him after you. If it's a boy. Either that, or I've always been fond a the name, Michael. *I* had a great-grandfather that went by *that* name."

"Hmm. Well . . . I do like the name Andrew. We have some time to ponder it. I reckon since you was dreamin' it, it might be some kinda sign from God."

"I don't think God works like that." She looked upward. *Are you tryin' to teach me a lesson?* "Let's wait an see what it is first, all right?"

"Reckon so. But a name is might important, Claire." He let the subject drop and got out of bed to get ready for work.

She sat there briefly, digesting their conversation.

Dear Lord, please make my baby a girl . . .

* * *

Andrew decided to ride out of town to Henry Alexander's blacksmith shop. He honestly had no idea what he'd do when he got there. More than anything he was curious. He had to see for himself what kind of man Claire had married.

Since she was acquainted with Sam, he rode Charger. If she were to spot the horse from a distance, she wouldn't recognize him. And even if she saw him on the horse, she might mistake him for someone else.

On the other hand, if she knew it was him, then he'd play it as it came. Truthfully, he didn't have a clue as to what he'd do.

I'm just along for the ride.

It was late morning when he approached Alexander's. Passing by a large house beside the shop, he assumed Claire would be inside. It was a beautiful home. The kind she deserved.

An older gentleman, presumably Henry Alexander, was hard at work on a wheel repair. He stopped when he noticed Andrew.

"Mornin'," he said with a warm smile. "Can I help ya?"

"Yes, sir. Would you mind taking a look at my horse? I believe his shoes may need replacing."

The man cupped a hand over his ear. "You say you need some shoein'?"

Understanding the man's impairment, Andrew looked directly at him. "Yes, my horse needs shoeing!"

He turned away. "Gerald! We got us a customer needs a shoein'!" He shifted toward Andrew again. "My nephew. He's real good at what he does."

Andrew couldn't stop the racing of his heart as he waited for Gerald to come out from the stable.

I'm about to see the man who holds Claire's heart and shares her bed.

The man approaching didn't look anything like what he'd expected. He was wearing coveralls and had straw stuck to his pant legs and in his hair. Though improper to judge another man's looks, Jake Parker's remark—as rude as it had been—made some sense. Not to that extreme, but Gerald Alexander wasn't handsome. The man couldn't have been more ordinary.

Sitting atop Charger, Andrew suddenly felt overdressed in his fine clothing and frock coat.

Gerald peered up at him and pushed his glasses up on his nose. "You need a shoein'?" he asked, then cleared his throat and coughed.

"Yes. My horse that is." He offered a smile, believing Gerald to be just as nervous as him.

But why?

He dismounted and extended his hand. "I'm Andrew Fletcher."

Gerald shook it. "Andrew, huh? Funny." He chuckled. "I'm Gerald Alexander. Pleased to meet you."

"I'm confused. Why are you laughing?"

"Your name. Just—never mind. Sumthin' my wife an I was discussin' earlier today." Gerald nodded toward Charger. "So, which shoe? Or do you want me to check 'em all?"

Andrew had to stay focused. Simply hearing the man refer to his *wife* had made him uneasy. "Why don't you check all of them? Charger's been through a lot over the years and I want to keep him fit." Gerald perplexed him. Why had Claire been attracted to him?

Gerald took the horses reins and led him into an empty stall. Then one-by-one he examined the shoes. "Ain't bad. Front ones are worse than the back. Your horse nervous?"

"Sometimes. He tends to paw at the ground when he becomes tense. He was in the war. A little gun-shy, so to speak. Usually gets skittish around new people."

"War, huh?"

"Yes. A man by the name of Jeremiah Campbell found him on an empty battlefield. He'd been left to die with multiple gashes in his flank. Jeremiah took him home and nursed him back to health. He gave him to me when I doctored *him*. Do you know him?"

"Uh-uh," Gerald said, wrinkling his nose. "But knowin' all that makes me understand why your horse gets nervous." He examined the hooves more closely. "I'd suggest you replace the front ones. Back ones should do for now."

"Very well. Thank you." This would give him plenty of time to ask questions.

Gerald set about taking care of Charger, beginning with the removal of the old shoes. "Is a cold fit all right by you? If not, it'll take a bit to heat up the embers for a hot shoein'. You in a hurry?"

"A cold fit will be fine. I trust you. You seem to have a way with him. I've not seen him so calm around someone new." Gerald's skill impressed him. "How long have you been working with your uncle?"

"'Bout six months now, I reckon. Came here in July. Awful hot then. Easier to work in this kinda weather. Though, when the rains come, it gets awful muddy."

"Yes, it does. At least we don't have to worry about snow here. I'm from Connecticut and the winters there can be brutal." There was so much more he wanted to know. Fortunately, the more they talked, the more relaxed Gerald became.

"What kinda work you do?"

"I'm a doctor. At City Hospital."

"A doctor, huh?" The man's face lit up. "That's good to know. My wife's expectin' a baby. Ain't seen a doctor yet. Said she don't need one. What do *you* think?"

Andrew's heart pounded once again. "Is this her first child?" Though he knew the answer, he wasn't about to let Gerald know that he knew.

"Yep!" He puffed out his chest. "I know. I look sorta old to be startin' a family, but we just got married, an well, it just sorta happened."

"Congratulations. On your marriage *and* the baby." Andrew meant every word.

"Oh, my wife an I was sweethearts since we was little. Just took me a while to get up the nerve to ask her to marry me. She's the most beautiful woman you'll ever see, an I ain't just sayin' that cuz she's my wife. Her name's Claire. Used to be Montgomery. Ever known any Montgomerys?"

"No, can't say that I have." *He thinks the world of her.* "Has she had any problems yet . . . with her pregnancy?"

"Not really. Less you count all the heavin' she was doin' up until 'bout a month ago."

"How far along is she?"

I have to know.

Gerald pushed his glasses up on his nose, then started counting on his fingers. "She's due June the second. We was married September second."

Exactly nine months from their wedding day.

Andrew nodded. "As long as she isn't having any pains or bleeding, she should be fine with a midwife. Do you have one in mind?"

"Nope. We hadn't thought that far ahead." He wrinkled his nose. "Bleedin', huh? Guess I'd better see to it."

"You might want to look into the Sisters of Charity in Mobile. Some of the nuns there are midwives." He wanted to see to it that Claire would be properly cared for.

"Thank you, Dr. Fletcher." After a broad smile, he continued to work with the hoof knife, trimming Charger's hooves to prepare them for the new shoes.

The way he handled the knife displayed a great deal of skill. "Ever consider becoming a doctor yourself, Mr. Alexander?" He couldn't help but return Gerald's smile. He'd begun to like the man.

"Heck, call me Gerald. *Mr.* Alexander is my uncle."

"Gerald it is then. You may call me Andrew."

"Naw. That don't seem right, you bein' a doctor an all. Mind if I just call you Doc?"

Andrew laughed. "Most people do. That would be fine."

Gerald held up the new shoes, then trimmed and smoothed the hooves until he seemed happy with the fit. Now and then, he'd give Charger a reassuring pat while speaking softly to him. He worked diligently and Andrew watched his every move.

They were silent for some time.

"Well, Doc." Gerald stood and rubbed his hands together. "These should do him for a good while. If you have any trouble at all out of 'em, just bring him back to me. I always stand behind my work."

"Thank you, Gerald. What do I owe you?" Andrew reached into his pocket for his money.

"Ever barter?"

"As a matter of fact, I do quite a lot of that." Andrew grinned. "What did you have in mind?"

"Would you consider comin' back here and deliverin' our baby when the time comes?" Gerald's brows drew in.

What could he say? This wasn't possible. He hesitated.

"I'm sorry, Doc," Gerald said, staring at the ground. "Guess that's askin' a might much from you."

"No. Not at all. It would be a fair trade. But I have obligations at the hospital and it's difficult for me to get away on short notice. I think it best if you acquire a midwife." He hoped he'd accept this as a valid refusal.

"I understand. Your work must be demandin'. A simple birthin' ain't as important as other things. Thanks for lettin' me know 'bout the midwife."

Andrew breathed a sigh of relief when Gerald told him how much to pay him. Much easier to pull money from his pocket than make a promise he couldn't keep.

Andrew was about to leave when Gerald stopped him short. "Say, Doc? It's 'bout dinner time. I reckon my wife has sumthin' good fixed to eat. Would you like to stay an join us for a bite?"

"Thank you, but I'd better be on my way." He mounted Charger, anxious to leave.

"Oh—Doc—there's my wife now! I'd like you to meet her." The man burst with pride.

Andrew wasn't ready for this.

Feeling the need to bolt, he glanced to where Gerald pointed. Claire had come outside with a basket of laundry. Fortunately, she'd been concentrating on her work and hadn't looked their way. With clothespins in her mouth, she began clipping the laundry onto the line. As she raised her arms, the swell of her belly shot like a knife into his heart.

Oh, God.

He couldn't bear the tightness in his chest. Pretending not to hear the man, he dug his heels into Charger's sides.

"Hey, Doc!" Gerald yelled, but Andrew had already headed down the road.

After rounding a curve, he stopped and turned to watch.

Gerald walked up behind Claire, put his arms around her and kissed her on the neck. She laughed and dropped the shirt she'd been holding in her hand. He spun her around and kissed her fully on the lips. She willingly returned the kiss.

They were happy and he was good to her.

I have to let her go.

Only her happiness mattered. Though he'd never have the answers to his questions, he'd learn to live without them. They *both* deserved happiness. She'd found hers, and now, determined more than ever, he'd find his.

* * *

"Gerald," Claire scolded with a laugh. "I need to get the laundry hung!"

"All right, Claire. But you look so purty, it's hard for me to leave you be."

With her ever-growing belly, she didn't quite believe him. But she appreciated his attentiveness. And being *overly* attentive, he helped her finish hanging the clothes.

"Tell Uncle Henry dinner's ready," she said.

"We'll be there soon as we wash up." He gave her a peck on the cheek, then left her to go to the shop.

She'd made a large pot of vegetable soup and baked some of her baking powder biscuits. Her strawberry preserves made them especially delicious and favorites of her *men*.

Once seated, she watched as they eagerly began to eat.

"We almost had an extra mouth to feed," Gerald said while munching on a biscuit.

"We have plenty." She happily served any of the customers Gerald or Henry asked in, and that happened frequently. Gerald had said her fine cooking had been good for business. "Always room for more folks at the table. What happened to him?"

Henry paid them no attention, lapping up soup and making happy sounds as he savored every bite.

"He left in a hurry," Gerald said. "Not sure why. But he was a doctor. Probably had patients to see." He popped the rest of the biscuit into his mouth.

She froze with her soup spoon in midair. "What was his name?"

"Kinda funny considerin' our discussion this mornin'." His words were almost unrecognizable with such a full mouth. He swallowed quickly, then drank a large amount of water. He smirked. "His name was Fletcher, Dr. *Andrew* Fletcher." He chuckled and wiggled his brows.

She didn't laugh. "What was he here for?" Her heart pounded.

"*Andrew* was here to have his horse shod. Why else do folks come 'round here?" He continued to chuckle, but *she* found no humor in the matter.

"Was there any other reason he came? Did he say anythin' unusual?"

I'm gonna be sick.

Somehow, she had to find out everything she could without making Gerald suspicious.

"That's a strange thing to ask. We just talked. I told him 'bout your baby—him bein' a doctor an all. Oh, an I told him 'bout us gettin' married in September. How we'd always been sweethearts, but you was so beautiful it took me a long time to get up the nerve to ask you to marry me. I told him your name. Said he never knew no Montgomerys." He continued to eat as if he didn't have a care in the world.

"You did what?" Claire stood and gripped the edge of the table, leaning toward him. "You told a complete stranger 'bout my baby—and—and how you *got around* to askin' me to marry you? How could you?"

He gaped at her, tipping his head. "He's a doctor, Claire. I figgered maybe he could help you. No need in gettin' all upset. It's not good for the baby. I asked him if he'd be willin' to deliver it for you, but he said he couldn't do it and suggested a midwife."

"If you don't mind, Gerald, I'd like to make my own decision as to who delivers my baby!" She fled from the kitchen and went straight to her room.

Unable to stop the tears from falling, she buried her face in her pillow.

Andrew had been there. At her home. And he'd met Gerald. Not only did he know that they were married, but that she carried Gerald's child.

Why does it hurt so bad?

She'd wanted him to forget her, so what better way could there be than to know she belonged to another man? Why did it also hurt having him *not know* that she actually carried *his* child?

Oh Andrew . . .

It had been quite some time since she'd cried over him. But she couldn't bear this.

It's too much.

"Claire?" Gerald cleared his throat.

Lifting her face from the pillow, she blinked slowly and tried to get her husband into view.

"Claire, I'm sorry. I didn't mean to upset you." Sitting beside her, he rubbed her back.

His concern made matters worse.

He's always so good to me.

"No, Gerald. I'm sorry." She propped herself up on one elbow. "I shouldn't have gotten so angry with you. I was just a little embarrassed is all. I didn't want a stranger lookin' at me—you know—especially a man."

He kissed her on the forehead. "I shouldn't a asked him without askin' you first. I just want you to have the best care possible. But I'll get you a midwife. Would that make you feel better?"

"Yes, it would. Thank you." She wasn't ready to go back downstairs. "I'm a little tired. I reckon I'll just stay up here and take me a nap. Do you mind?"

"Not at all. Henry an I can clean up the dishes." He kissed her again, then left the room, shutting the door behind him.

How could she ever forget Andrew when every time she turned around he seemed to appear in one way or another? She feared one day she'd have to confront him with the truth.

CHAPTER 25

Saturday, the twenty-third of December. Gerald had left early in the morning to get Beth so he could bring her home to Uncle Henry's. Claire expected them back by mid-afternoon, so she busied herself with the finishing touches on the house for Christmas.

The tree looked beautiful in the corner of the living room. Henry presented her with a box of ornaments he'd found in the attic. He'd told her Sarah had hung them on their tree when the boys were growing up. Some of them were store-bought and very fine, and others were hand-made, holding even more memories.

Claire added a few hand-made ornaments of her own. She'd crocheted some small snowflakes that she'd starched and dried, then hung with tiny strings onto the tree.

When Beth arrived, she'd pop some corn to make garland, knowing her best friend would want to help her string it. They'd done it as girls and she was certain Beth would enjoy reliving those special times.

Henry had cut some boughs for her to use to decorate the stairwell and the mantel of the fireplace. The woodsy aroma filled her with Christmas spirit. She bound them together with twine, then crafted some large red bows to give them an elegant final touch. Lastly, she carefully fit the boughs to the railing of the stairway, by reaching over the top of it and tying it underneath.

Henry stood at the base of the stairs, watching her. "You be careful now, Claire!"

"I'm just fine, Uncle Henry. Doesn't it look pretty?"

"Might purty."

He remained at the bottom of the stairs as she worked her way down. When she reached the final step, she misplaced her foot and stumbled.

Right into Henry.

With a pounding heart, she lay across his arms looking up at him. "Oh, my! Thank y—"

His lips covered hers with a kiss more passionate than she'd ever received from Gerald.

What?

Horrified, she smacked his chest. "You had no right!" She pushed away from him and got back on her feet, breathing so hard she feared she might faint. Once she'd steadied herself, she slapped him hard across the face and began to cry.

He reached out to her. "Oh, Claire, I'm sorry. Don't know what came over me. Can you ever forgive me?"

"What were you thinkin'?" Not only did her voice shake, but her entire body as well. "I'm your nephew's wife!" She ran to her room and slammed the door.

What would she do? She'd known of Henry's attraction, but never dreamed he'd act on his feelings. She hadn't encouraged his affections, but she hadn't been distant from him either. All she'd done was treat him like a family member. One whom she happened to be taking care of.

What will I tell Gerald?

If she told him what Henry had done, he'd want to leave. They couldn't do that. Not now. They needed the money and a place to live. Most importantly, they needed a home for the baby.

Composing herself, she made up her mind to go down and confront the situation head-on.

She marched down the stairs. Not finding Henry in the living room, she went to the kitchen. She found him there with his head in his hands.

"Henry Alexander!" She pounded her fist on the table, drawing his attention.

He raised his head and met her gaze.

Has he been cryin'?

It didn't matter. No tears would keep her from giving him a piece of her mind.

"What you did had best NEVER happen again!" She looked straight at him. "I'm GERALD'S WIFE and don't ever forget that! I know you're his uncle and he RE-SPECTS you. However, if he KNEW what you just did, he'd NEVER FORGIVE you for it!"

"Oh, Claire. Please—*please* don't tell Gerald! I swear to you it won't happen again." His chin quivered and his eyes were filled with fear.

Would it be right to keep another secret from Gerald?

Why's my life so complicated?

She sat across from him at the table. "Why'd you do it, Henry?" Tears misted over her eyes.

He hesitated, but then leaned back and licked his lips. "I love you, Claire. I know it ain't right, but I do." He frowned and closed his eyes, then covered his face with his hands.

She sat back. He'd admitted what she'd feared.

Reaching across the table, she pulled his hands away from his face.

His eyes opened wide.

She would try to be understanding, but she had to be reassured he'd never make advances again. "You can love me as your niece, but nothin' more. Do you understand me?" She enunciated every word.

"I do."

Though it was wrong to keep this from Gerald, she believed she had no choice. "I won't tell Gerald as long as you behave yourself. This would hurt him terribly and I don't want him hurt!"

"I really am sorry, Claire." His face softened and his words *seemed* sincere.

She believed him.

* * *

The mood in the house changed when Beth and Gerald walked through the front door. There were hugs all around and many *Merry Christmas* greetings.

Henry built a fire in the fireplace and Claire made a large pot of spiced cider, which had the whole house smelling Christmassy.

The weather had turned much colder, but snow was doubtful. Claire put extra blankets on the beds to keep everyone warm and cozy. The day would've been perfect had it not been for the incident with Henry. She'd try to put the thoughts of that aside and enjoy her time with Beth.

Beth brought in several packages that she placed under the tree, then Claire showed her to her room.

"Beth, I'm so glad you're here." Claire gave her a warm hug. "I think you'll be comfortable in here."

Beth sat down on the bed and scanned Gerald's old room. "I can tell a woman's livin' in this house again. You've really fixed things up nice. New winda dressin's and beddin'. I'm sure Uncle Henry appreciates you."

"Yes, he does." She'd never tell her just how much. "I'm happy here. Gerald, too. And with the baby comin', things couldn't be any more perfect."

Claire took her into *her* room to show her their pine bed, pointing out Gerald's intricate carving.

Beth fingered the lettering. "My brother's learnin' all kinds a new things. I'm really happy for you, Claire. You deserve this. All of it." Beth hugged her again. "How are you feelin' these days? Is everythin' all right with the baby an all?"

"Yes, I'm feelin' just fine. Mornin' sickness has finally passed, which I'm thankful for. Now I just have to get used to this growin' belly." She pulled her dress taut against her stomach.

"Oh my, Claire! You look awful big for just four months. Reckon you're gonna have twins?"

"Don't even say that! I'm nervous enough 'bout just one, let alone two."

Being that she was truly *five* months along, she assumed her size appropriate. However, she fretted about pulling off the delivery and convincing everyone the baby was premature. But as long as the baby was healthy, she could deal with anything else. Including suspicious folks.

They went back downstairs to visit with Gerald and Henry, shared a nice supper together, and then Claire popped the corn to make the garlands for the tree. They stayed up late working on them, giggling so much that the men finally excused themselves to bed.

Gerald kissed Beth on the forehead, then gave Claire a more loving kiss on the lips. Henry also kissed Beth on the forehead, and when he came to Claire he merely said, *goodnight*. Had the event of the morning not occurred, Henry would have kissed her forehead as well. Had Gerald noticed the difference?

Things had changed in the house and would never be the same again.

* * *

Claire loved having Beth with them. She'd laughed more than she had in a very long time.

It was Christmas Eve and they were enjoying their noontime dinner. They sat at the table and talked about past Christmases.

Since the shop had closed for the holiday, a knock on the door surprised them. The only one at the table oblivious to the sound was Henry.

He looked at them, questioning with his eyes.

"Someone's knockin' on the DOOR!" Gerald yelled in Henry's direction.

"Oh," Henry said, raising his brows. "Don't know why you're all just sittin' there. I'll go see who it is."

Beth giggled. "Shame you hafta yell at him."

"I know," Gerald said. "But for some reason he don't hear me as well as he hears Claire. Even when I'm lookin' right at him."

"I think he hears better than he lets on," Claire said. "He likes messin' with you."

"MERRY CHRISTMAS!"

Claire froze at the unmistakable voice. "Aunt Martha?" She glanced at Beth, who immediately slumped down in her chair, frowning. And then, when she looked at Gerald, she thought he might cry.

"It's all right, Gerald. She's my aunt after all." She jumped to her feet and headed for the front door with Gerald traipsing behind her.

Martha held up a turkey, dangling by its feet. "Hope you ain't got your Christmas dinner all planned out just yet!"

Claire hugged her. "Merry Christmas, Martha. I can't believe you're here."

Beth entered the room. "Neither can I." The frown hadn't left her face.

Martha ignored her. "I know I wasn't invited, but then, when does family have to be invited to pay a visit? I just had to come an see my favorite niece."

"I'm your *only* niece, Aunt Martha."

"Makes all the more reason to come. Now how 'bout invitin' me in? It's a might chilly standin' in this here doorway."

Henry motioned her inside. "Forgive me. I forgot my manners." He took the turkey from her and carried it to the kitchen.

"Nothin' to forgive," she replied, then turned and yelled out the door. "George! Bring them packages in here an my bag, too!"

George came inside in mere moments. When he saw Claire, he lowered his head and turned away from her. He set the bags on the floor close to Beth, then gaped at her for several moments before turning and bolting out the door.

Martha shook her head. "Man seems a might taken by your friend, Claire. Hell if I know why." She moved to the door and braced her hands against the doorframe. "Be sure to be back here day after t'morra to fetch me!"

"Day after t'morra?" Beth mumbled.

Martha slammed the door and clapped her hands. "Yep! Day after t'morra."

Obviously, Martha would be staying. She walked further into the house gazing at the decorations, mumbling her approval.

Claire bit her lower lip and attempted to smile at Beth. She loved Aunt Martha, but hadn't expected her. Not now. Not without forewarning.

When Henry came back in from the kitchen, they all just stood there looking at one another.

"So, you'll be stayin' with us a few days then?" Gerald asked, while scratching the back of his head.

Martha glared at him. "That all right with you?"

"Course it is!" he replied cheerfully, but Claire knew him well enough to know he was likely shaking in his boots. "We always have room for family."

Will you ever forgive me, Gerald?

There wasn't a lot she could do. After all, as Martha had said, *she's family.*

Typical of her aunt, she had a cheek full of chaw. Claire had become familiar with this particular look on her face. She needed a place to spit. At home Martha simply spat on the floor.

Claire twisted her hands into a knot. Not only did she fear Aunt Martha might say something she shouldn't, she also didn't want Martha's nasty spit all over the house.

"Aunt Martha," Claire said as sweetly as she could. "It's best you not spit on the floor here. Can you go outside and do it?"

"Outside? It's freezin' out there." She crossed her arms over her sagging breasts.

Uncle Henry abruptly left the room.

"He mad or sumthin'?" Martha asked.

"I don't know," Claire replied. "He usually doesn't just walk out like that."

"I'll go an check on him," Gerald offered. But before he left the room, Henry came back in.

"Had to get this from my room," he said, wiping the dust from an old spittoon. "My eldest boy, Hank, used to like havin' a good chaw now an then. This was his." He handed it to Martha.

Martha grinned. "That's right thoughtful of ya, Henry. Thank you!" She spit. "Works just right!"

Beth released a heavy sigh.

Claire had to do something to make her feel better. She put her arm around her, trying to reassure her. "We're gonna have a lovely Christmas, Beth." Maybe by saying it, she'd convince herself.

They all went into the kitchen to finish their meal, though Beth muttered something about losing her appetite.

Claire made some sweet tea punch for Martha, and Martha made herself right at home, content with her chaw and favorite beverage.

The upstairs had three bedrooms. They used the third room mostly for storage, but when Gerald had made the pine bed for them, the wrought iron bed had been moved into that room. Claire fixed it up for Martha and everything came together for her unexpected stay.

It felt good to have her aunt to herself while she helped her get settled in the little room.

"Claire Belle," Martha sighed. "I hope I ain't intrudin' on ya. I just missed you so much, an figgered this would be a good time to visit."

They sat on the edge of the bed. Claire nestled against her. "You're welcome anytime. Don't you ever think twice 'bout that. I'm glad you're here."

Martha patted her hand. "I'm glad, too." She peered into Claire's eyes. "You look good, Claire. Gerald treatin' you all right?"

"Yes, he is. He's a fine husband. And he's real excited 'bout the baby comin'." She tenderly rubbed her belly.

"He better be. You should be due 'bout the end of April. Ain't that right?"

"Yes, but please don't say that in front of the others." Claire twisted her fingers with worry. "I know you understand we don't want them to know things happened 'fore we were married."

"I won't say a word. But I'd like to kick Gerald in the tail for puttin' you through this."

"Please, Martha, don't be so hard on him. He really is a good man." *Why'd I ever hafta tarnish his image?* "And we're very happy now."

"All right then. I'll go easy on him. Long as he shows me he's takin' care of ya. That's all that matters."

"Thank you, Aunt Martha." She hugged her neck. "We'd best be gettin' back downstairs. I'm sure they'll be missin' us."

"Glad to." Martha wiggled her brows. "I like lookin' at that Henry Alexander. He's a fine lookin' man."

"I thought you didn't like men much," Claire teased. "Didn't you call them all *dog meat* at one time?"

Martha laughed heartily. "Some dogs are better than others. I ain't dead yet, girl."

As they descended the stairs, Claire's tension eased. A *bit . . .*

If she could survive this Christmas, she could survive anything.

CHAPTER 26

Claire woke early Christmas morning with Gerald snuggled against her. The house was cold, but the bed and their bodies were warm. Though she didn't want to get up, she knew she must. She'd do all she could to keep everyone happy for the Holy day of Christmas. That meant starting early.

Gerald stirred. "Stay here with me a little longer, Claire."

"No, Gerald. I've gotta get up. I've gotta get that turkey in the oven, put the rest of the presents under the tree, and start a fire first an foremost." She was already stressed and the day hadn't even started.

"Henry will start the fire. Don't you go doin' that. An you let Beth an Aunt Martha help you with the dinner an all. Don't try doin' it all yourself. Not in your condition."

"I'll be fine. I just wanna make this the best Christmas ever."

He placed his hands on her belly. "It is. You already gave me my gift."

She rolled over and kissed him. "You've given me much more." She caressed his cheek. "Oh, Gerald. I'm sorry Aunt Martha dropped in like she did. But she *is* family, and I couldn't ask her to leave."

"I wouldn't expect you to. I just can't figger out why she dislikes me so much."

"Pay it no mind." She had to reassure him. "She doesn't like many men."

"Seems to like Uncle Henry well enough. Treats him like he hung the moon." His mouth twisted into a frown.

"She's just a funny old woman, but she's very sweet. You just gotta give her a chance."

"I'll try. Can you ask her to stop glarin' at me?"

"I think she'll be friendlier today. Bein' it's Christmas an all." She attempted to get out of bed, but Gerald pulled her back down.

"Merry Christmas, Claire." He ran his fingers through her hair, then gave her a sweet kiss.

"Merry Christmas." She rested her hand on his cheek and stared at him for several moments. *I don't deserve you.* After giving him a kiss of her own, she got up, dressed, and left the room to begin her chores.

She chuckled hearing Martha's loud snoring seeping into the hallway. Even though she doubted anything could wake her, she tiptoed down the stairs and went to the kitchen.

As Gerald assumed, Henry had started a fire and was most likely out tending the horses. Her spirits were lifted further when Beth came in and offered to help.

"I love havin' some time alone with you, Beth," she said, and gave her a Christmas hug.

Beth returned it, then clapped her hands together and set to work.

Henry had been kind enough to pluck and clean the turkey for them the night before, so all they had to do was dress it and get it in the oven.

They chatted and laughed, just like young girls again.

"You know, Claire," Beth said. "When I was little, I felt like a princess comin' to this house."

"You did?" Claire sat down, content that the meal was well on its way.

"Yep." Beth ran her hand over the wood table. "Henry's things was always nicer than ours. When my daddy died, Henry asked us to live here, but Mama didn't think it'd be proper. So we moved into the boardin' house."

"I'm glad you did. If you'd lived here, we might a grown apart." She reached out and squeezed Beth's hand.

"So tell me, Claire." Beth looked sideways at her. "What's it like sharin' a house with two men?"

Claire laughed. "You wouldn't wanna know." Then she became serious. "Honestly, I enjoy havin' someone to care for. It's nice not bein' all alone."

Beth's face fell and she stared at the table.

"Oh. I'm sorry, Beth." *How could I be so unfeelin'?* "I know you live by yourself, and it must be hard for you bein' alone in my old house."

"I like bein' alone. Most a the time. Sometimes I think it'd be nice to find a man to share my life with. Someone *real* good lookin'." She grinned, looking Claire in the eye. "Someone like that handsome doctor."

Claire's breath hitched. "What doctor's that?"

"Oh—that's right—you always seem to have a hard time recollectin' him. You know, that Dr. Fletcher you was gonna make them shirts for." She rested her cheek against her palm and sighed.

Good thing they were alone. If Beth had mentioned his name in front of Gerald, he'd wonder how Beth knew him. Then, if he realized Claire knew him as well, how could she ever explain herself? Especially since Andrew had told Gerald he didn't know of any Montgomerys.

All these secrets were becoming overwhelming. How could she ever keep them all?

"Oh. Yes. *That* doctor." Claire spoke with as little emotion as she could.

Beth sat up straight and her eyes drew open wide. "He came by lookin' for you again shortly after you an Gerald was married. You know, after you came and seen me an told me 'bout the baby."

Claire swallowed hard. "He did?"

"Yep. Sure did. He even recalled my name. Oh, Claire. I'd give anythin' to have a man like him."

"What did he want?" Claire's heart raced.

Beth shrugged. "Reckon he was still lookin' for them shirts. I told him you moved away. That you an Gerald got married an was gonna have a baby. He didn't stay long. Said he wasn't feelin' well an had to leave. I told him you gave away them shirts, so he said you no longer had any business to discuss. Then he said I didn't even need to tell you he came by. Kinda strange, if you ask me."

"He wasn't feeling well?" *Me neither.*

"No. He looked kinda pale, too. Oh, an when he said he was gonna go back home to Mobile, I told him that was where you and Gerald live now. Told him he should see Gerald if his horse ever needed a shoein'. Maybe I got you some future business." Beth sat erect with her chin raised, obviously proud of her accomplishment.

Her words sank in deep. Andrew had come intentionally to their home. He knew he'd find her there with Gerald and came to see for himself. He must have wanted to know more about the man she'd married.

Andrew was checkin' up on me.

"Beth, if you don't mind, please don't mention this to Gerald, all right?" *It'd ruin everythin'.* "He tends to get a little jealous."

"If he ever seen Dr. Fletcher, he'd be a man to be jealous of. He makes me sweat just thinkin' 'bout him." Beth wiped her brow, then patted her face.

"So, you won't say anythin' to him then?" She needed reassurance.

"Course I won't. He won't know anythin' of Dr. Fletcher 'til the day I marry him." She winked. "A girl can wish, can't she?"

Claire forced a smile. "Course she can."

Henry walked in the back door. He stared momentarily at Claire, then quickly looked away. "Merry Christmas, Beth. Claire." He hugged Beth, then nodded at Claire.

"Merry Christmas, Uncle Henry!" Beth chimed. "Why don't you go get GERALD up an tell him we're ready to open some PRESENTS?"

"Yes, Henry," Claire added, looking straight at him. "You could always beat your cane on the stairwell for old time's sake." Knowing how uncomfortable he'd become around her now, she smiled at him, trying to ease his discomfort. "Aunt Martha might appreciate it, too."

"You bein' serious, Claire? Or just joshin' me?"

"Oh, I'm very serious. First time *I* heard you beat that cane, I woke straight up."

He moved to the stairwell. "Gerald! Martha! It's Christmas! These girls wanna open presents!" He beat his cane soundly against the stairs.

Claire and Beth stood behind him, waiting.

"What in tarnation? Is the house on fire?" Martha appeared at the top of the stairs in her bed clothes, wild-eyed and with her hair sticking straight on end.

Henry winked at her. "Merry Christmas, Martha!"

Martha's eyes popped open wide. She glanced down, then rapidly covered herself and raced back to her room.

Henry chuckled and went to the living room, taking a seat on the sofa.

Relieved that the mood of the house seemed to be headed in the right direction, Claire returned to the kitchen with Beth to check on the sweet breads and hot cocoa. This would be the start of an Alexander family tradition.

Gerald walked in, surprisingly dressed, and gave Claire a kiss on the cheek. She repaid him with a cup of cocoa.

Martha came in, scratching herself and yawning. "Boy, oh boy, I like that there bed you had me sleep on! I slept like a baby. Though I'm not too fond of your rooster."

Though Martha fussed, Claire knew she was teasing. Martha was *quite* fond of Henry. "Take the rooster some cocoa, Martha, and wish him a Merry Christmas." Claire handed her a mug.

Martha chuckled and walked out, and Gerald stood back shaking his head. Yes, it would be a memorable Christmas.

They gathered in the living room, each finding a comfortable place to sit, then Gerald patted Claire's lap and crossed to the tree.

He cleared his throat. "I just wanna say I'm thankful y'all are here to share Christmas with us." He motioned to Claire to join him.

This was highly unlike him. He always shied away from speaking in groups such as this. Claire took her place next to him and he wrapped his arm around her waist.

"I know Claire feels the same." He gave her a squeeze. "We love y'all very much and hope next year we can do this again. It'll be even more special cuz next year we'll have our little baby with us." He placed his hand on Claire's stomach. "That's really what Christmas is all 'bout. A baby and the gift we were given in Him. I'm thankful for the gift of a baby Claire gave me. I don't never need any-thin' else."

He kissed her on the cheek and she wiped a tear from her eye. He'd touched her heart. It had undoubtedly been the biggest speech he'd ever made. He didn't hesitate over any of his words and never once touched his glasses. Every-thing came directly from his heart.

Martha smiled at him for the first time. "Now that's the sweetest thing I ever heard."

Claire couldn't have been more touched. She cast her eyes around the room. Beth also had a smile on her face, but Henry's eyes were focused on the floor.

Must be hard for him to look Gerald in the eye.

Gerald clapped his hands together. "All right, then. Let's open presents! I wanna give mine first!"

He reached under the tree and pulled out a rather large package wrapped in brown paper and tied with twine. He handed it to Claire, then she took a seat on the sofa on the opposite end from Henry.

Excited, she tore it open. "Oh, Gerald! It's beautiful!"

She examined the porcelain pot. It had a rose pattern that matched the porcelain comb and brush set Henry had given her. "Is this for soup? It only has one handle."

Gerald laughed and Henry chuckled.

"No, Claire," Gerald said. "You don't put soup in it. It's a chamber pot."

"What's it for?" She'd never heard of such a thing.

"It goes with the set in our room—the porcelain bowl and pitcher that are on the stand. Have you ever noticed the stand has a little cabinet door under it? You keep this in there." He leaned in, and nodded, raising his brow.

She still didn't understand.

"Claire, lately you've had to use the outhouse more than ever. I hate to see you hafta get up in the middle a the night an go out there. 'Specially since it's so cold now. You can go in here instead." He pointed to the pot.

Heat rose into Claire's cheeks. "Oh, my. But it's so lovely. I can't imagine doin' *that* in there."

"That's why it has a lid. You do your business, then put the lid on it, set it in the cabinet, and empty it later. Saves you a lot a trips outside. Henry said Aunt Sarah used it all the time. Oh, but don't you worry none. I cleaned it out *real* good for you."

Martha snorted. Even Beth couldn't contain herself and burst into laughter.

Gerald hung his head and pushed his glasses up on his nose.

Claire's heart ached for him. "Gerald, I love it." She hugged him tight. "It's the most *thoughtful* gift I've ever been given. I'll use it well."

He perked up again and kissed her on the cheek.

They continued to exchange gifts, but none quite as exciting as the chamber pot. Beth loved her angel ornament, and Henry and Gerald were pleased with their flannel shirts.

Aunt Martha gave all of them some of her homemade preserves, and Uncle Henry gave Gerald some new tools for work. Beth had embroidered *his and hers* pillowcases for Claire and Gerald, and gave Henry some of her special family recipe dill pickles.

Since Martha had arrived unexpectedly, they didn't have gifts for her. But she told them not to worry and they could give her something later. All she really wanted was for them to come for a visit after the baby was born.

They promised they would.

Henry hesitated before handing Claire a small box. She timidly took it. Her stomach fluttered. This didn't feel like any of the other gifts they'd exchanged.

Opening the box, she removed a necklace made of silver with a golden rose hanging from the chain. The same necklace that graced Sarah's neck in the portrait over the fireplace.

She shook her head, then looked straight at Henry. "I can't accept this. It's too much." She put it back in the box and extended it toward him.

"I want you to have it," he insisted. "Sarah's gone. It'd mean a lot to me to have *you* wear it."

Claire looked at Gerald, then back at Henry. "I don't know . . ."

"Claire, it's a gift," Gerald jumped in. "He *wants* you to have it. Just say *thank you.*"

Claire dutifully told Henry, *thank you,* and moved to put the box away.

"You should put it on, Claire," Beth said. "It's lovely. We all want to see it on you."

Claire reopened the box and Gerald helped her put on the necklace. The smile Henry gave her made her mouth dry. If Gerald knew what had happened, he'd never have let her keep it. Truth be told, he never would've remained in the house to celebrate Christmas with Henry at all.

Claire sighed.

Why does everythin' hafta be so hard?

Gerald stepped back and grinned at her, wide-eyed, bursting with excitement. "We got one more gift, Claire!" He raced out of the room and returned, carrying a beautiful cradle. It had a large green and red bow tied around it. "Uncle Henry an me made this for the baby."

Claire covered her mouth with her hands, not believing the incredible surprise.

The cradle perched atop a pedestal and had been built so it could rock. They'd paid a lot of attention to the detail. Gerald had used his carving skill to carve *Baby Alexander* on one end. She ran her fingers over the carving and started to cry.

"It's perfect, Gerald." She hugged him tighter than ever. "This has made our Christmas so special. Thank you so much." She didn't want to let him go, but realized she also needed to thank Henry.

Releasing Gerald, she walked over to the man, but kept her distance. "Thank you, Henry."

"You're welcome, Claire." He briefly met her gaze, then looked away.

They spent the rest of the day laughing, talking, and eating. As evening fell, Beth led everyone in singing *Silent Night*.

Regardless of how it had started, Claire would never forget this wonderful Christmas.

CHAPTER 27

Andrew couldn't erase the memory of Claire and Gerald. Claire at the clothesline, laughing, then kissing her husband so lovingly.

But even more prevalent—the vision of her swollen belly. Why couldn't it have been him there with her? *His* child within?

He'd continued getting out of bed each morning as he'd promised himself. Every sunrise marked one more day further away from his time with her. Perhaps eventually he could forget her.

She's happy. That's all that matters. Maybe if he thought about it long enough it wouldn't hurt so much.

Alicia Tarver had invited him for Christmas and he'd gladly accepted her invitation. He'd purchased candy sticks for the children, a warm blanket for the baby, and a new quilt for Alicia and Elijah. Though store-bought, it had been made by a local seamstress and very well done. Of course, it had also made him think of Claire, *his* seamstress.

Alicia prepared a wonderful meal of baked chicken, stewed potatoes, fried corn, turnip greens, and fried apples. For dessert, she baked a sweet potato pie. Having more than he'd ever need, Andrew had contributed the chicken, and the rest of the food they'd grown themselves.

He enjoyed watching the children play. They had very little, but it didn't seem to bother them. He had no doubt the children didn't realize they were poor. They'd never known anything else. They were loved and that's all that mattered. Alicia and Elijah were fine parents, raising exceptional children.

"Thank you again for inviting me to share Christmas with you," Andrew said. They were all seated around the table, relaxing after the wonderful meal.

"Glad to have you here, Doc," Elijah replied.

"That's right," Alicia chimed in. She held Betsy over her shoulder, getting ready to lay her down for the night. "We wanted to be shore you got a good meal."

Andrew smiled and rubbed his hands over his stomach. "It was delicious."

"I see you's gainin' back some a that weight you lost," Elijah said with a laugh. "Good thing, too. If you wanna find you a good woman, you cain't be skin an bones."

Alicia narrowed her eyes and shook her head at her husband.

"It's all right, Mrs. Tarver," Andrew said. "I know he's right. Honestly, I'd *like* to find a good woman. Since *you're* already taken, I'll need to look elsewhere." He winked.

Alicia chuckled. "Behave yourself now. And please, long as we've knowed each other, I wish you'd call me Alicia. I consider you my friend."

"Thank you, *Alicia*." Her words touched him. "You two are the finest friends I believe I've ever had."

"What 'bout me?" Clay asked.

"You, too." Andrew laughed. "Just remember, I'm still your boss."

"I cain't never forget that, Doc. I like the money you pay me too much. Not to mention the book learnin'."

"You just keep coming by. I'll make a doctor out of you yet." Andrew meant every word. He gave Clay opportunities none of the other boys in the shanties had, but he saw Clay's potential and wouldn't have it any other way.

"Wouldn't that be sumthin', Lijah?" Alicia asked. "Our boy a doctor?"

"He can do it," Elijah said, proudly raising his chin. "He gots smarts I never had." He patted Clay on the back. "You can plan to take care a us when we gets old an feeble."

Clay responded with a grin.

Old and feeble. Who will I grow old with?

Andrew wanted what they had. A long-lasting love.

"I want to tell you something." Andrew folded his hands on the table and spoke almost in a whisper. "I saw the woman again."

"Oh, Lawdy!" Alicia scolded. "You chasin' after her?"

"No. It was nothing like that. I found out where she lives. It's just north of the city about a mile. Her husband shoes horses. I had to see for myself what sort of man she'd married."

Elijah frowned. "You shore that was a good idea?"

"She never saw me. I talked to *him*. Had new shoes put on Charger. He's a fine man and it's obvious he loves her."

"You could tell all that just by havin' him shoe your horse?" Alicia asked.

"Yes, I could. I asked the right questions and he opened up to me. I'm certain he has no idea Claire was ever with anyone but him." He looked at the floor. How could she have so easily erased him from her life?

"Sad thing. Woman keepin' things from her husband." Alicia shook her head in disapproval.

"I don't blame her," Andrew said. "She's probably ashamed of what we did." He took a deep breath. "Anyway, I'm telling you this because I made up my mind that day to let go of her. She appears to be happy. I saw them together before I left. The way they kissed told me they were lovers."

"Musta been hard on you seein' all that," Elijah said.

"Yes, it was. But I'm glad I saw it. Makes it easier letting go."

Alicia stood and laid the baby in her bed, then returned to the table. "I's proud a you, Doc. We want you to stop moanin' all the time. This is a good start." She clapped her hands together. "Now, how 'bout another slice a my sweet potato pie?"

"I'd love one," Andrew replied with a smile.

They ate more pie and continued talking and laughing until well after dark.

Sam knew the way home, so Andrew had no problem getting there. As he put her in the barn, a strange chill ran down his spine.

He looked in both directions sensing he was being watched.

"Hello?" he called out, but no one responded. "Who's there?"

He jerked around to the sound of snapping twigs and something shuffling through the leaves. Someone or some-*thing* ran off into the trees.

Human or animal?

It didn't sound like an animal, but who would be watching him?

His stomach fluttered. Something didn't feel right.

Cautiously, he went into his home. Everything appeared to be where he'd left it, but someone had been inside. A number of muddy footprints had been tracked across the floor.

His doors had no locks. Never before had he felt a need for them. But now he'd give the idea a second thought.

With a wrench in his gut, he closed the door and pushed a chair up under the knob, wedging it solidly into place.

He'd always listened to his inner voice.

It was screaming louder than ever.

* * *

Dr. Mitchell's office door had been left wide open, so Andrew rapped, then stepped inside. The man looked up from a medical book.

"Good morning, Dr. Fletcher." He set the book aside. "Did you have a pleasant Christmas?"

"Yes, I did. Thank you. You?" Andrew gestured to a chair and was affirmed with a nod to take a seat.

"We did. Though we missed not having Hannah with us. She spent the holiday with her husband's family in Memphis."

"Unfortunately that's what happens when your children marry. At least you're fortunate she lives here. Her husband could have chosen to remain in Memphis."

Dr. Mitchell removed his glasses and polished them on the corner of his white coat. "True. Donald loved her enough to move. And with their baby coming, I couldn't be happier."

"So giving her up for a holiday seems fair." Andrew stared at his hands. The mention of Hannah's baby reminded him instantly of Claire.

"Andrew?"

Since Dr. Mitchell seldom called him by his given name, Andrew immediately raised his head and was met with concern. "Yes?"

"I know you've been troubled. Are you still having difficulty with Mr. Schultz? I assume you didn't come to my office to hear about how I spent Christmas."

"You know me well." How much should he say? "I believe I've worked out the issues with Mr. Schultz. My troubles have been of a personal nature. But it seems I've got those matters under control. I came to apologize for being out of sorts. I've tried to keep my difficulties from affecting my performance."

"I have no complaints about your skill as a doctor. But I must say I'm glad to see you've been eating again—put on some of the weight you'd lost. I've been worried about you."

"I was worried about myself. Please tell your wife that I'd be honored to take her up on her offer for dinner. I've managed to find my appetite again."

Dr. Mitchell smiled with a nod, then looked at Andrew over the top of his glasses. "Please don't hesitate to come to me if you ever need to talk. About anything."

Airing his personal issues to the Tarvers had been hard enough. Andrew preferred to keep matters private. "Thank you." Though he didn't want to trouble Dr. Mitchell with information about Claire, he had to tell someone about the incident at his house. "Have you ever had problems with intruders at your home?"

The man's brow crinkled. "Intruders? No. We've always felt safe where we live. Why?"

"Someone was in my house yesterday while I was away. When I came home, I had the feeling someone was watching me, then heard them run off into the woods. Then I noticed muddy footprints on my floor. I don't know what reason they'd have to go inside. As far as I could tell, nothing was missing."

"Hmm. They may have been looking for money, or perhaps even medicine. I imagine most everyone who lives around you knows you're a doctor. Do you keep any there?"

"I store some general medications in a spare bag in my pantry. But nothing had been disturbed. I just had this horrible feeling inside . . . It's hard to explain."

Dr. Mitchell stood from his desk, then moved closer to Andrew. "It's always wise to listen to those feelings. Since you didn't indicate that they'd *broken* in, can I assume you left your door unlocked?"

"There is no lock."

"Then I'd suggest you install one."

Andrew nodded.

"Andrew—you're not in the best part of the city." Dr. Mitchell perched on the edge of his desk and crossed his arms over his chest. "Have you ever thought of moving closer to the hospital?"

"Yes, but I love where I am. The land suits me. I need the acreage for my horses. Besides, I like being close to the shanties. They need me."

"I've never known a man so dedicated. But it still concerns me. Have you made enemies?"

"None that I know of."

"Well." He let out a pronounced breath. "Take care. And buy a lock." The look he gave him reminded him of ones he'd gotten from his father. "Oh—I've been meaning to ask you about that horse of yours. The white stallion."

"Charger? What about him?"

"I knew a young man—actually my son-in-law's brother —who used to own a white stallion, but lost him during the war. When did you acquire yours?"

"Shortly after I arrived here. He was payment for my services. Do you remember when I was treating Jeremiah

Campbell for his snake bite?"

"Yes, I do."

"He gave me the horse. Said he'd found him on a battle-field. Charger still has scars from wounds he'd received. The poor horse had been through an ordeal. You don't suppose he belonged to your relative, do you?"

"I doubt we'll ever know. But would you mind showing him to my son-in-law when he returns from Memphis?"

"Not at all. I just hope he's not the same horse. I'd hate to have to give him up."

Dr. Mitchell chuckled. "It's unlikely. But even if it turns out to be their horse, I'm quite certain you could work out a deal. Perhaps another barter?"

"Charger sired a beautiful colt. Maybe they'd consider taking him."

"We'll have to wait and see. As I said, the likelihood of your horse being Cotton—Billy's horse—is slim."

"Cotton? A soft name for such a fiery stallion. Someday you'll have to tell me about Billy and how he lost him."

"I will. When you come for dinner. That way my family can add *their* recollections. It's quite the story."

"I'll look forward to it. Thank you for always listening to me." Andrew stood and extended his hand.

Dr. Mitchell shook it firmly. "I may be your mentor, but I'm also your friend. I'm grateful to you. You've taken a lot off my shoulders here."

"I'm happy you feel that way. Now I'd better get busy or I may have more issues to overcome with Mr. Schultz."

Dr. Mitchell patted him on the back and sent him on his way.

Andrew headed down the long hallway to see to his patients. After work, he'd pay a visit to the mercantile and buy a lock.

CHAPTER 28

Victoria O'Malley lived in one of the finest homes in all of Mobile. A full two stories with four large sculpted pillars adorning the front. It had a peaked roof and housed a small attic with a door leading to an outside widow's walk. Black wrought iron fencing bordered the widow's walk, which made it look even more elegant.

There were four bedrooms on the upper floor, a wide cascading stairway descending from it, and a large candelabra hanging over the stairway from the high ceiling. The lower floor had two bedrooms, a large kitchen, living room, dining room, study, and sitting room. Her daddy used the study for an office. She rarely bothered him when he locked himself away, documenting items for the bank.

They'd special-ordered everything they owned from overseas. Fine paintings hung on the walls, and they had a mural painted in the dining area depicting an Irish seascape. Her daddy had told her he wanted something to remind him of their homeland.

Victoria grinned devilishly, staring at herself in the mirror. Wealth suited her. The dress she'd picked for the occasion was perfect, fitting her voluptuous curves in a manner she had no doubt would please. And pleasing a handsome doctor was exactly what she had in mind.

Having just celebrated her eighteenth birthday, her daddy now recognized her as a woman and old enough to marry. Of course, she couldn't marry just any common man. Her husband-to-be had to be someone of stature and obviously great worth.

Character had its importance, but above that, she wanted him to be fine to look at. She wasn't about to share her bed with someone like Herman Flint, the attorney her daddy kept pushing her toward. The man's nose covered most of his face, and he had a horrible habit of scratching himself in inappropriate places when he thought no one was looking.

God, no!

Regardless of how much money the man had, she would never allow him to touch her. And certainly not *bed* her.

Being an only child had great benefits. Spoiled? Yes, she admitted it. And she loved it. She got anything and everything she asked for. If her mama said *no*, she would go to her daddy. He always said *yes.*

Two months had passed since she and Penelope had seen Dr. Fletcher walking down the street. Her heart fluttered at the mere thought of his form. Tall, broad-shouldered, and an incredibly handsome face.

Mmm . . .

She shuddered, dabbed a small amount of cologne in her cleavage, and giggled.

You're in for a treat, Dr. Fletcher.

Since that very first sighting, she and Penelope had been spying on him. They knew what time he arrived at the hospital and what time he normally left. They also knew he had dinner at the little café by the hospital. Sylvia's Pantry, a small eatery owned by Sylvia Watson, a local widow. It adjoined the Mobile Hotel.

What better day to approach the love of her life than on Valentine's Day? She'd turned eighteen the day before and wasn't about to waste time. Having been given permission to wed, why wait?

She'd never been more ready.

Noon. Andrew would be arriving at Sylvia's any moment. He arrived on time nearly every day. On occasion, he wouldn't be there at all. On those days, Victoria assumed him to be tied up with patients and unable to take his regular meal break. She hoped that today would *not* be one of those days.

She and Penelope hid around the corner of the building.

"How do I look, Penny?" she asked, turning in a circle.

"Stunnin'. If he doesn't fall at your feet, then sumthin' must be wrong with him." Penelope took a step back, smiling.

Victoria had chosen the perfect Valentine's-Day-red dress, trimmed in white lace. The low neckline accentuated her large bosom. Her other *asset* had been well defined by an overly large bustle. Her corset held her tight and firm, making her more than ready to make a remarkable first impression on the doctor.

Since the weather was still a bit brisk, she wore a knit shawl over her shoulders. It had been out of the question to cover her body with a coat. The good doctor needed to see what he had in store for him. If only he'd be willing to play.

Her final touch had been a matching hat, held on her head by a wide satin ribbon that tied at her neck with a large bow. Her red ringlets bounced off her shoulders. Picture perfect.

They peeked around the corner.

Victoria's heart raced. "Penny," she whispered. "There he is."

"Shh . . ." Penelope scolded.

"Have you ever seen a man more exquisite?" Victoria held her hand to her breasts, then glanced down to make certain they were still perfectly in place.

"Never," Penelope replied. "Now don't forget what we planned."

"I won't. I've been goin' over this in my mind since Christmas." Her palms sweat and her heart pounded, but she didn't care. She would finally meet him.

"Go on then." Penelope nudged Victoria's back. "Your future husband is waitin' for you."

Normally, nothing made Victoria nervous. Accustomed to getting her way, she had little to be concerned with. But this attractive man had her in knots.

She gained her composure and sauntered toward him. He'd taken his seat in the far corner of the café and was reading a newspaper. She stood in front of his table and cleared her throat.

He looked up and smiled.

"Excuse me," she said. "I was told you're a doctor."

"Yes, I am," he replied and stood. "Dr. Fletcher. I work at City Hospital."

"Yes, that was what I heard. I'm Victoria O'Malley." She touched her white-gloved hand to her bosom, drawing his eyes.

"I'm pleased to meet you, Miss O'Malley. Would you like to have a seat?" He moved toward a chair, ready to help seat her.

"No. I'm afraid I can't stay. Please sit down. You didn't have to get up on my account." She cast one of her best smiles and slowly batted her eyes.

He sat and smiled again. They were off to a very good start.

Perfect smile. Perfect teeth. Perfect man.

Exactly what she deserved.

"I could use your opinion on sumthin'." She was ready to make her move.

"How may I help you?" Another gracious smile.

"I've been havin' this awful pain. Right here." She touched her fingertips to her right breast, then leaned in toward him. Glancing down briefly, she affirmed he'd gotten the view she'd prepared for him.

"I see." He let out a pronounced sigh.

She remained bent over, then lifted her eyes and looked directly into his. The spark she'd hoped for wasn't there. She stood upright, confused.

Doesn't he like lookin' at my breasts?

She would *not* give up. "So, what do you think could be wrong with me, Dr. Fletcher?" She breathed heavily, heaving her bosom to the best of her ability.

"I think perhaps your corset is too tight," he chided her, then snapped open his newspaper and began to read.

"Well!" She huffed and started to walk away.

"Miss O'Malley, you'd best be careful with that corset."

She leered at him over her shoulder.

He lowered his newspaper and raised his brows. "It can also cause constipation." After saying something so revolting, he had the nerve to start reading again.

"Oh!" She stormed out of the café and back to her friend.

"What happened?" Penelope asked, grabbing her arm.

"I've never been so humiliated!" Victoria cried. "I believe you may be right 'bout that doctor. He obviously doesn't appreciate women."

Victoria went home, defeated and angry. But she wasn't finished with Dr. Fletcher. It may have been a bad start, but eventually, she'd get what she wanted.

* * *

The nerve of some women!

Andrew read the same line in the newspaper at least ten times. Though he had to admit Victoria O'Malley was stunning and he'd found her sophisticated southern drawl appealing, he'd been appalled by her blatant display.

Her breasts were nearly in my face.

Granted, they were exceptional-looking breasts, but no matter. Women should never flaunt themselves in such a way.

With every intention of looking for a woman to share his life, times like this discouraged him. No woman would ever measure up to Claire, so why should he even try?

Victoria O'Malley had acted just like all the other women in Mobile, throwing herself at his feet with hopes of becoming a doctor's wife. But how had he never noticed her before? An attractive woman like Victoria would be hard to miss.

None of it mattered. He'd never align himself with such a woman. As his father had written, he needed to find a woman of stature. Victoria may have been finely dressed, but her actions were that of a prostitute.

No, he wouldn't give Victoria O'Malley another thought.

* * *

A loud rap on Andrew's door brought him out of his thoughts. His mind hadn't rested over the encounter with the beautiful redhead.

He swung the door wide. "Dr. Mitchell?" The man had never come to his home before and was accompanied by a younger gentleman. Very tall, well-dressed, and by all accounts handsome.

"Good evening, Andrew," Dr. Mitchell said. Andrew appreciated his informality. "I hope we're not intruding." He looked beyond him, into his home, as if expecting to see someone else.

"Not at all." Andrew motioned them inside. "Please come in."

They didn't move. "I don't believe you've met my son-in-law." Dr. Mitchell beamed. "This is Donald Denton. Hannah's husband."

Andrew extended his hand and gripped Donald's firmly. "I'm pleased to meet you."

"You as well," Donald said, dipping his head. "I've heard great things about you."

With raised brows, Andrew eyed Dr. Mitchell and grinned. "Great things?"

The man chuckled. "I told you I appreciate having you at the hospital. I don't keep my feelings from my family."

His praise and affirmation was just what Andrew needed to hear. At least he had his professional life headed in the right direction. His personal life was an entirely different matter.

"I assume you've come to take a look at Charger," Andrew said. "Is that right?"

"Yes, sir," Donald said. "I wired my brother and told him about your horse. He's hopeful."

Andrew's stomach knotted.

Hopeful? Will he want to take him away?

Donald smiled. "Don't worry, Doctor. Billy simply wants to know he's all right."

His face must have given away his concerns. "Well, then. Let's go see him."

He pulled the door shut and they followed him to the barn. Then he led them to the pasture where Charger was grazing.

"The colt is Patch," Andrew said, pointing to Charger's offspring. "I'm not very clever with names."

"It fits," Donald said.

The white patch across the horse's nose had been the reason for the name. He'd rather give *him* up than Charger. He'd become attached to the stallion.

Charger lifted his head, then trotted toward them.

"That's odd," Andrew muttered. "He's usually skittish around strangers." The horse moved beside him and butted his shoulder with his nose.

"He undoubtedly loves his master," Dr. Mitchell said.

"He wants an apple." Andrew chuckled, then stroked his nose. "Sorry, boy. I don't have any right now."

Donald approached the animal cautiously. Charger snorted and pawed the ground, but otherwise stayed still.

"He's beautiful," Donald whispered, gingerly setting his hand against the stallion's side. He then traced one of the scars with his finger. "The wounds had to have been deep."

"They were. Luckily, the man who found him knew how to doctor him."

Donald examined him closer, paying extra attention to his hooves. He knelt down near his back left hoof, then stood with a smile that lit up his face. "I think it's him."

"How can you tell?" Andrew asked. His heart sank into his boots.

"His hoof." He pointed. "Cotton's hooves were all cream-colored, with the exception of the back left. His had the same black stripes running down the back of the hoof. A unique trait. Billy told me it would be a way to know for sure. From this, and what you've said regarding his age, I believe wholeheartedly that this animal belonged to our family."

"I was told your brother's story. It's a shame they never discovered who tried to kill him."

"We were at war," Donald said. "Horrible things happened to many men. But good came out of all of it."

Andrew nodded. Sadly, a good outcome cost countless sacrificed lives. "You wouldn't have met Hannah had it not been for Billy's unfortunate accident."

Donald grinned, then looked at his father-in-law. "You told him everything?"

"Margaret and the girls helped," Dr. Mitchell said. "They love to tell that story."

Sam trotted by in the distance and Charger took off after her.

"It seems he prefers someone over you." Donald gestured to the horses.

"She's coming in heat," Andrew said. "I'm hoping for another exceptional foal." The small talk only prolonged the inevitable, so he decided to push things forward. "When does your brother want to come for Charger?"

Donald gasped. "Oh—*no*. As I said, Billy only wanted to know he's all right. We don't want to take your horse."

Andrew's heart finally returned to a steady beat. Even though he'd said it, he hadn't believed it. An animal with Charger's breeding was priceless. He'd assumed the young man had simply been trying to appease him until he knew for certain. "No? But I thought—"

Donald waved his hands. "My father has plenty of horses. More than he needs. We gave up hope a long time ago that Cotton would be found. But it always bothered Billy. He felt guilty for taking him and running away. Father had planned to breed him, but that was almost eight years ago. And even though *Charger* is still young and quite capable . . ." He glanced over his shoulder to where Charger and Sam were becoming familiar. "He belongs to you now. It's as it should be."

"Would you like his colt?"

"Patch?" Donald shook his head, laughing. "No. He's a fine animal, but he, too, belongs here."

"Can I pay you?" Andrew needed to do *something*. Horses were much too valuable to simply give at will.

Dr. Mitchell gripped Andrew's shoulder. "Douglas Denton is one of the wealthiest men in Memphis. He doesn't need your money."

Andrew's mouth dropped, causing Donald's grin to grow even larger.

"I can speak of him openly," Dr. Mitchell said. "Douglas is one of my best friends. Besides, if you lived in Memphis, you'd already be aware of his wealth. It's no secret."

Andrew had always been familiar with great wealth. He'd been surrounded by it his entire life. It appeared the matter had been settled and no more would be said.

Since the sun had started to dip low on the horizon, they began walking back toward the house and the doctor's waiting buggy.

The two men climbed up, ready to leave.

"You should come for dinner again soon," Dr. Mitchell said, grabbing the reins. "Rachel and Elizabeth can't stop talking about you."

The girls were nineteen and eighteen respectively. Both attractive in their own right, but becoming involved with his mentor's daughters wouldn't be wise. All he needed were more troubles involving women.

"Thank you," he said, politely.

"I'll wire Billy right away," Donald said. "If he wasn't living in Kansas, he'd probably want to come and see Charger."

"That's a long way to travel to see a horse. But let him know he's welcome any time."

Andrew stood outside and waited until their buggy had gone out of sight. With a lifted spirit, he returned inside and shut the door.

Victoria, Rachel, and Elizabeth.

Three beautiful young women who were obviously interested in him.

But none of them were Claire.

CHAPTER 29

Spring approached. The trees had started to bud, the ground had gotten muddy, and in her eighth month of pregnancy, Claire had become enormous.

Since Christmas, she'd been feeling quite well. Henry had remained distant from her, but that was for the best. Gerald, on the other hand, had become more and more attentive, helping her with chores as much as he possibly could. Because of her size, she'd found it difficult to bend.

It was late March and a rather warm morning. Claire got out of bed to get dressed and began removing her gown. As she lifted it up, she stopped and gazed at herself in the mirror.

Whose body is this?

Her breasts were larger and her hips had widened. Of course, her exceedingly large stomach seemed completely foreign-looking. She stood sideways and rubbed her belly, watching herself all the while.

I'm absolutely huge and I still have a month to go.

She faced forward again with her gown raised above her belly. Her eyes widened with horror.

"Gerald, Gerald, wake up!" She didn't shift her gaze from the mirror.

He jumped out of bed and raced to her side. "What is it, Claire? What's wrong?"

"Look at me. Look at my belly," she whimpered.

"What? It's big. But we knew that was gonna happen."

"I'm not talkin' 'bout that. *Look!*" She pointed to her lower abdomen.

She'd always looked directly down at her stomach and had never seen what had been going on beneath the large bulge. Her reflection revealed something horrid—like someone had taken their fingernails and dug deep into her flesh, then slowly drew them up toward her navel. The marks were dark and purple. Permanent scars. She couldn't help but cry.

"I look so ugly." She covered her face with her hands. "Now I have these marks that'll never go away."

"Claire, come on now." He caressed her back. "You're beautiful to me just as you are. Those marks are part of the love you've given carryin' our baby. They're nothin' to be ashamed of."

"Oh, Gerald." She hugged his neck and continued to cry. "You're much too good for me."

"Don't you say that now, Claire. I'm the lucky one. I hate you hafta go through all this just to have a baby. Don't seem quite fair. If I could, I'd gladly wear them scars for you." He held her tight. "Come on now. Why don't we get back in bed so you can relax? Might be kinda nice snugglin' a little."

She smiled and complied, lying flat on her back. At this stage of her pregnancy, it had become the only comfortable position.

Gerald lay on his side next to her, caressing her skin. He lifted her gown and exposed her belly, then rubbed it tenderly. Then he repositioned himself and laid his head between her breasts, right above the bulge.

She ran her fingers through his hair as she'd grown fond of doing. Her feelings for him had certainly deepened.

He continued to stroke her belly. He glanced up and grinned, then looked directly at her stomach. She had no doubt what he planned to do. He intended to talk to their child again. This had become something of a ritual. The first time the baby had kicked and Gerald had been able to feel it, he'd become even more drawn to his conversations with the child.

"Once upon a time," he whispered.

Claire giggled. Today's conversation would be slightly different.

"Once upon a time . . ." Having been interrupted, he started over. This time he spoke a little louder. "There was a sorta handsome prince named Gerald." He winked at her. "The prince had fallen in love with the fairest . . ." He paused, wrinkling his nose. "No. *Beautifulest* woman in all the kingdom named Claire. The prince needed to show her just how much he loved her, so he decided to slay the evil dragon." He stopped, looked at Claire, then shook his head.

"Sorry, Claire. That's a might too scary for the baby." He patted her stomach. "Sorry, baby." After taking a deep breath, he went on. "He decided to bring her a rare flower from the royal garden. When he gave it to her, it made her so happy she gave him a kiss." He looked at her once again.

Completely enthralled with his story, she continued it for him. "And when he kissed her, she saw he was not *sorta* handsome, but the most beautifulest man in all the kingdom."

He gazed at her with love-filled eyes. "And they lived happily ever after."

He kissed her belly, then raised himself up to her, kissing her on the lips.

"I love you, Gerald Alexander," she said with tears streaming down her cheeks. It was true. She'd fallen in love with him. He'd won her heart.

And yet, she still thought of Andrew. Couldn't let him go. How could she possibly love two men?

"Why me, Claire?" He cried, too. "How did I ever get so lucky to have you love me?" She'd never seen him cry before.

"We were meant to be, Gerald. We were *always* meant to be."

They kissed passionately, then lay there together snuggled in each other's arms. The baby inside kicked and would soon be born.

* * *

The final month of Claire's pregnancy passed much too quickly. Even though she was more than ready to have the baby, she needed to stretch the time out as long as possible.

She'd grown tired of carrying around the extra weight. Her back hurt, her feet hurt, and her hands were so swollen she no longer needed the yarn around her wedding ring.

Though she felt *physically* ready, mentally, she wasn't certain of anything. She still feared the child might not be right when it was born. Every night she prayed for a healthy intelligent baby, and hoped God in his goodness would bless it with that simple request.

But what would she do if folks suspected something when it came early? She'd cope with everyone else, but didn't know what she'd do if Gerald had any doubt he was the baby's daddy.

Gerald had arranged for a midwife from the Sisters of Charity. They were only a mile away. They told him to send someone once her labor started, and they'd send a proper midwife. At least that had eased one of her worries.

On Wednesday evening, the twenty-fourth of April, they'd just finished eating supper when she felt a sharp pang in her belly. She thought at first her digestion was giving her difficulty, but then about five minutes later it happened again.

Not now. It's too soon . . .

She groaned.

"You okay, Claire?" Gerald asked.

"I reckon I'm fine. Just crampin' a might." It couldn't be the baby. Not yet.

"Don't look fine. Reckon you should go lie down? " He got up from the table and placed his hand on her back.

"That's a good idea." She let him help her to her feet and he escorted her up the stairs to their bedroom.

"Gerald. I'm scared." As she lay down on the bed, her hands shook.

He kissed her forehead. "You'll be fine."

Another pain came. Even harder than before. "Oh, no! I think the baby's comin'."

He fled from the room and flew down the stairs. "Uncle Henry! The baby's comin! Get the midwife!"

The slamming of the door assured her Henry was on his way.

Gerald returned to her side. "You're sweatin' sumthin' awful, Claire. I'll get some cool water."

Again, he bustled out of the room and faster than a hare came back with a pitcher of water. After dampening a rag, he wiped her brow.

She closed her eyes. "Gerald, we never decided on any names for the baby."

The past months she'd worried over every detail. They'd converted his old room into a nursery, she'd sewn clothing for the baby, made more diapers than she could count, and even made some stuffed animals for the child. Everything had been done except choosing the name.

"Let's not worry 'bout that right now. You just worry 'bout yourself." He held her hand, then raised it to his lips and kissed it.

"Oh!" She grimaced. Another pain.

"Oh!" Gerald cried and grabbed his stomach.

Has he lost his mind?

"You makin' fun a me?"

"No, Claire. It hurts. It *really* hurts." He doubled over.

She stopped worrying about her own discomfort and worried about him instead. Taking the cool rag from his hand, she wiped his brow. "Gerald? You need to lie down?"

"Yep. Reckon I better." He climbed into bed beside her.

An hour later, Henry arrived with the midwife. He introduced her as Sister Mary Margaret O'Casey, a nun from the Sisters of Charity. She was short and plump and entered the room carrying a small canvas bag. She wore a simple habit and sensible shoes.

Mary Margaret's head drew back and she pointed to Gerald. "What's wrong with the lad?" Her brogue was as thick as her waistline. "I thought I came to deliver a babe, not find the two of you in bed together."

"He's not feelin' well, Sister," Claire explained. "Havin' pains just like mine." The moment she said it, another pain struck. "Oh!"

"Oh!" Gerald echoed her and doubled over again.

"Saints, no." Mary Margaret placed her hands on her hips. "This won't do. You'll have to move yourself to another room, lad. Let me do me job here with the misses."

She hoisted Gerald from the bed and ordered him out of the room. "This is no place for the menfolk. Go boil some water or something." She shooed him away.

It was becoming dark, so Mary Margaret lit the lantern on the stand next to the bed. Gerald had brought a rocking chair to their room, preparing for the baby, and she scooted it next to the bed stand.

"Now then, dearie. Let me have a look at you." She pulled back Claire's blanket.

Have a look?

Claire had never met this woman before. This *stranger* intended to look at her in a very private area. Now she truly felt ill.

Mary Margaret stared at Claire's bulge. "Your Uncle tells me you aren't due for another month. But don't you worry that pretty head of yours. If I believe there will be any trouble at all with the babe, I'll take you to City Hospital."

That was the last place Claire wanted to go.

She lifted Claire's gown. "Oh my, lass. Why are you wearing your knickers? How can you expect to have the babe with knickers on?"

Claire's cheeks became warm and she looked away.

Mary Margaret patted her leg. "Now, dearie. I've seen more than one of these in my day. I've birthed nearly fifty babes over the years. You'll have to get over bein' shy. When you have a babe, your modesty needs to be thrown right out the window."

Her sing-song voice had started to grate across Claire's skin. However, she had no choice. The baby intended to be born and she either had to do it on her own or let this strange little woman help her.

Claire reached down to remove her undergarment and Mary Margaret didn't hesitate helping her.

"That's a good lass." Mary Margaret blew on her hands. "Me hands tend to be a wee bit cold."

Claire inched backward. Her hands *were* cold. And how on earth did such a plump woman have such hard bony fingers?

Mary Margaret removed her hand and wiped it on a cloth. "One finger," she proudly proclaimed.

"What are you talkin' 'bout?" Claire found the entire experience appalling.

"It's one finger. The opening for the babe. Once you get to five fine fingers, then it will be nearly time to push." She smiled, lifted her hand, and wiggled her fingers at Claire.

Claire felt another pain and tensed.

"Now, dearie. You must learn to breathe with the contractions. Like this. In through the nose and out through the mouth." Mary Margaret demonstrated.

All Claire could think about were the woman's five fingers. The pain subsided. "You aren't really gonna put your entire hand all the way up in there? Are you?"

"Oh, my! Little lass, you shouldn't worry yourself over the size of me hand. The babe's head is much larger."

Claire flopped her head back against the pillows. Certainly, God *had* decided to punish her.

He sent me the nun from hell!

Mary Margaret got up from the rocker. "I think I'll let the menfolk know it's going to be a while." She excused herself from the room.

A while?

How long would a while be?

When the woman returned, Claire lay there, breathing as she'd been instructed. It definitely helped.

"Ah . . . Now that's a good lass," Mary Margaret chirped.

"How's Gerald?" Claire let out a long slow breath, having just had another contraction.

"You'd think *he* was having the babe," she tittered. "But the lad will be fine. Still having pains."

"He is?"

"Aye. I've seen it before. Sometimes fathers feel the mother's pain. He must love you very much."

Claire nodded and smiled.

Mary Margaret took a seat in the rocker and opened her canvas bag. Claire had assumed it contained things to help with the birth, but the woman pulled out a ball of green yarn and some knitting needles.

"What are you doin', Sister?"

"I'm knittin' a sweater for me brother. His birthday is next month. He lives up north where it's much colder." The needles clicked as she moved them back and forth, continuing an arm of the sweater.

"But I'm gonna have a baby. How can you be knittin'?" Claire had to be dreaming. Real life couldn't be this strange.

"What else should I be doin' right now? You've got a long way to go before I need to help you. You just keep breathin' and I'll keep knittin' and before long we'll have us a babe." She rocked in the rocking chair in time with her needles.

Hours ticked by. Since Claire had never given birth before, or witnessed a baby being born, she had no idea how long it could take.

"Sister? I don't reckon my water broke. Does that mean sumthin's wrong?"

"Oh, no, lass. Nothing is wrong. It's best that way. If you're water breaks too soon, you can have a dry birth. *Very* painful. But if the water breaks as the babe is coming, it's like a slippery slide and the babe comes right out."

"Oh. All right, then." Claire laid her head back. She didn't want any more pain than necessary. Maybe God had decided to help her a might.

"I'd best check you again. It's been a while." Mary Margaret set aside her knitting and blew on her hands.

Claire grimaced, waiting for the inevitable.

"Oh!" Mary Margaret shrieked. "Three fingers!"

Claire huffed. *I'm ready for five.*

The clock kept ticking away. Well past midnight. Thoughts of Gerald and Henry came to mind and she wondered what they might be doing.

Most likely they're both asleep.

About two in the morning her pains intensified. They were closer together and strong. Her controlled breathing became panting.

"Careful, lass," Mary Margaret said. "You don't want to hyperventilate." She set down her knitting and blew on her hands. "Oh, dearie! We're at five fingers!"

Claire would have cheered, if she'd had the strength, but she was nearly spent. "Is it time to push, Sister?"

"Heavens, no! It could be several more hours." The woman had the nerve to chuckle.

Claire huffed hard through another contraction. "But you said it was five fingers. I thought we were done."

"No, dearie. I said five *fanned* fingers. Me fingers are still tight together. You'll be ready when I can fan them wide." She demonstrated with her hand, showing her fingers together, then spread wide and fanned out.

Claire frowned. "I thought you said five *fine* fingers, not *fanned*." She dropped her head back onto the pillow, shaking it from side-to-side. "I can't do this, Sister."

"You're doing fine, lass. Keep breathin'. Me and me *fine* fingers will keep you going." She laughed softly at Claire's misunderstanding.

Since Claire's contractions were harder and stronger, she progressed a bit quicker. However, Mary Margaret had been correct. Another three hours passed.

An intensely hard contraction gripped her, as though her entire abdomen had been ripped wide open. Her fingers dug into the sheet. "I hate men!"

Loud footfalls pounded up the stairwell.

"What's wrong?" Gerald cried out from the other side of the door. "What happened?"

Mary Margaret went to the door, opened it a crack, and peered out. "Well, lad. Just so you know . . . It may have been a fine time you had puttin' it in there, but not so much fun gettin' it out. She's fine. It's just about time. Now go away and let me finish me business." She fluttered her fingers at him and shut the door.

She came back to Claire's side. "Now then. Sit up and bend your knees."

Claire panted hard and gripped the bedding.

Mary Margaret patted her leg. "Don't you go a hatin' the men folk. If you want to blame anyone for your pain, blame Eve."

In utter agony, Claire had no intention of arguing with Sister O'Casey. "Who's Eve?" she managed to ask through gritted teeth, between breaths.

"From the Bible. From Genesis. Adam's wife. If she hadn't given him that fruit, God would never have condemned her to pain in childbirth. So, like I said, don't hate the men. Put your anger on Eve."

A Bible lesson during childbirth?

Claire closed her eyes, praying it would end soon.

Another contraction and her water broke.

"Saints be praised!" Mary Margaret cried, raising her hands in the air. It seemed all they'd needed was the gush of water.

Mary Margaret checked her progress one last time, just to be sure. She pulled her hand away, raised it in the air, and fanned her fingers wide. "Five fine fanned fingers!" she cried out, chuckling all the while.

Claire used some of her energy to grin at the woman.

After returning her smile, Mary Margaret's face hardened. "Now, lass, this is where you're going to have to work hard. When I tell you to push, you must push. But if I tell you to stop, you'd better stop."

Another hard contraction. Claire's face curled up and her eyes squinted from the pain.

"It's time for the pushin'!" Mary Margaret knelt between her legs. "Now, push!"

Claire bore down with all her might, pushing with her remaining strength.

"The head is coming out now." The woman gave her every detail. "Once we get past the shoulders, then we'll have smo-oo-ooth sailing."

Another contraction and another push from Claire and the shoulders came through.

"Now, stop your pushin', lass."

Mary Margaret pulled the baby from Claire and prepared to cut the umbilical cord. She wiped the child clean with a cloth, then slapped it on the behind. It let out a loud squall.

"You have a little lad," she said softly, her voice sounding soothing and warm. "He's perfect. Ten fingers, ten toes, and pardon if I say it—a rather *gifted* endowment."

Completely exhausted, Claire could hardly sit up to look at him.

She had a son.

Andrew's son.

"Can I come in?" Gerald asked, pounding on the door. "I heard the baby!"

"Give us but a minute please!" Mary Margaret hollered. "Bring up some of that water and some fresh bedding."

Within moments, Gerald knocked again. "I have the water."

Mary Margaret opened the door and took it. "Just a little longer and you can see your wife and child."

"The beddin' is in that there wardrobe over yonder."

"Thank you. Oh, and by the way . . . the babe's a lad."

"Huh?"

"'Tis a boy! The babe's a boy!" She shook her head and closed the door.

Gerald let out the biggest yelp Claire had ever heard. He sounded even happier than the day she'd agreed to marry him.

Mary Margaret helped her sit up in bed and propped pillows behind her.

Claire watched her closely as she bathed the baby, then wrapped him tightly in a blanket. After helping Claire clean herself, she moved her into the rocking chair so she could change the bedding.

Mary Margaret placed the baby into her arms and she finally got a good look at her son. His full head of dark hair and eyes as dark as the night, took her breath away.

Tears welled in her eyes. "He's so beautiful."

"Lass, if I may say so, your babe is *not* premature as you feared. This child is full term." She rested her hand on Claire's shoulder. "It may be none of me business, but you may not have calculated your time properly."

Claire guessed at her suspicion. "Please, don't say anythin' to Henry. Don't let on 'bout the timin'. He wouldn't understand."

"And your husband? Will he understand?" Her eyes narrowed, peering into Claire's.

"Yes, Gerald knows."

"Well then, that's all that matters. What happens between you and your husband is your business. Now, I know he wants to see his son. Why don't you get back into bed? You'd be much more comfortable there."

Claire eased out of the rocking chair. Though sore, the child in her arms had been worth the pain. She crawled between the clean sheets. "Thank you, Sister. For everythin'. Yes, please bring him in." She couldn't stop her tears.

Mary Margaret opened the door and Gerald rushed in. He cautiously sat beside her on the bed and kissed her face. After looking at the little life in her arms, he started to cry.

"He's so beautiful, Claire." He wiped his tears, then kissed the child on his tiny head.

"Be careful now," Mary Margaret said. "That babe is delicate."

"You don't have to worry 'bout Gerald, Sister," Claire said. "He's the gentlest man ever there was."

"I'll leave you three alone for a time. I'll come back shortly to make sure you know how to feed him." She left the room, shutting the door behind her.

"Claire," Gerald said, sniffling. "I can't believe it. We have a son." He counted his toes and fingers. "Look at all his hair. I never knew your daddy, so I reckon he must get this from him."

"Yes, Gerald," Claire lied. "I remember seein' pictures of him my mama had. He had a full head of dark hair and very dark eyes."

"I'm just glad he took after your side a the family. He's a fine-lookin' boy."

"What are we gonna call him?" She had to know.

"I still like Andrew."

She deflated and whimpered. Without saying a word, she'd indicated it wasn't such a good idea.

"Or, Michael's good, too." Gerald grinned after seeing her perk up. "How 'bout we call him Michael Andrew Alexander? Would that suit you?"

"That's perfect. And very dignified." She hugged his neck as she gently rocked the baby.

Michael squalled.

Mary Margaret pushed open the door, while knocking at the same time. "I think the babe is hungry."

Claire's breasts had already swollen with milk. It wasn't difficult to get Michael to nurse.

Gerald stared, open-mouthed. "How's he know how to do that?"

"It's nature at its best," Mary Margaret said. "God created us perfectly. It's a babe's instinct to know exactly what to do. Now, lassie, you be sure to switch sides. Let him drink from both or you'll be lopsided and your milk will back up. You don't want that to happen."

"Yes, Sister." Claire trusted her. She may have been a strange little woman, but she knew what she was doing. She couldn't have done any of this without her.

Gerald escorted her from the room.

"Gerald?" Claire stopped him.

"Yeah, Claire?"

"Is Uncle Henry still awake, or are *you* gonna take Mary Margaret home?"

"Henry's been up with me all night. He heard the baby cry, but didn't reckon he should come up. Said he'd see him t'morra. He's plannin' to take her home."

"Oh, all right, then." Claire looked down at Michael. "You're comin' back to our room, aren't you?"

Gerald stood up tall. "Course, I am. Soon as I see the sister downstairs. I'll just be gone a few minutes."

"Good." As he closed the door, Claire's heart fluttered.

Gerald returned as promised and slipped into the bed beside them. Eventually, they fell asleep with their son between them.

It didn't last long. In no time, Michael began crying once again, wanting to nurse. It had been a brief three hours. The crying woke Gerald, too.

Claire started to get out of bed for a clean diaper, but Gerald stopped her.

"I'll get it, Claire." He yawned, got up, lit a lantern, and went to the nursery. He came back waving a diaper.

Though small, Michael was strong and healthy. Gerald changed him proficiently, as though he'd done it all his life. He then placed him in her arms so he could nurse.

She sniffled. "Oh, Gerald. He's so small an innocent. I can't bear the thought of him havin' to grow up in such a mean world with wars an hatin'. What if he gets hurt? How can we ever protect him?" She'd never been responsible for another life before. She'd only ever had to worry about herself. Now she had a tiny little life completely reliant on her for everything. He'd die without her. Was she ready for that responsibility?

"That's why he has both of us, Claire." He kissed her forehead. "We're in this together, to make sure he's safe an loved. We won't always be able to protect him from everythin'. That's part a life. But he'll always have us here for him. To catch him if he falls. He'll know his mama an daddy love him more than anythin'." He cuddled down next to her with his head against her waist.

Michael's tiny heart beat rapidly as he lay at her breast. She placed a tender kiss on his head and swayed back and forth, rocking him with motherly affection. She'd never forget this moment.

Gerald dozed off. Her rocking had lulled him as well.

She'd succeeded in convincing him Michael was his son. He had no doubts. No suspicions that she'd ever been with another man.

He's happy. Isn't that a good thing?

Was she wrong to mislead him as she had? To seduce him and marry him just so she could have a daddy for her son? And now, she truly loved him.

But what about Andrew? He had a son and would never know.

Am I bein' fair to him?

Her mind wouldn't rest. She had to let go of the guilt and continue the lie.

Gerald was a good man and would be a wonderful daddy.

CHAPTER 30

Emerald green. The perfect color to offset Victoria's red hair. Today, she'd show that uptight doctor just what he needed—*her*.

Thank God for Izzy.

Isabella had worked for the O'Malley's since the war. Victoria's daddy owned slaves prior to Izzy, but once they were set free, he'd succumbed to having to pay a salary for good help.

After cooking him a meal, he'd hired Izzy on the spot. No one cooked like her. Her size indicated just how well she cooked. She sampled most everything, delighting in her own work.

"Miss Izzy?" Victoria rushed into the kitchen and took a seat in the far corner.

Izzy shot her a sideways glance. "What you doin' in my kitchen lookin' so fine?"

"We still have some a those canned cherries in the pantry, don't we?"

"We does. What you wantin' now, Miss Victoria?" Izzy pushed on the rolling pin, making breakfast for her parents.

"Well . . ." She flashed a smile. "I was wonderin' how hard it would be for you to bake a nice big batch of those cherry tarts I like so much?" She tilted her head slightly to the right. It had always worked when she was a little girl and she still managed to get results from doing so.

"And who might those tarts be for? Hmm?" Izzy questioned her without looking up from the dough she'd been rolling out to make biscuits.

"A handsome doctor who looks like he might enjoy them." Victoria had already confided in Izzy regarding the good doctor. The woman knew her intentions. For years, Izzy had been caring for her every need, and this was one secret Victoria had been bursting to share.

"Lawdy, child! You's just gonna get your heart broke messin' with that man. He already put you in your place when you barely said *hello*. You lookin' to get knocked down again?"

"Please, Izzy?" Victoria stuck out her lower lip and pouted.

"Well. All right then." Izzy's eyes narrowed. "But don't come runnin' back here when he throws 'em in your face."

Victoria sprang from her chair and wrapped her arms around the woman. "Thank you!" After kissing her cheek, she fled to her room to finish primping while Izzy made the tarts.

The final touch. She penned a note on an expensive piece of stationery that she sprayed with perfume.

Dr. Fletcher,
I hope you like Cherry Tarts. I worked very hard making them just for you. I have been told I am very talented in the kitchen. It will please me knowing you have enjoyed something I have made with my own two hands.

I would like to thank you for the advice regarding my corset. I have loosened it and am feeling much better.
   With Sincerity,
   Victoria O'Malley

She folded the note, kissed it, tucked it into an envelope marked with his name, and headed to the hospital. A wicker basket filled with the freshly baked tarts swung from her arm.

She walked through the front door and approached the desk clerk.

"Please give this to Dr. Andrew Fletcher," she said and handed the basket to the clerk. Without waiting for a reply, she turned and left.

* * *

Andrew finished his morning rounds and was preparing to go to Sylvia's for his midday meal.

He'd been about to leave when the clerk called him to her desk. "Dr. Fletcher, a woman brought this by for you earlier today." She smiled and batted her large blue eyes at him.

"Thank you," he said and took the basket.

Her heavy sigh followed him out the door. He couldn't help but grin. It was flattering having one of the hospital employees find him attractive, but she was much too young for him.

It was a beautiful sunny day in May. Not too warm. The perfect time of year.

He sat down on a bench just outside the front entrance and opened the note that had been resting inside the basket. He couldn't tell which smelled stronger; the perfume from the note or the cherry tarts.

For a moment, he couldn't recall Victoria O'Malley, but her comment about the corset reminded him. *The attractive redhead from Sylvia's on Valentine's Day.*

He chuckled.

She's certainly trying hard.

It couldn't hurt to sample her cooking, so he took a bite. The tart tasted delicious.

Hmm. This is promising.

It would be improper to carry a basket of food into the café, so he took it back inside and handed it to the clerk.

"Could you hold this for me, please?" Though embarrassed to admit it, he didn't know her name. After working with her for several months, why hadn't he asked? He leaned in. "Miss? I'm ashamed to say, I don't know what to call you."

Her lashes fluttered. "Sally. My name's Sally." Her words came out breathless.

"Sally." He smiled. "Do you mind?" He extended the basket to her.

"Not at all, Dr. Fletcher." She took it and set in on her desk.

"Thank you, Sally. Oh—there are cherry tarts inside. You're welcome to have one if you'd like. They're quite good." He smiled once again, leaving Sally speechless.

He walked the short distance to Sylvia's. As he rounded the corner, Victoria stood there waiting for him.

She looked ravishing, but that came as no surprise. Her dress was *slightly* more conservative than her Valentine's Day attire. And though he'd chided her for wearing her corset too tight, she'd not shed the thing. The cut of her dress revealed she took pride in her bosom.

As he approached her, she smiled coyly. "Did you like my cherry tarts, Dr. Fletcher?" She didn't even bother saying *hello,* but her eyes had already said the words.

"Good day, Miss O'Malley." He gave her a polite nod. "And yes, I enjoyed them very much. Truthfully, I only had *one*. I didn't want to spoil my dinner."

She sauntered up to him, invading his personal space. He backed away.

She pouted and tilted her head. "Don't you like me, Dr. Fletcher?"

"Miss O'Malley." Her behavior had already caused him to lose his patience. "I don't even *know* you, so how am I to know whether or not I *like* you?"

She stuck her lip out further.

She's a child.

"How old are you, Miss O'Malley?"

"Why, Dr. Fletcher! It's impolite to ask a woman her age."

"Forgive me, but *are* you a woman? The way you've acted during our encounters, I have assumed you to be a mere girl." He was more than ready to go inside and have his meal. She bothered him.

"I happen to be eighteen," she huffed. "And if you can't tell by lookin' at me that I am a full-fledged woman, then I believe you may need to have your eyes examined!" She stormed away in a fit of rage, shaking her fists.

He shook his head and went into Sylvia's.

Almost a year had passed since he'd met Claire at the bay. And though he'd sworn to move on with his life and let go of her, he doubted he'd ever find anyone like her.

Worse yet, he still loved her.

* * *

Victoria returned home, ran up the stairway to her bedroom, and flung herself face down on the bed.

"Did he throw 'em at ya?" Izzy asked, entering the room.

Victoria flipped over and sat upright, pouting. "No. But he called me a *mere girl*! How can he look at me and not realize I'm a woman?"

"Maybe you needs to start actin' like one. You pout too much. You ain't a baby no more." Izzy had her hands on her hips, shaking her head. "No man wants a little girl in his bed. He wants a woman. Best you start learnin' what that means."

Victoria knew exactly what she meant, but didn't know what to do. She'd never had any trouble getting the attention of men. All she had to do was walk by them and show her cleavage. It wasn't complicated. She didn't know why it hadn't worked with Andrew.

Though she'd failed twice, she would not give up.

Sooner or later, he'd see her differently.

ACKNOWLEDGMENTS

In November of 2010, I had a dream that I was attending a college writing class and was given an assignment to write a romance novel based at a time of civil unrest. In my dream, I went home and started to write. When I woke up, I remembered everything. The plot, the setting, the characters. *Everything.*

The next night the dream continued. Very odd. Especially considering I rarely remember fine details about my dreams. When I shared the story with my co-workers, Kim Gray and Bobbie Bauer, they were intrigued and encouraged me to write it down. Thank you both for pushing me on! Until that time, I'd never written a novel. I'd written songs, a bit of poetry, a few plays, and some children's stories. But I'd never even *considered* writing a novel.

I believe in my heart that God inspires us in every aspect of our lives. Waking *and* sleeping. That being said, I thank God for inspiring me through my dreams and showing me a new path for my life. Ever since I wrote those first words, I've not stopped writing.

Deceptions is my fifth release, but it's actually my first book. My firstborn in many ways. It's had numerous edits and changes since that first draft, but it's still the same story. The one I dreamed. Claire and Andrew are dear to my heart, and I hope you'll enjoy reading more about them in the rest of the series.

A special thank you goes out to my friend, Dr. Amy Weeks. She helped me tremendously with the details of the childbirth chapters. We also had some enjoyable dinners together, plotting a number of medical issues that arise in the upcoming books.

Thank you to my editor, Cindy Brannam, who always smooths out my rough edges! I'm extremely grateful that she's sticking with me through this series.

Rae Monet captured Andrew and Claire perfectly! The first time I saw the cover, it brought tears to my eyes. Thank you Rae! I'd also like to thank Karen Duvall for the flat design and Jesse Gordon for formatting. You all helped me produce a beautiful book.

Thank you to my many Beta readers who took the time to read such a lengthy piece of work. Whew! And Mom, you can put up that heavy binder and share this version now.

Thank you to my fellow authors at Music City Romance Writers. You've taught me a lot in the last four years, and I'm forever grateful.

The books in the *Southern Secrets Saga* are not typical romances. I've tried my best to capture the emotions and difficulties of the time period and the conditions in the south at that time. Our country struggled during reconstruction after the Civil War. Things that happened weren't always pleasant, but one thing remained constant. The ability to love. When love is put first, anything can be overcome.

Thank you for reading my stories. I promise to keep writing books you can hold in your heart as well as your hands.

Coming soon!
Consequences
Southern Secrets Saga, Book 2

Dr. Andrew Fletcher can't bring himself to let go of Claire Montgomery, despite knowing she's settled into life with her blacksmith husband and newborn son. No one can measure up to her standards, yet every woman in Mobile is determined to take her place, trying everything imaginable to win his heart.

After a near-death illness requires Andrew's bedside care, Victoria O'Malley finally has him just where she wants him; she's first in line to become a doctor's wife. Exactly what she deserves—she'll let nothing get in her way now.

But someone is determined to ruin everything. A series of tragic events will bring everyone together again, and things once meant to be hidden will rise dramatically to the surface.

Deceptions, no matter how slight, always have consequences.

The RIVER ROMANCE Series
By Jeanne Hardt

Step back in time to 1850 and travel along the Mississippi
River in the *River Romance* series!

Marked
River Romance, Book 1

Cora Craighead wants more than anything to leave Plum
Point, Arkansas, aboard one of the fantastic steamboats
that pass by her run-down home on the Mississippi River.
She's certain there's more to life out there...*somewhere.* Besides, anything has to be better than living with her pa who
spends his days and nights drinking and gambling.

Douglas Denton grew up on one of the wealthiest estates
in Memphis, Tennessee. Life filled with parties, expensive
clothing, and proper English never suited him. He longs
for simplicity and a woman with a pure heart—not one
who craves his money. Cora is that and more, but she belongs to someone else.

Cora finally gets her wish, only to be taken down a road of
strife, uncertainty, and mysterious prophecies. When she's
finally discovered again by Douglas, she's a widow, fearing
for her life and that of her newborn child and blind com-
panion.

Full of emotions, family secrets, and the search for true
love, you'll find it's not just the cards that are marked.

Despite her new position as manager of the *Bonny Lass,* Francine DuBois doubts her abilities. After all, the only skill she's ever been recognized for is entertaining men and giving them pleasure. But she'll never let her insecurities show in the presence of the new captain. He's too young to be a pilot and he'll never measure up to his predecessor. However, just below the surface, there's something about him she can't ignore.

Luke Waters may be young, but he's determined to prove he's more than capable. He'll show everyone he's the best pilot the Mississippi River has to offer. His only problem - the new crew manager. His religious upbringing taught him to frown on women of her profession, so how can he bring himself to overlook her way of life and give her the respect a workable relationship requires? Especially when he can't stop dreaming about her.

Which is worse? A tainted past, or a tainted opinion?

Forgotten
River Romance, Book 3

Rumor has it, the war is about to end. But that doesn't stop Billy Denton from running away to enlist. He's lived a privileged life on the Wellesley estate, where slavery is seen as a necessary means to operate their textile production. Believing no human should be enslaved by another, he's willing to fight—and even *die*—to change the future of the woman who holds his heart.

Living and working at the estate is all Angel knows. When Billy tells her he's joining the Union army, she begs him to stay, fearing she'll lose her best friend ... the only man she's ever loved. She'd rather remain a slave, than have him harmed in any way.

Angel attains freedom, but time passes and there's no sign of Billy. In her heart, she believes he'll come home to her. Their love may be forbidden, but can never be forgotten.

Holding on to hope ... Angel waits.

jeannehardt.com
facebook.com/JEANNEHARDTAUTHOR
amazon.com/author/jeannehardt

61801090R00185

Made in the USA
Lexington, KY
20 March 2017